In The Foothills

A Collection of short fiction and poetry

Michael C. Cordell

Foothills Villa Publishing

For information, contact the author at mcordell2@gmail.com or visit www.michaelcordellauthor.com.

ISBN: 978-0-6152-1679-9

First Edition: July 2008

Printed in the United States of America
Book and cover design by Michael C. Cordell

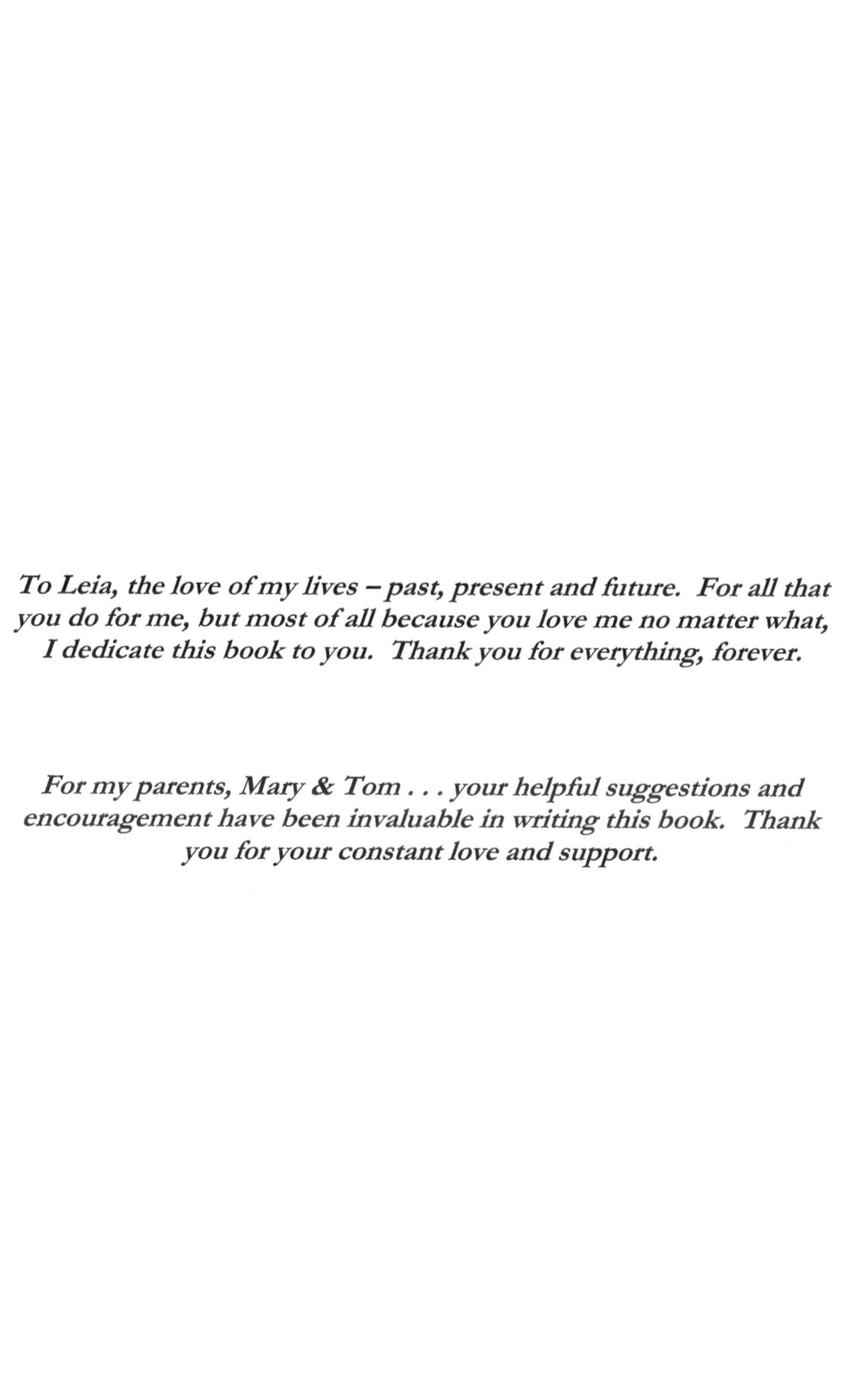

To Leia, the love of my lives – past, present and future. For all that you do for me, but most of all because you love me no matter what, I dedicate this book to you. Thank you for everything, forever.

For my parents, Mary & Tom . . . your helpful suggestions and encouragement have been invaluable in writing this book. Thank you for your constant love and support.

CONTENTS

INTRODUCTION

If someone told me I would be a writer back when I was still in high school, I probably would've smiled and disagreed politely.. At sixteen, I was less enamored with fluid prose than I was with a hot guitar lick or a clever turn of phrase by the day's baddest rock lyricist. Who knew what the future held?

I write this as sit in my study in Glendale, California, looking out our window-framed western exposure over the Verdugo Mountain range. It's just about time for sunset and the "six o'clock bird" – as I like to call him – is chirping staccato beats as he sits in the holly tree to my left. This same bird greets me in the morning . . . same monotone melody, same rhythm. Constancy, sweet constancy.

It's been an interesting year and a half since I began this collection of stories and poetry. Heck, up until then, I hadn't read any poetry except for that found on greeting cards and e-mailed jokes since English Lit. Somehow, the writing bug bit me and in a big way. Several stories, poems and three screenplays later, I find myself craving more hours in the day to be able to put down what's in my head to "paper."

In The Foothills really is an ode to the place we find ourselves in California, the source of my inspiration many times . . . the eternal muse, in mountainous form. Though I've lived on the west coast since I was in my late twenties, it is only here that I truly find myself at home. That's a long time to be searching for something intangible and unseen.

All of these pieces have a story behind them . . . some reflect the mood of the moment, others are mutations of real life events . . . others still were dredged from thin air, merely pure imagination. The muse is out there, but she's sometimes hard to catch and hold for very long. You have to find her first.

Shad Fishing In Northern Connecticut

The magazine article that catches my eye is entitled "Shad Fishing In Northern Connecticut." By sheer coincidence, this is a subject of which I am most familiar having been reared in that part of New England. From my earliest memories, my father would boast how he could land shad without losing a drop of sweat.

"The trick's in the bait, boy," he growled at me where we stood riverside, laden with all of our tackle and a small cooler of Coke that was supposed to last us the entire day. "You can catch shad with any kind of hook or net, but you have to make the fish want to jump into the boat … and you know how to do that, boy?"

Of course, my father knew I learned this already, but he tutored me like it was brand new every spring as we drove from East Granby to the Farmington River near Windsor.

"Yes, Dad, I know. It's the brandy, right?" I'd burble dutifully.

"You got it, boy!" he'd cackle, always pleased with my response. "Soak anything in brandy and those shad crawl up your line just to get into the bottle."

According to family legend, Dad's grandfather's grandfather, Josiah Cyrus, discovered this little secret when he first settled in the area now called East Granby, Connecticut, which he named after the road to the Chicopee River where the shad ran hard early in the season. The details of how he actually stumbled on the fishes' predilection for the vine were never recorded in the family archives. It didn't matter, though. He passed it on to his son and all the way down the line to me, at the venerable age of eight years old.

Strangely, I am both pleased and disappointed not to see even the slightest mention of this time-honored technique in the in-flight magazine that I'm browsing to kill time from Los Angeles to Hartford. Every few paragraphs, I get distracted from my reading by one of the four or five overzealous or under-medicated children who manage to slip the steely bonds of motherhood and careen down the narrow aisle intent on going God knows where.

I take note of my other fellow travelers, each with that same expectant, yet bored, look that I'm sure is frozen on my own face. I am startled from my reverie by the sudden shriek of an infant in obvious distress. The baby's mother stands up to cradle her child on her left shoulder, caressing the small creature on its back to calm it down.

A young girl I had noticed standing in line at the gate catches my attention again. She is wearing a canvas green backpack, a keepsake from some space camp she must have just completed as evidenced by the Challenger-like mission patched hanging from the bag's zipper. In her hand is an oversized Sudoku puzzle book. She can't be more than ten or eleven, but she has that determined look of a child already prepared to break free of parental controls. I empathize with her plight. At this particular moment, though, she's nothing more than the face of the ennui all air travelers share.

Before my great-great grandfather Josiah met the woman he would marry, he could have rightfully called himself a "gentleman farmer" (though he never would've phrased it that way, I'm sure). But once he wedded Amy MacPherson, by God, he decided it was time to start getting serious and find a cash-paying job. As luck would have it, the local grain mill was hiring and Josiah's brother (my great-great-great Uncle Caleb) got in there first. Soon after, Josiah himself signed up, followed quickly by the third brother, Matthias. The Cyrus brothers, as they were known, were industrious workers and business savvy to boot. Within a few years, they bought the Mill and began to expand the town. Soon after, Josiah became East Granby's first mayor in a landslide.

I look up again to catch sight of the girl genius walking toward me, backpack still firmly attached to her small frame. I suppress a smile as I think back to myself at that age - so adult, so childlike, so impatient to get on with my life. The flight attendant observes me watch the girl and for a moment, I get the sense that I'm being assessed as a potential threat to the kid. I force myself to look down on the magazine and eventually the child's ad hoc guardian continues her rounds.

The Granby Mill was one of the largest in Northern Connecticut and did a fair amount of milling for that part of the state. Josiah and his brothers built a fine business for themselves and by the time they were ready to turn the mill over to their sons, the Cyruses were the most prosperous family in the county.

When my dad was born on same day the Great Depression began, East Granby had grown from a little mill town to a thriving community of close to five hundred souls. The country's economic plight hurt our modest town only slightly, at least compared to the rest of the nation. When WWII broke out, the Granby Mill was a major provider of grain to the armed services and before long, any reversal of fortunes East Granbians suffered during the Crash were left far behind.

Dad was all of twelve when the Japanese attacked Pearl Harbor. To hear him tell it, East Granby reacted just like the rest of America did, with shock, anger and a strong sense of vengefulness. No one attacked our ships and planes, by God! My father had to turn that anger somewhere and because he was too young to enlist (though if he could've gotten away with it, he would've signed up), he directed his energies toward working harder than ever in the mill. As it turned out, his efforts were much needed since Granby Mill loaned many of their young men to Army. The mill had to keep producing, though, so the townswomen and older children assumed the positions opened by the heroes that left them behind.

Sadly, few of the Granby Mill contingent (as they were called locally) made it home undamaged by the terrors of war, if they returned at all. The mill's foreman, Hiram Beckham, came back with one less arm than he carried with him to the Pacific theater. At first, he tried to pick up where he left off at the Mill, but it was too difficult for him to learn how to be a lefty. There were few physical therapists around East Granby (and no therapists of the cerebral kind) and Hiram eventually quit even though my grandfather did whatever he could to accommodate the man's handicap. Three months after leaving Granby Mill for good, a neighbor found Hiram dead on his back porch, the shotgun he used to end his misery still locked between his clenched legs.

The 767 shudders briefly courtesy of a late summer storm and the sudden motion stirs me from my uneasy slumber. I usually do not sleep soundly on airplanes, even in my rare travels in first class. I look around at my fellow coach passengers and don't detect any real alarm at the turbulence, so I turn my head toward the window and close my eyes again.

My father was of drafting age by the time America got involved in Korea. He avoided active duty thanks to hearing loss from a near-fatal case of infantile influenza. My future existence was nearly assured by that fortuitous turn of events, though at the time, Dad was nonplussed with the Army's easy dismissal of an otherwise flawless specimen of manhood. He returned from Hartford after his failed physical like a whipped dog to face his parents' disappointment.

Instead of chastising the boy, my grandfather hugged Dad long and hard once he stepped off the train, duffel bag hanging by his side. My grandmother stood by, wiping tears away from her foamy blue eyes and waited patiently for her turn to greet the returning soldier. It was a wonderful homecoming, my father told me.

After his abbreviated tour of duty with the Army, Dad settled back into his life in East Granby, learning the business of running the Mill just like his Grandpa learned from his own father. Knowing Dad, he was a dedicated and no-nonsense pupil. Mom told me of times during their first years of marriage where she'd be waiting for him to come home until just before sun up, just to see him get two hours of sleep before returning to his desk.

With Dad's dedication to the Mill, it's a mystery how my parents were able to meet and get married, let alone have time to raise six of us to happy, healthy adulthood. The Korean War had just ended and the town was having its annual holiday celebration. Back in those days, East Granby residents would festoon the town with red and gold bunting and trim every standing pine tree as though it would be the featured evergreen in their own houses on Christmas morning.

On Christmas Eve, there would be a community skating party at the town center which was flooded into a massive rink for the occasion. Parents would take their families down for a turn around the ice and unattached young singles would choose their New Year's Eve dates from those standing around the giant bonfire that illuminated the skaters.

Dad didn't have much skill on the ice, my mother told me, but she herself had been practicing with skates bought for the occasion on the old pond behind her house. According to Mom, she was out there every day early in the morning until the noon sun turned the slick surface to slush. So when the night of the big skate came, she was ready to impress the most eligible of the town's young men.

Both of my parents swear that they never set out to meet each other that night and I believe them. They knew of each other, of course - everyone knew the Cyrus family, they were the town's civic and business leaders. My mother's Uncle Jack was employed at the Mill long before she was born, so she already was part of the extended Mill family. The two of them just never talked to each other before the fateful night of the holiday skating party.

As my mother was gracefully skating around the rink, she kept an eye out for any bachelors who were watching her. Back in her day, Mom was a looker and she didn't have to wait too long to attract interested parties. My dad apparently wasn't one of them, though, that is until she hit a rough patch on the ice and literally fell head over heels, almost on his lap.

Thankfully, Mom only banged her knee up a little, though her ego was more bruised by her rough and tumble interruption of dad's conversation with one of his co-workers. Always the perfect gentleman, he helped my mother up, brushed her off and sat her on the bench to warm up. Soon, they were talking about everything under the sun and when the townspeople left to spend the rest of the evening with their families, my dad drove his new friend to her home. Before he left her there, though, he secured his first date with her for New Year's Eve.

Their courtship was a short one. Both of them knew they found their "other" and there was no reason to waste time with a protracted engagement. Their wedding was the talk of the town for days before and after the event. Everyone in East Granby was invited and with the exception of the sickliest residents of the town, the entire populous turned out for the event. My hometown never would see the likes of such an affair again.

The flight attendant startles me awake and I rub my eyes to see her handing me a hot cloth wet with lemon-scented water. I gratefully take it from her and wash away the sleep. It's too dark outside to discern where we are, but my watch tells me we have at least another hour before our final descent. Most of the cabin is unlit, though I can see the stray reading lamp on here and there. I close my eyes again.

My brothers and sisters preceded me on the family tree and by the time I was born, the oldest already had done their tour of duty at the Mill and were off to college. I started working in the family business when I was twelve. As soon as school let out, I rode my bike over to my father's office and got my assignment for the day. I had to start at the bottom like every other Cyrus child, which usually meant sweeping floors and cleaning out trucks. I didn't mind it much, since it gave me time to ponder the stories that were always popping up in my imagination. I'd then rush home to write them down before I did my homework, the only distraction in my life that would cause me lose the whole tale in a flash.

My father noticed my propensity for writing at a young age. He wasn't much for composing letters and was always asking my mother how to draft business correspondence just the right way. Once, she suggested he ask me to help him since I was doing so well in my English classes. Dad shrugged and posed the question to me. I thought for a few minutes, then wrote down some tentative sentences for his edification. He read them a few times, crossed out one or two words, then told me I was on the right track. Encouraged by this, I finished the letter and handed it to him proudly. I could almost see a slight smile on his normally inscrutable face as he read my handiwork. He thanked me and put the folded paper into his jacket pocket.

The next day, I arrived at my father's office to find a small typing table set up near his desk, a charcoal gray Smith-Corona sitting on top of it. Next to the machine was a small pile of typing paper and the original letter with my dad's edits scrawled across it. I had taken a typing class in school, but hadn't used those skills much since then. Undaunted, I sat down in front of the typewriter, slid a piece of paper into place and began pecking out the final draft of the letter.

It took me two or three tries to get it looking like a professional job and when I was finished, I placed it on my father's desk with the handwritten version next to it. I then rushed out to do my regular chores and waited for the verdict. About an hour later, I saw him standing at his office window reading what appeared to be my letter. If Dad knew I was watching him, he didn't given any indication. Instead, I observed him fold the letter and put it into an envelope. He walked out of his office to find me, but I beat him to it and met him at the door. Without a word, he handed me the envelope and went back to his desk.

I ran down the stairs to my bike and pedaled as fast as I could to the mailbox down the street. Just as I was about to drop the enveloped in the box, I realized I hadn't addressed it! I rode back like a madman to the Mill and bolted up the stairs. My father only briefly glanced at me before returning his attention to other paperwork. I sat in front of the Smith-Corona again and carefully typed the address on the envelope, then took off for the mailbox again.

The bike trip back to the office the second time wasn't as frenetic, but I knew better than to dawdle. Once I returned, I grabbed my favorite broom and got to cleaning out the back of the trucks as I did daily. That was the last time I was to do that chore. Beginning the next day, I was my father's office assistant and so began my education in the business end of the Mill. This early elevation was unprecedented in the Cyrus family, but I think my father recognized a special talent in me that my siblings didn't share. Such as he was, Dad was duty-bound to nurture my innate ability.

No one in the family seemed miffed that the baby was learning the family business on a fast track. Most of my siblings were already pursuing other careers that would take them away from the Mill and two of them out of East Granby itself, another first in our extended family history. The problem was I didn't think that Granby Mills was my calling either, but I didn't have the heart to tell my parents. So, I dutifully learned how to run a grain mill from my father until it was time for me to go to college myself. Neither of my parents were surprised that I decided to become a professional writer after I graduated. I think my father was even proud of himself for being my first client.

As a result of his business acumen, Granby Mill grew to over 800 employees under my father's reign. The progressive medical plan he implemented was hailed as the best in the grain processing industry. This kept the unions at bay and engendered even more loyalty with the Mill's already stalwart employees. Simply put, the Cyruses took care of their workers like they were their own family and all of us thrived as a result.

In 1981, we were all dealt a serious setback. My mother was diagnosed with stage III breast cancer and even though she underwent an aggressive course of chemotherapy and radiation, the doctors said she didn't have a chance in hell of making it. My mother was a fighter, though, and outlived the most optimistic prognosis by several months. In the end, though, the specialists were right and it was that terrible disease that finally took her from us.

The entire town, including many who had moved away years ago, attended the memorial service at the First Lutheran Church that rainy Wednesday night. Each one of Mom's kids stepped to the podium to thank those attending for their sympathy and to share a humorous story about our her. When it came to my turn, I didn't think I would be able to hold it together long enough to relate my memory, but after pausing to look up at the sky for her strength, I told the story about how my parents met. When I finished, I looked over at my father and saw him sobbing quietly into his hands, stopping only for a moment to look at me gratefully. I nodded his way and made my way back to my seat.

My father didn't really have it in him to carry on as though nothing had changed after that. He tried to bury himself in his work, but all who knew him well saw he was only going through the motions by then. So no one was surprised that when he was approached for the hundredth time to sell the Mill to a huge granary, he finally agreed. By Christmas 1983, the Granby Mill was no longer owned by the Cyrus family. By agreement with the new owners, all of the Mill's employees were kept on if they chose to stay or received a generous buy-out if they didn't. Most opted to remain, but the oldest of the crew decided to follow my father out the door.

Dad's retirement was mostly uneventful. He took a long trip through western Europe, something that he and my mother planned to do together when he finished working. He mostly traveled on trains, he told me, stopping in the small towns to buy food for his solitary meals onboard. Even on vacation, Dad did things frugally.

With a surplus of time on his hands, Dad's sole distraction brought him back to the river. Fishing seemed to be my father's grasp on one last thing he could call his own on this earth and he enjoyed it almost every day when the shad were in season. Though I worried about him spending so much time alone, I was glad he had that to cling to.

With a jolt, the plane comes down hard on the runway and brakes even harder before the pilot serenely taxies to our gate. I wait until everyone else gets off before grabbing my overnight bag and exiting, smiling at the flight attendant who had earlier startled me out of my sleep.

It doesn't take me long to get my rental car and make my way out of Bradley International to CT-20. Soon, I'm driving down East Granby's old Main Street. I pull into the long driveway and park.

"Hi, Dad," I said kissing his grizzled cheek and sit down next to him.

"Who's that? Billy?" he asks, staring me in the eye.

"Yeah, it's me, Dad," I reply, "You're sharp today."

My father chuckles a bit, but is interrupted by a mucousy cough I never heard before. He settles down after a minute and looks at me again.

"Who's that? Billy?" he asks a second time, screwing his face up as he tries to recognize me.

"That's right, Dad, it's me," I answer him. Just as a second coughing jag starts, the nurse comes in. She hands him some tissues to catch the phlegm and checks his pulse. With a curt nod to me, she exits the room as efficiently as she entered it.

"Billy, is it time to go to work? We've got to get to the Mill early today," he inquires, then settles back in his bed to watch TV.

"Dad, I brought something for you," I said to him, handing him the in-flight magazine I was reading. "There's an article in there about shad fishing I'll read to you if you want."

At that, my father perks up right away. "Shad fishing?" he shouts, eye shining. "You know, boy, it's been a long time since I did that." His voice trails off as he tries to remember his last time on the river.

"The trick's in the bait, boy," he says, smiling. "Did I ever tell you about that?"

I smile. "Yeah, you did, Dad, but tell me again."

He chuckles, this time without hacking. "It's the brandy, boy. It's all in the brandy."

And he tells me all about how to catch those shad without breaking a sweat and I listen like it's the first time.

Monuments

Bleak, winding roads lay before me,
No one in sight as I hug each bend on this journey.
I exist, I don't live, yet I have the one thing only I can lose, hope.

Nothing about this daily subsistence is life-affirming.
I go through the motions without emotion.
I strain even as I am constrained by my self-created prison, walls.

The dragon dares me to dance, but I demur.
I stand ready, but for what? For whom?
How I will get there is for greater minds than my own, self.

I'm only the docent on this tour I've chosen.
Standing perfectly erect, yet imperfect as I am.
I hear words murmured all around, still I walk purposefully, away.

Animal Control

Officer Lucinda Dreyer carefully examined the remains of a Master lock, her fingers running over the shredded metal casing. The device was torn in half, leaving nothing more than two jagged pieces. How could this be, she asked aloud.

"What was that, Lu?" her partner, Elmore Greely, called out to her.

"I said that I don't know how this could have happened," she answered in a shout. From her vantage point, she could see Greely poking around the inside of the animal pen with a piece of discarded lumber, gingerly exposing possible places for hidden creatures.

Greely heard Lucinda's laughter down the hill. He shot her an annoyed scowl and continued his search. The veteran police officer hated animal-related calls more than any other. To him, people were a known quantity, even if they were drunk and brandishing hunting rifles. Wild animals were completely unpredictable and for Greely, that made them the worst kind of foe.

Lucinda was nothing like her partner, at least on that score. She dreaded violent confrontations with people, but she was the first one on the scene if an animal was involved. At one time the rookie strived to become a veterinarian, but she just couldn't stomach animal vivisections any longer. After two years at veterinary school, she called it quits.

"Any sign of the critter that got away?' Greely yelled.

"No, nothing over here. Whatever it was, I doubt it did this kind of damage to the lock. Any sign of the owners?" Lucinda began walking toward the house.

"Nope. The place looks pretty torn up. Our perp certainly knew what he was doing."

"He? Or 'it'?" Lucinda teased.

"Cut that out, Dreyer! You know how these creepy crawlies spook me."

Lucinda just rolled her eyes and continued looking around for any clue that would lead them to whoever or whatever it was that caused this mess. She walked to the rear of the house and started searching the master bedroom.

"I already went through there," Greely called loudly, but Lucinda ignored him. She peered under the partially collapsed bed, shining her flashlight back and forth beneath the sagging box spring. On the third sweep she spied something odd, but it was too close to the center of the bed to reach easily.

Laying the black barrel of the flashlight on the ground and aiming it at the object that caught her eye, Lucinda eased along the floor until the unknown item was within her grasp. With one yank, she detached it from the loose metal spring that had hung near the floor. She shimmied her way back out and stood up, grasping the flashlight in her free hand.

"Greely, you got to see this," she announced as she examined what was in her hand. At first, she thought it was a piece of ripped stained cloth, but then decided it was actually a flap of skin and hair. A closer inspection confirmed the stain was actually congealed blood.

"Greely?" Lucinda shouted again, her voice a little shaky. Thinking that her partner was too far from the house to hear her, she stepped over to the bedroom window.

"Hey, Greely, are you there?" Lucinda shouted through the opening. "If you're screwing with me, so help me there will be payback!"

She waited a few moments before trying to call him on her walkie-talkie.

"Greely, this is Dreyer. What's your 10-20?" Lucinda said into the mike. "Greely, do you copy? Over!"

The only sound she heard on the radio's speaker was static. She tried to raise him again, but he didn't respond. She was now officially spooked and tried to think what she should do next. The fact that it was almost sunset didn't help her shakes.

Lucinda reached into her pocket and pulled out a plastic bag, sliding the bloody piece of skin inside it. She slipped the sealed bag into her pocket.

Drawing her service revolver, she eased out of the master bedroom into the hallway. She shined the flashlight in each room she passed, but there was no sign of her partner. Lucinda swore to herself that if this was Greely's way of getting even for her teasing him about creepy crawlies, she'd never do it again. She'd just have to think of some other way to pay him back.

When Lucinda reached the front door, she could see the sun just drifting below the horizon. She called out Greely's name several times, but heard nothing in reply. The walkie-talkie just spewed static.

It took another few minutes before Lucinda reached the police car, but there was no sign of her partner anywhere. She picked up the police radio, but much to her chagrin, it was dead. She reached in to turn on the ignition and found the key was missing.

Running out of options and worried that her flashlight batteries would give out soon, Lucinda decided to risk walking to the next door neighbor's house. She crept along the side of the building to the pen where the destroyed lock was found. No further than ten feet from the privacy fence, she spotted it.

On the ground lay a freshly killed deer. To be exact, the front half of a doe, the edges of the carcass frayed like torn leather. Next to the animal's remains she saw the dark fabric of a police officer's cap, the brim soaked with blood.

Lucinda covered her mouth to stifle the scream.

Weapon in hand, Lucinda inched slowly to where the hat rested near the deer. She squatted next to the dead animal and carefully reached to pick up the cap. Except for the blood, the hat looked perfectly intact. Lucinda held out hope that this meant Greely was unharmed.

Lucinda stood and aimed her flashlight around the general vicinity of the slain doe, but saw nothing else. She made her way to the privacy fence again, this time looking around all sides as she approached.

The gate in the fence was loosely latched. Lucinda removed the bent wire that served as the lock and stepped onto the neighbor's property. From where she stood, she could see one lamp illuminated in the back of the house. She holstered her weapon.

Feeling more confident now that the deer was behind her, Lucinda headed up the steep hill to the neighbor's front door. She pushed the doorbell, but did not hear it ring. It took several knocks before someone answered it.

The man who stood before her was clearly unhappy to be disturbed. He was dressed in thick corduroy pants, flannel shirt and work boots. The hair on his head was matted. He looked like he hadn't shaved in days.

"Can I help you?" he growled.

Lucinda kept her right hand on the service revolver in her holster as she was trained to do.

"Sir, I'm Officer Dreyer and I need to use your telephone."

The man raised an eyebrow.

"I'd sure like to do that, officer, but my phone's on the fritz right now. I was going to wait until morning to run down to the liquor store to call Ma Bell about it. There's a phone booth there, you know."

Lucinda shined her flashlight in the man's face, startling him. He shielded his eyes from the bright bulb.

"Sir, I'm here in my official capacity as a peace officer investigating an animal-related call next door. I'm asking you again to use your telephone for police business." The firmness in Lucinda's voice surprised both of them.

"Officer, why would I lie? If I had a working phone for you to use, believe me, I would let you. The liquor store's your best bet."

Lucinda sighed before responding.

"My police cruiser is currently inoperable, sir. My partner apparently took the key before searching the other side of the premises we're investigating and he hasn't returned to our rendezvous point yet."

Lucinda inspected the man's face to see if he had any reaction to her partner's disappearance, but saw nothing.

"Well, officer, you're free to use my truck to get to the liquor store. I was about to go to bed when you knocked and I'm fixing to do that right now. I have to wake up at four in the morning and I can't be gallivanting all over God's half acre toting you around because your partner got lost."

The man almost spat the last word out in disgust. Lucinda did not rise to the bait.

"Thank you, sir. If you could lend me the keys, I'll let you get back to sleep."

Without another word, the man returned to the darkened room behind him, then reappeared clutching a key ring. Lucinda could clearly discern the Ford decal on the fob as he handed it to her.

"Be careful with the clutch, she has a tendency to grind when you go into second."

"Thank you, sir. I'll leave the keys --"

"Just slip 'em inside the mail slot. Good night." He closed the door without another word.

Lucinda eased the Ford onto the main highway and drove as fast as she dared in the old truck to the liquor store. The parking lot of The Lucky Strike was empty. She found the public phone and dialed her precinct.

"Beecher Falls Police, can I help you?"

"Officer Dreyer here, Sergeant. I have a, um, a situation," she stammered.

Sergeant Dave Bladow was a twenty year veteran of the Beecher Falls police force. He was known as a level-headed, thoughtful man and a favorite among the rookies.

"Lu, calm down. Why are you calling on a land line?"

Lucinda swallowed hard before reporting the bad news.

"Sergeant, I was just at the Kessinger home on that animal-related call we got. Greely's missing."

"Missing? What are you talking about, Lucinda?"

Lucinda proceeded to tell Bladow about all that happened since they had arrived at the house.

Bladow paused for a moment. Lucinda Dreyer was a first rate officer, but she was still green. It wasn't unheard of for Greely to pull pranks on his rookie partners.

"Look, Lu, are you sure he isn't messing around with you?"

Irritated, Lucinda snapped, "How would that explain the deer?"

"Relax, Lu, relax. You're right, partial deer carcasses just don't show up out of the blue. I'll send a car over there right away. They'll meet you back at the house."

"Thanks, Sergeant. Sorry I yelled at you like that."

"Don't sweat it, Lu. Look, be careful over there, okay? I don't know what the hell you're dealing with, but just keep your eyes open and don't take any foolish risks."

"Thanks, I'll remember that," she answered and hung up the phone.

Lucinda quietly parked the truck back on owner's property and deposited the keys in the mail slot as requested. There were no lights on at all in the neighbor's house now.

It took more than twenty minutes for her back-up to arrive. They met Lucinda on the road and followed her to the Kessinger house. Officer Michael Kim aimed the squad car's bright spotlights on either side of the building and followed his partner and Dreyer to where the deer lay.

"Geez, what the hell did this?" Officer Bill Grisham grunted as he shined his flashlight over the dead animal.

"Beats me, but I certainly wouldn't want to meet up with that beast!" Kim declared. He shined his flashlight around the perimeter of the house, but saw nothing except the gate in the fence.

"Did you talk to the neighbor?" Kim asked Lucinda, slowly walking to the gate.

"Only briefly. I was more concerned about getting to a phone to get back-up out here."

"Maybe I should go over and have a chat with him. Why don't you and Grisham search inside the house?"

Lucinda nodded and led Grisham to the front entrance. Seeing their flashlights inside the place, Kim walked over to the fence.

"You take that side, I'll take this one," Grisham directed. Lucinda went where he pointed.

"Dreyer!" Grisham called out moments later.

Lucinda ran from a walk-in closet in the guest room to the kitchen where Grisham stood. In the glow of her flashlight she could see him standing in front of the open refrigerator, a grimace etched on his face. She was afraid to look at what he was staring at.

Crammed inside the large appliance were the remains of a Doberman pinscher. There was a large quantity of pooled blood coagulated on the bottom shelf, some of which was now spilling on the floor. Someone had stuffed a hand towel in the dog's mouth, perhaps to prevent it from screaming during its final moments.

"I guess we can rule out another animal doing this," Grisham quipped. He stepped away from the grisly sight.

Lucinda stared in disbelief at the poor animal and all the blood that collected below it. For a moment she felt dizzy.

"Lu, are you okay?" Grisham asked her, quickly at her side.

"Yeah, yeah, I'm okay. I just need to get some air."

Lucinda almost ran through the living room to the front door. She sat on the stoop and took several deep breaths to clear her head.

"How are you feeling?" Grisham inquired, stepping outside.

"Better now, thanks. I guess I'm just not used to seeing so much blood in one place." Lucinda took her police cap off and wiped her damp forehead.

Grisham sat down next to her.

"Where did the Kessingers disappear to?" he wondered aloud. "They just took off. Poof!" He gestured as though the family just vanished into thin air.

"People just don't disappear," Lucinda muttered. "And they don't leave dead pets in their refrigerator, either."

Grisham shined his flashlight in front of him.

"Lu, I think we found everything we can in here until daylight. I don't know how long the electricity's been off either, but we can check with the utility company when we get back. Maybe the family couldn't pay their bills and took off."

Lucinda stood up and tested her balance. Satisfied she wasn't going to fall over, she followed Grisham back to the where both squad cars were parked. As they neared the side of the house, they heard Kim's panicked shout from next door.

Grisham broke out in a dead run with Lucinda close at his heels. They raced to the rear of the neighbor's house toward the direction they heard Kim's shout, service revolvers ready.

"Don't you think we should call this in first?" Lucinda said.

"What's Bladow going to do? He's the only other cop on duty tonight. Briggs and Martin are both on sick leave right now."

Lucinda looked helpless for a minute.

"Chin up, Lu. We'll find your partner -- and mine!" Grisham assured her and led the way down the hill.

The yard was littered with old junk of all types, including what looked to be a 1969 Chevy Camaro. Its rusted hulk stood as a testament to the muscle car's former primacy and the ravages of time mixed with neglect.

Lucinda and Grisham called out to both missing officers, but did not get a response. After searching the grounds and coming up empty, they looked for a rear entry to the house.

"Here it is!" Lu shouted, her left hand holding the edge of a dilapidated screen door. A larger wooden door was behind it. Paint was peeling off in large sheets from its surface. The metal doorknob was just a ball of rust.

Grisham rushed to her side and investigated the entrance.

"This door doesn't look like it's been opened in years," he concluded, pulling the corroded handle. Fine dust fell on both of them as he shook the door hard. A cobweb clung to Lucinda's uniform.

Grisham put his ear to the door and listened, but after a moment, he shook his head. Lucinda followed suit and drew the same conclusion.

"Look, Lu, why don't you search the rest of the perimeter and see if you can find an open window or something. I'm going to go around to the front of the house and see what I can see."

Grisham left her and quietly scaled the hill to the front of the house. Alone for the first time since her back-up arrived, Lucinda found she was shaking uncontrollably.

Get a grip, she told herself and edged her way along the exterior of the house, her flashlight casting its bright beam ahead of her. She kept an eye out for gopher holes and general debris that would catch her feet. The moonless night wasn't helping her see.

There were few windows on the bottom floor. Lucinda figured that at least half of it was a closed off basement, probably housing a large furnace and a central air conditioning unit.

As Lucinda turned the corner along the western wall of the house, she could feel she was being watched, even hunted. Cold sweat dripped down her back, chilling her even more. She shook off the jitters and looked carefully for a way into the basement.

"Ululululululululululululu!"

Lucinda almost jumped out of her skin. She aimed her flashlight above her. The light reflected the two yellow orbs of a Northern hawk owl staring suspiciously at her. Lucinda could make out the thick black stripes framing its whitish face. She shook her head and continued her search.

Finally, she came across a narrow window. She scanned the edges of the frame, trying to find a place she could access, but years of caked on dirt obscured any opening. After pushing on the glass itself and finding there was no give whatsoever, she shined her flashlight inside.

There was not much there to see except a couple of stacked cardboard boxes and a rickety wooden chair, the latter standing in the corner of the small room. The floor was unfinished, just cracked cement with streaks of old gray paint.

Lucinda started to walk away from the window, but then stepped back and put her ear against the pane. At first, all she could hear was the faint rumble of what was probably the ventilation system. She listened for a few moments, but there was no other sound.

Suddenly, Lucinda heard something inside the basement drop with a dull thud. She aimed her flashlight inside the room again and saw nothing obvious. Then, very faintly, she could see a dim light along the entire bottom edge of the opposing wall.

A hidden room!

Lucinda tried pushing on the window again, but it didn't budge. She had to get into that house now!

Quickly, she followed the western wall up the hill until she found another window. This one was higher than Lucinda could reach. She looked around for something to step on and found a wheelbarrow a hundred yards away.

Lucinda positioned the cart, tray side down, and climbed up. At that height, she was able to just see inside, her flashlight illuminating the dark room. It took her a few moments, but then she started recognizing shapes.

In the center of the room stood a large and ornately carved armoire. An antique, Lucinda guessed. Behind the armoire were stacked several cardboard boxes. Next to the stack she saw a large cedar chest, also antique. Several nondescript posters without frames hung on the walls.

"Did you find anything?"

Lucinda jumped at the voice and lost her balance. Grisham's strong arms caught her before she fell to the ground.

"Jesus Christ!" she hissed when she regained her composure.

"Sorry about that, Lu," Grisham smiled sheepishly. "So, did you?"

"Did I what?"

"You seemed to be looking at something interesting."

"Yeah, I was." Lucinda stepped off the wheelbarrow and gestured for Grisham to look around.

While he peered inside, she told him about the hidden room that she may have spied.

"I think it's time we disturb this neighbor again, Lu," Grisham concluded. The two policemen walked around to the front entrance and knocked on the door.

This time, no one came no matter how hard they knocked. After fifteen minutes, they decided to try the handle, but it held fast.

"We could break in, but do we really have probable cause right now? I mean, the only thing you saw, Lu, was what may be a false wall in a basement. That's not necessarily something a judge would look at as a good reason to bust someone's door down."

Lucinda didn't respond right away. Instead, she ran back down the hill, leaving Grisham standing on the front porch. In a minute she returned with a long length of stiff wire.

"What are you going to do?" Grisham asked her.

Lucinda ignored him. She bent the wire at one end, then fished the crude hook she made into the mail slot. As

Grisham watched her questioningly, she moved the wire along the inside of the house until she found what she was looking for.

Slowly, she pulled up the hook. Attached to the end was the set of keys she had earlier dropped inside. On the same key ring, there were a number of Schlage keys. She tried each of them until one successfully turned the lock.

"Come on," Lucinda gestured to Grisham and the two walked quietly into the darkened house.

The foyer was little more than a utility room. Two tattered parkas hung from improvised coat hooks nailed to the wall. A rectangular storage closet stood in one corner.

"Gun case," Grisham whispered. "No lock on it. Hope there aren't any kids around."

Lucinda opened the door to the case. Mounted carefully were two 30-06 Springfield rifles, both in fine condition. Stacked on the bottom of the case were several boxes of cartridges.

"Deer hunter, huh?" Lucinda asked.

"Seems like it." He pointed at the camouflage pants and jacket stowed in an open box near the case.

Lucinda moved into the adjoining hall. Grisham continued looking around the dimly lit foyer.

How can someone live in such a dreary place, Lucinda wondered as she inspected the dark kitchen. Everywhere she looked, there were boxes half-filled with mostly junk. The sink was overflowing with dirty dishes and tin cans from past eaten meals.

She could barely hear Grisham moving things around behind her. Did she dare turn on the light?

Lucinda was reaching for the switch when she heard a muffled bang at the other end of the house. Grisham was at her side within moments, pointing down the long hallway. Lucinda nodded and drew her service.

The two cops walked quietly past smaller rooms until they reached the end of the hall. The master bedroom, Lucinda guessed, looking at the closed door in front of her.

Grisham reached for the doorknob, looking back at her to make sure he was covered. With a jerk, he pushed open the door, weapon raised.

"Police! Don't move!" Grisham shouted. Lucinda stood to his immediate left, her gun pointed on the opposite side of the bedroom.

Not a sound could be heard in the unlit room. They shined their flashlights all around, but saw nothing unusual. The queen size bed sat against one wall.

"Hey, if this guy was in bed, why the hell is it still made?" Grisham wondered aloud.

"Exactly," Lucinda said. The two officers walked carefully into the room, but seeing no one, they holstered their weapons and proceeded with the investigation.

While Grisham checked the dresser drawers, Lucinda opened the closet door. There were few clothes hanging from the rack. On the floor of the closet were two pairs of work boots and a set of hip waders.

"Nothing here," Grisham called out.

"Same in the closet," Lucinda replied. "What about that cedar chest in the corner?"

Grisham walked over to where the oversized container sat. A combination lock held it fast.

"Should I break it?" Grisham asked Lucinda. She stood behind him, aiming her flashlight beam along the sides and top of the chest.

"Let's see if we can move it first," Lucinda finally answered.

The two cops grabbed opposite sides of the container and lifted simultaneously. The chest barely budged, even with all their strength.

"What the hell is in this thing?" Grisham said, scratching his head with the butt of his flashlight.

"No idea," Lucinda grunted. Something about the lock caught her eye and she bent down to look at it.

"Blood. There's blood on here," she said simply. "Look."

Grisham inspected the lock and wiped the red sticky fluid with his finger and then smelled it to be sure.

"Yeah, it's blood alright. I guess we better force ourselves into it."

Lucinda looked around for something to pry open the lock and spied a small toolbox in the corner. She rummaged around until she found a screwdriver.

It took their combined strength, but finally they wrenched the lock off. Grisham swung open the top of the chest. Lucinda gasped, covering her mouth to keep from screaming.

The stench that rose from the chest was enough to make them both gag. On top laid a police uniform wrapped in cellophane.

Grisham removed the packaged uniform. A brief glance at the jacket pocket confirmed that the clothing belonged to Greely. Underneath the carefully preserved packaged they found the missing rear half of the deer carcass.

Lucinda stepped out of the bedroom before she got sick from the smell of decaying deer flesh. Grisham joined her, looking concerned.

"Are you going to get sick?" he asked her.

"No, I'm going to be okay. Let's just keep looking."

The two cops searched the rest of the bedroom, but found nothing else worth a further inspection.

"Okay, now what?" Lucinda asked.

"Let's see if we can get downstairs," suggested Grisham. He led the way back down the hall.

They checked two doors until they found the one to the basement. Grisham flipped on the light switch at the top of the stairs, but nothing came on.

"My kingdom for a working light in this neighborhood," Lucinda muttered as she followed Grisham down the dark staircase. Despite the brightness of their flashlights, the lack of ambient light was disorienting. Grisham had to feel his way along the cellar corridor. Lucinda followed his lead and did the same.

Grisham led them to where Lucinda saw the light under the wall. As they approached the vicinity, Lucinda stopped suddenly.

"Did you hear that?" she whispered. She aimed her flashlight to her right. "I thought I heard a voice."

"No, I didn't hear anything. Come on, this way."

Lucinda stayed less than two steps away from Grisham, moving her lantern back and forth around the dark cellar. She stopped a second time.

"Don't tell me you didn't hear it that time," she insisted.

"Yeah, I think I did. Over here!" Grisham pointed to one corner.

As the pair neared the far side, the faint voice got louder. Soon, they could hear more than one person talking. Lucinda felt along the wall. Grisham watched as her hand grasped a recessed handle.

"Found it!" Lucinda exclaimed and turned the knob.

The bright light from inside the room almost blinded them at first. As their eyes adjusted, they saw a round table sitting in the middle of the room surrounded by several wicker chairs.

"Officer Dreyer, how nice of you to drop in," said the man who she recognized as the owner of the house. "The name is Michael Carlisle. Officer Grisham, it's nice to see you again."

Lucinda looked puzzled, but did not reply. Grisham shook Carlisle's hand and moved to the rear of the room.

"Hi, Lu," called Greely, smiling broadly. He was shuffling a deck of cards.

"Greely! You're alive!" Lucinda shouted, elated. "Why are you wearing a bathrobe?"

Before he could answer, a tall man stood up and approached her.

"Officer Dreyer, my name is Stephen Kessinger," the man said, shaking her hand.

"Kessinger? You're the neighbor, right?" Lucinda was thoroughly confused now.

"Yes, I own that house next door," Kessinger acknowledged and sat back down. "Don't live there anymore since my wife left me, though."

"Hi, Lucinda," Kim said to her, waving from his seat at the table. "Glad you finally stopped by."

Lucinda was dumbstruck for several moments. It was Kessinger who spoke up first.

"Officer Dreyer. Lucinda. May I call you Lucinda?" he asked her.

"Sure, whatever," she mumbled. Kessinger led her to his chair.

"You see, Lucinda, I'm afraid you were the victim of a somewhat elaborate practical joke," he began. "Shall I explain?"

Lucinda didn't reply.

"Your partner, Officer Greely here, felt you were long overdue for a hazing. The challenge was to figure out what would be the most appropriate one under the circumstances."

Lucinda nodded. "So all this was a joke on me?"

"That's right, Lu, but I certainly couldn't have done it without the help of my friends here," Greely said.

"So, that deer --" Lucinda started.

"That deer is mine," Carlisle offered. "I donated it for the cause … as well as my house, of course."

Lucinda shook her head. "But the dog --"

"Oh, I'll explain the dog in a minute," Kessinger interrupted.

Greely continued. "First, I disabled the radio in the squad car and took the keys with me. Oh, and I laid my hat next to that deer carcass. You didn't get blood on it, did you?"

"A little."

"That's gonna cost you, Elmore," Kim joked.

"At least I made sure my uniform didn't get bloody in that chest," Greely retorted.

All the men laughed at the joke. Lucinda still looked stunned.

"Now about the dog, Lucinda," Kessinger said. "You probably didn't know I was the local animal control officer, did you?"

Lucinda's eyes opened wide. "NOW I remember where I heard your name," she exclaimed. "You're the one I wrote to before I took the job on the force."

Kessinger nodded, smiling. "Yes, that was me."

Lucinda stared at her partner. "So you did this to teach me a lesson?"

Greely shrugged. She looked over at Kim and Grisham for some explanation, but they looked at their feet, mouths closed.

"Why did you guys do this to me? Hazing? Why, because I'm a woman?" She was now getting angry.

"Calm down, Lucinda. It wasn't because you're a woman. It's just that, well, getting into animal control is all you ever talk about. You never act like you're happy to be on the force at all. So, the boys and I decided to show you a different side of animal control." Greely smiled innocently.

Lucinda looked around the room, but did not see a sympathetic face among them.

"About the dog, Lucinda," Kessinger spoke up. "That was just the one I had to put down a few days ago because it contracted rabies."

"Did you keep it in that pen on your property?"

"Yes, of course," the animal control officer responded. "I certainly didn't want to keep it at the main facility. I had that pen put in my property years ago especially to hold any potentially dangerous animals away from the rest."

"What about the blood in the refrigerator?"

"That's deer blood, of course," Kessinger chuckled. "I poured a large quantity of it in there for effect."

Lucinda shook her head in amazement. "What about the lock? You tore that lock in half?"

"Not quite. I actually had a destroyed lock for several years now. I just planted it at the scene, knowing you'd surmise something escaped from the pen." Kessinger looked at her matter-of-factly.

Linda paused. "Was Bladow in on this, too?"

"Not at first, but we called him after you did. We had to make sure the watch captain wasn't going to call out the National Guard looking for a kidnapped cop or something," Greely answered.

Just then, Linda remembered the flap of skin she found. She reached into her pocket and pulled out the still sealed bag.

"Then what the hell is this?" she shouted, shaking it in Kessinger's face.

Startled, Kessinger asked, "Where did you find that?"

"Under your bed, hooked to a damaged spring. What's this all about?"

Kessinger did not answer. "Let me see that, Lu," Greely asked. He inspected the skin and hair closely. "This is human!"

"Now, wait, let me explain," Kessinger started.

"I think we better go next door to see if we can get our own explanation," Greely said to Kessinger. "Officers Kim and Grisham will escort you with us."

Greely led the others back to Kessinger's house.

"Carlisle, flip on the master circuit breaker, will ya?" Greely asked. A few minutes later, all the lights came on in Kessinger's house.

Greely and Lucinda methodically searched each room. Kim and Grisham waited with Carlisle and Kessinger in the kitchen.

"Greely, come here, quick!" Lucinda shouted

Greely rushed to where Lucinda was standing. In front of her was a bedroom closet, but didn't seem deep enough to be practical.

"Help me, Greely" Lucinda grunted as she tried to pry away the rear wall. Greely joined her, grabbing the edge above her. Several tugs later, the piece of plywood came loose. They peeled it away from the back.

Behind the false wall lay what simply looked like a rolled up carpet. They dragged it outside the closet and carefully uncovered the contents. Inside they found the decomposed body of a human adult. From the remaining hair on the head, it appeared to be a female. A large wound on the back of her skull suggested she was bludgeoned to death.

Greely and Lucinda walked into the kitchen and looked at Kessinger. He immediately broke down in tears.

"I didn't mean to kill her," he sobbed, his hands in his face. "I didn't mean to."

Lucinda look around the room at her fellow officers, but not one of them was man enough to look her in the eye.

"Look at you!" Lucinda yelled, pacing back and forth. "Instead of doing what you were hired to do and solve crimes, you go ahead and waste everyone's time and the taxpayers' money playing silly games."

No one replied. Carlisle just looked down at Kessinger, crying without pause below him.

Finally, Grisham spoke up. "I admit what we did was pretty stupid, Lucinda, but we really didn't mean any harm."

"Look, guys," Greely interrupted. "Lucinda's more of a cop today than any of us has been for a long time. She's solved a murder that was sitting right under our nose for months. Hell, we played cards here just last week!"

The men nodded, but Lucinda was unimpressed.

“You’re all pathetic,” she spat and left the room.

Kim and Grisham led Kessinger outside and put him in the back of their squad car. Lucinda could hear their siren screaming as it headed down the main highway.

"Lucinda, I --" Greely started.

Lucinda held up her hand and walked away from him. He followed her outside.

"Lu!" he called out to her. "I'm really sorry we pulled that on you, okay?"

Lucinda kept walking down the driveway.

"You're a great cop, Lu! I'm proud to be your partner!" Greely shouted.

Lucinda stopped and turned. "But I'm not proud to be yours. See you later, Greely."

As she passed their squad car, Lucinda took off her badge and flung it in the open window. Animal control, my ass, she thought to herself as she left her innocence behind.

Beyond Measure

Depths of doubt occupy
true and honest hands,
Fingers splay and stretch with
no strings attached.
A welcome song, a lover's kiss unites
both time and the timeless,
Neither hears nor sees nor thinks,
but both simply feel.

Willowy tendrils,
no more than dust,
Sheaves, freshly gathered,
once dispensed without despair.
Until the day breaks anew,
each moment growing distant,
The embers quiet,
lingering strains alight no more.

Will there be again,
the well-learned pas de deux?
What once passed between,
is now kept within.
No dirges play,
nothing more than silence
Sacred and refined,
Sealed until night comes again.

Street Life

Even at his best, Malone had never been described as "boundless," but today was a low water mark. As he took those first tentative steps away from the County Hospital's cheerless entryway, Malone judged he was at about sixty percent of capacity no matter what the underpaid intern told him. That's how Malone always referred to his current condition - in percentages only he understood.

With his bag announcing "Patient's Belongings" in tow, Malone trudged to the sidewalk and rested on the first bus bench he saw. It wasn't long before the 5:01 to downtown arrived. He eased himself up the vehicle's five steps and after a few minutes of fumbling for his change, he slumped into the empty seat behind the driver. He was asleep before the next stop.

Malone didn't know how long he was snoring before he was startled back to consciousness by the blare of the bus's horn. For a moment, he thought he was back in the hospital again. Once his senses returned, he faced the adjacent window and watched the rest of humanity slog their way up and down busy sidewalks and through jammed intersections.

For the second time since he was released, Malone inventoried his personal effects. The surgical scrubs he was given to use for pajamas were his new favorite possession, but the paper thin slippers would last only a few days of regular use before disintegrating. At least I got a free water pitcher out of the deal, Malone mused.

Satisfied his worldly goods were accounted for, he settled back into his seat and waited until his stop. Other passengers got on board, but all avoided sitting next to him as though he were diseased. It must be the hospital bag, Malone convinced himself.

When the bus stopped at Broadway and 8th, Malone limped his way to the exit and down to the street. He looked up and down the expanse of Broadway and decided it wasn't yet time to meet up with his friends. Instead, he pointed himself toward 8th street and shuffled along the irregular sidewalk. From time to time, he would hold his hand out to passing strangers, but was rebuffed each time.

It took more than a half hour for Malone to make it to the Subways he usually frequented. He sat down at one of the café tables outside the store and observed the bustling crowd that brushed passed him. Few turned their heads his way and the one or two that did either looked disgusted or annoyed. Malone learned to ignore the displeasure of others a long time ago and just smiled each time a stranger glared at him.

The smells from the restaurant escaped each time the door swung open and before long, Malone felt the familiar cramping of his empty belly. Familiar like an old friend that you'd like to say good-bye to forever, he grumbled out loud. Without warning, his face was contorted by unseen forces as he shouted obscenities while he twisted his neck at extreme angles. Observing his abrupt actions, strangers skittered past him, their panic obvious on their faces. In time, the outburst subsided and Malone emitted a labored sigh of relief from the effort.

He stood up from his chair and walked to the window to watch the Subways customers order their sandwiches. Maybe he could catch the eye of some warm-hearted soul and get a few cents toward a bag of chips. One after another, patrons hurried past him as they exited without even glancing at his open palm he pushed into their face.

This is going nowhere, Malone finally thought to himself. He picked up his bag and headed north on Flower Street to where he normally took shelter in a parking garage. Many of his friends slept in the same lot. The owner didn't mind as long as they stayed out until the garage closed. Malone was thankful that there was at least one human among all the zombies he encountered every day in this city.

There were only a couple of the regulars at The Palace (as the street people called it) and a couple of guys Malone never saw before. That's the way it was living in Los Angeles. You had your permanent residents and then you had your vacationers, the latter floating between homeless meccas in hopes of finding a sanctuary where police would leave them be.

The cops and the street dwellers had a love/hate relationship if there ever was one. If you didn't harass the paying residents of the newly developed apartments and condos and stayed out of the way of those who worked in the city - and most importantly, let the shop owners run their businesses - the cops didn't hassle you. It didn't hurt to buddy up with them when you encountered them, either. Familiarity was a homeless person's best protection on the streets. The LAPD didn't like strangers and would roust many a newcomer from a sound sleep to relocate them to a more accommodating city.

Malone preferred being closer to the big office buildings than the bodegas over on Broadway (or even worse, down on Skid Row where every night someone was killing somebody else while others were just dying from whatever makeshift medication gave them peace). At least the daily commuters were usually quick to pull change out of their pockets or on a good day, a dollar bill or two. Whether it was out of pity or guilt made no difference to Malone. A meal was a meal.

His usual spot at The Palace was occupied by a visitor, but Malone didn't mind too much. The second best spot in the place was free and there was already a blanket there just waiting for him. There was no sign of rats today, thanks to a series of fresh traps laid out by the parking lot attendants. He just hoped none of the newcomers got the bright idea of eating the bait from those traps. Malone had seen what happened to others who made the fatal mistake and it was too horrible a sight to recall.

He curled up on the cardboard matting and wrapped the blanket snugly around him. He didn't fall asleep immediately. The angry shouts of The Palace's visitors at passersby keeping him on edge. Eventually, the trauma of his hospital stay caught up with him and he was soon deeply asleep.

How he actually ended up in the hospital still wasn't clear to Malone, but the fact he had to go was obvious to him even if he didn't remember all the details. If Malone only avoided

Mad Max like he always did, he never would've taken that knife into his side. Instead, he made the mistake of telling the crazy old man to shut up that night so he could sleep. The Palace was particularly crowded then and even though Malone was occupying his favorite place, he had to stuff wet newspaper in his ears to quiet down the din of the occupants.

Mad Max was the loudest of all of them, screaming at anyone in his general vicinity and when everyone steered clear of him, he targeted imaginary intruders with his vile abuse. It was during the height of his screaming that Malone shouted to Max to settle down, adding it was too late to listen to his nonsense. The next thing that Malone knew, Mad Max was sitting on top of him, throttling him by neck.

The skinny old man may have lived on the streets forever, but he was still had strong hands and Malone finally had to toss Max off of him to save himself from being choked to death. That didn't deter his opponent in the least. Mad Max attacked Malone again, this time brandishing a small pocket knife. It was lucky for Malone that he saw the shiv before it went into his throat because that was the first place that the old man aimed.

Malone grabbed Mad Max and threw him to the hard concrete floor, allowing all of his weight to fall on the old man. He struggled to grab the knife from Max but lost his grip on the old man's wrist in the struggle. The stab in his side came as both a shock and a relief. Malone vaguely recalled some of the other regulars pulling Max away from him, but things kind of went dark. Only when he woke up in the hospital did he realize he survived a serious wound and lost a lot of blood en route to the hospital.

The Palace was normally as safe a place as you could find in the city. The regulars watched out for each other and the occasional bad ones, like Mad Max, were banished to Skid Row if they stepped out of line. Dangerous characters were usually brought to the attention of the cops who had ways of making the problem go away for good.

Malone woke up with a start with visions of the crazy old Max on him again. He turned to the left and found a fast food bag sitting within a few feet of him. Curious, he looked inside and found several McDonald's hamburgers, still warm in their wax paper wrappers. For a moment, he hesitated, looking around him in all directions to make sure that no one saw his booty. The rule of the streets was you eat what you find and if you want to, share it with others. There were a few regulars that would share the little they had with their closest friends, but not Malone. The way he looked at it, he never knew how long it would be before he got his next meal, so it made little sense to share what he had in hand.

Satisfied he was alone, Malone extracted the first burger and almost inhaled it in three large bites. He chewed several times and swallowed hard to avoid choking. That's the way it was when you haven't eaten in a long time, you're like a feral animal when you find something edible. He ate the second and third burgers more slowly, savoring their taste this time. His belly full, he decided to emerge to score something to drink. Before getting up, Malone did a quick self-check and figured he was at seventy percent, thanks to this largesse of some passing stranger.

Malone's first stop, as always, was Subways. The workers there were usually good for a glass of water or even ice tea if he asked nice. Today, they were too busy to give him anything more than an empty cup, so he poured himself water from the beverage dispenser and quickly walked outside. Malone didn't want to hurt the rapport he had with the staff by sitting inside and scaring away paying customers.

"Thomas!" he heard as he walked out the door. He turned expectantly to the greeter and saw a familiar face. Malone shook the extended hand and said hello.

"Did you get the burgers?" the bearded man asked, smiling.

"That was from you?"

"Yeah, I know where you hang out when you're not here." The man gestured to the table in front of the store.

"Thanks, the food was just what I needed," Malone replied. "I just got out of the hospital, you know?"

"Oh, that's where you've been," said the man. "I hope it wasn't serious."

"Nothing that a few stitches and some extra blood couldn't cure," Malone joked.

The man laughed politely. "Well, take care of yourself, Tom."

"What's your name again?" Malone asked, extending his own hand.

"Tom, just like yours, my friend. Be well." Shaking Malone's hand, the man crossed the street and walked into the loft apartment building on the corner. Malone would remember him as Loft Guy.

Malone sat down at one of the café tables and after setting his cup aside, he pulled out the hamburger bag and systematically began to eat the remainder. Normally, he would keep some food for another time and spend a fitful night of sleep guarding it from the others. He was already too hungry to wait this time and finished the rest of the sandwiches in less than ten minutes.

From time to time, Malone interrupted his dining to spew an outburst of angry words directed at no one in particular. During these episodes he would shake his head in fury, eyes blinking spasmodically. Then the moment passed as quickly as it started. Too much stress and not enough sleep make the devil dance, he thought, exhausted from the effort.

Finished, Malone began his evening trek throughout the rest of the city. The Wilshire Grand hotel guests were usually good for a hand-out at this time of night. After that tour, he headed up to the Main Library and then down Grand Avenue past the Biltmore. Sometimes there would be a film shoot there he could watch. Maybe some day he could get lucky like The Quarter Man and earn real money appearing in a film, just playing himself.

By the time Malone completed the circuit back to his corner it was almost 7 o'clock. He was cold from the night air and tired from his walk and his recent injury. At The Palace, he settled down in his favorite spot - now opened up for the night. For the first time since he left the hospital, he checked the area where he got stabbed. There was some blood still oozing from the wound, but the doctors told him that it would do that some until he healed. Malone reached into the hospital bag and pulled out one of the large bandages they gave him. He found the small bottle of sterile wash and cotton pads and cleaned up the area where the knife went in him.

Satisfied that he was healing just like they told him, he rebandaged the area and zippered his heavy jacket. Using the hospital bag as a pillow, he laid down on the cold cement, the flattened cardboard having since been taken by another resident. Sleep found him soon enough.

"Tom?"

Malone opened his eyes to see Loft Guy staring down at him, the morning sun behind him.

"Hey, Tom, sorry for waking you. I thought you may want some breakfast over at Subways. I'm buying." Loft Guy smiled.

"Sure, I'm up for that," Malone replied, taking a moment to shake the sleep out of his foggy brain. He picked up his hospital bag and followed Loft Guy out of The Palace. As they walked, Malone noticed the other residents giving him the green eye. Adopted street dwellers don't have many friends on the street. Aware of this, Malone kept a respectful distance from his patron as they walked down Flower Street.

Loft Guy was holding the door of the restaurant open for him when he arrived. Malone gave the counter man his order - foot long meatball with provolone cheese - and watched him assemble the sandwich, pointing to the vegetables he wanted added. Loft Guy told Malone to grab a bag of chips and fill his soda cup while he paid. They met back outside.

"Thanks a lot," Malone said gratefully.

"My pleasure, Tom. I hope you have a Merry Christmas," Loft Guy replied.

"Christmas? It's Christmas already?" Malone asked, somewhat confused.

"Christmas is tomorrow, Tom. Be well," Loft Guy said, patting Malone on the shoulder and crossing Flower to the apartment building.

Malone looked around and saw all the café tables were taken, so with his sandwich clutched in his hand, he walked back up to The Palace. His favorite spot was unoccupied, so he sat cross-legged on the concrete and set his meal down on the ground. Looking around to make sure he wasn't being eyeballed, he unwrapped the sandwich and took a huge bite. It tasted like heaven! For the first time since he was stabbed Malone gauged himself to be at a strong eighty percent.

The sandwich was huge and Malone could only eat half of it along with the chips and drink. He wrapped up the remains of his breakfast and stored it securely in his hospital bag. After throwing out the trash, Malone made his way out into the late morning sun. It was Christmas Eve which meant that the Mission would be handing out meals to street people starting at sundown and continuing all through Christmas Day. Malone tried not to miss the Mission meal days and decided to walk around today to build himself up a good appetite.

Over at the park, he saw some of the regulars sitting around, hustling pedestrians for money. From what Malone observed, they weren't having very much luck. He greeted his friends and wasn't surprised he didn't get a warm welcome in return.

"What you did to Mad Max wasn't right," Scarab announced when Malone sat down next to the group. "He's gone."

Malone shook his head and looked in the general direction of Skid Row.

"No, he ain't there, fool," Scarab spat. "The cops got him. He was telling them it was your fault you got yourself cut, but they didn't listen."

Malone shrugged in response and got up. Clearly, he wasn't going to win any arguments today. It was like that a lot out here. One day a guy's your best friend, the next day he hates your guts. None of it made any sense, but neither did living on the streets.

After leaving the park, Malone made his way to Broadway to check out the action. There were always a lot of shoppers around the day before Christmas and they were always in a giving mood. With any luck, Malone could pull down enough to get himself a few nights in the SRO place on Hill and three squares each day besides.

As he walked north on Broadway, he called out Christmas greetings to the regulars, but no one seemed to be in the holiday spirit. Thankfully, the shoppers weren't of the same mind. Within an hour, Malone panhandled close to twenty dollars, a personal best. Eighty-five percent! Despite his elation, he knew better to flash his cash later at The Palace, though, especially with the strange mood he had been sensing all day.

When he got back to the parking garage, he found his favorite spot was taken, this time by one of The Palace regulars. Malone wondered if his brief stay at the hospital lost him some respect because to have your spot taken by a regular wasn't normally done without it sending a message. Or maybe it was the special favors that Loft Guy was doing for him that had everyone suspicious. It didn't take long on these streets for the crowd to turn against you. That is, until another one of them did something stupid to take the heat off of you. Everything in life is fleeting, Malone concluded, all of it.

He looked over and saw the only spot that was free was where Mad Max stabbed him. Street people were a superstitious lot and Malone was no exception. However, Christmas Eve was the most difficult night to get a room at the SRO. It was either stay here or stand in line for nothing at the hotel. He opted to stay.

With a sigh, Malone walked over to the place where he and Max had their last encounter. Wrapping himself with a scrap of plastic sheeting left behind by one of the other residents, he quickly fell into a deep sleep. Vivid dreams haunted his slumber. Dreams of empty Christmases as a child, neither of his parents able to do much more than fight with each other. Disturbing visions of fighting with rats to get a morsel of food to sustain him for just another day. Recollections of fighting to survive in a city that wanted nothing more than his kind to just disappear.

At first, Malone thought the dark figure standing over him was another dream. He couldn't make out the face or the words the visage mumbled.

"Who are you? What do you want?" Malone stammered, more than a little spooked. The figure didn't respond but came closer.

Before he could react, Mad Max descended upon him brandishing a kitchen knife. The old man's weight dropped on Malone, the knee landing directly on Malone's wounded side. As he screamed in pain, he saw the glint of the knife as it cut through the air toward his neck. This time the shiv found its mark.

Malone struggled viciously, but the old man's knee successfully tore open the stitched area near his kidney. He could feel the blood pouring out of him from both wounds. He screamed obscenities, his head twisting back and forth and his torso trying to throw off the attacking creature on top of him.

Fifty percent ...

Some of the residents of The Palace gathered around the death struggle, but no one was brave enough or even willing enough to get involved. Maybe one of them would be adopted by his benefactor once Malone was gone, some thought. Malone cried out for help, but no one moved. They just watched and waited.

Thirty percent ...

Malone lost all his strength now and stopped struggling under Mad Max. The old man felt his foe's defeat and eased off Malone's limp body, brandishing his knife as a warning to the crowd that they would be next if the cops brought him in again. The residents ignored him, focusing their attention on the wounded man lying prone below them.

Twenty percent ...

Tomorrow's Christmas and I'll never see it, thought Malone as the darkness descended. Everything in life is fleeting, everything.

"Thomas?"

Malone opened his eyes. He could barely hear the sound of a siren in the distance.

Loft Guy was looking down at him, smiling. "Don't worry, we're almost there."

Walls of Brilliance

Senses rendered by silent throes;
Vengeful sorrows at desperate night.
Awaken Spirit in guiding song;
Unlearn the hand that lays unmoved.

From where do such thoughts procreate?
And whence they peek at my first call?
A well-worn course I must devise.
To know both well this love and lust.

Within my grasp I feel her now.
Alight upon this fevered breast
My mind is yours, do not hold back.
Please! Oh no! Your light's grown cold.

Much more awaits, of this I know;
Unless, of course, she does demur.
But if this loss indeed does stand,
I left too soon, and thus, too late.

Baylor

No matter who met Baylor Thompson, their first impression was he could probably snap a man's neck in two at the slightest provocation. It just wasn't his mere size that led one to that conclusion, though that fact certainly could not be ignored. Baylor was described by his closest friends as a "man mountain" - taller than a tree and twice as heavy, some said.

Baylor did nothing to dismiss those first impressions, either. He eschewed the razor at an early age, growing a thick, bushy beard he rarely trimmed or even brushed. Strangers, old and young, would just stare at the huge man with fiery red hair sprouting in untamed clumps from the top of his head and continuing down to the middle of his chest. It grew unfettered as wild brush through the open neck of his shirt.

He was an imposing presence. That much was certain.

However, Baylor's size belied the man underneath. His most closely guarded secret of all of his secrets was that harming another living soul was always the furthest thing from his mind. Only Baylor knew that if push came to shove, he would walk away from a fight rather than injure someone. Baylor Thompson had a heart as big as the body that cocooned it, something that his late wife nurtured.

Maddie was gone for a little over three years now, but to Baylor, the pain of that loss was as fresh today as it was the day he found her collapsed on the floor. The emergency room doctor told him it was a brain aneurysm and tried to assure the blubbering hulk of a man that she went quickly and without pain. Baylor had no cause to doubt him, but the words did little to ease the incredible loss he felt then and still felt.

Every Sunday, Baylor would climb to the very top of Mount Eli to lay a dozen white roses at the grave of his beloved. He would then sit down next to the pale white headstone and talk to his wife about the past week's events. Baylor would share his joys and sorrows with Maddie, carrying on the conversation as though they were sitting next to each other on a park bench. After an hour, Baylor would stand up, shake the dirt from his church pants, and slowly make his way down to the base of the hill where he would climb into his truck and head home.

Baylor's garage was principally his place of work. Every morning, he would don a flannel shirt and well-worn overalls, put on his Chicago Cubs baseball cap and slip on his steel-toed work boots. After feeding his dog Buster, he would make a pot of coffee and take a steaming mug with him to the garage. Working as a blacksmith was lucrative employment these days … after all, he was the only one within a hundred miles of town.

Before doing anything else, Baylor would load coal into the forge and ignite it for the day's firing. Some blacksmiths preferred the gas-powered forges, but Baylor swore by the heat a coal unit would generate. As the fire got hot enough, Baylor would plan out his day's work, laying out pieces of wrought iron and raw steel as inspiration came to him.

Baylor then would grab his trusty tongs and picked up a large slab of iron. He would hold it in the forge until the metal glowed yellow-orange and then slam it on top of the anvil. It didn't take but a moment to bring the heavy hammer down on the softened steel, smashing and shaping it with each swing of his well-muscled arm. With his vast strength, Baylor could easily stretch a one foot piece of wrought iron to two feet in fewer than twelve good strokes.

People who commissioned work from him would watch in amazement as the huge man pulled, bent and shaped plain pieces of metal into unique works of art in a short amount of time. When Baylor had a number of rush projects, he would work well into the dark, sometimes not shutting down the forge until after midnight.

There were days where Baylor had no commissioned work, too. During those rare times, he would search the countryside for scrap steel to take back to his workshop. Sometimes he would drive two or three hundred miles to scavenge fifty pounds of abandoned steel blocks or a truck full of pure galvanized pipe removed during a building remodel.

Once a year, Baylor would trek to the Army surplus store to replenish his tool supply and perhaps pick up new overalls. Old Zeke who owned the place would wait on the big man hand and foot no matter who else was in the store. Baylor's annual trips to his establishment usually meant a big pay day for him. It was worth it to Zeke to make sure his best customer was well tended to.

It wasn't too long after his most recent visit to see Zeke that Baylor became reacquainted with Laura Lawson. Laura was the daughter of Mayor Samuel B. Dawson, the town druggist and the local high school football coach the years Baylor was in school. Despite the fact that he and Laura lived a few miles apart these days, the two never saw each other except occasionally at Sunday worship.

Baylor was hammering heated iron as he usually did, so he didn't hear Laura's car pull into the driveway or the car door slammed. She watched him pound on the anvil for a good fifteen minutes before Baylor took a break and saw her standing at the garage door. For a moment, he didn't recognize her in her John Deere cap. But finally, a glimmer of recognition washed over him when she smiled shyly in his direction.

"Baylor Thompson, you're going to work yourself to death if you keep that up," she giggled as she sidled toward him. Buster rose from his usual place by the forge and trotted over to inspect their guest. After a thorough review, he lay back down again.

"Laura," he replied politely, turning back to his work on the anvil. He paused a moment to wipe sweat from his brow before picking up the iron creation he was forming and inspecting it carefully. He then turned his full attention to her. Baylor's intent gaze amused Laura.

"Now Baylor, don't glare at me like that," she laughed. "I came here because I would like to hire you to make something for me. Do you have time to talk about it now?"

"I guess so."

Baylor resumed his inspection of the hot steel clasped in his tongs. He placed the partially completed work back in the forge and held it there until it reached the right temperature. He then thrust the superheated metal into a large bucket of water, quickly placing the cooled iron on the anvil and hit it several times with the hammer until he was pleased with the shape.

All the time he worked, Laura watched his glistening biceps flex and flinched each time the hammer struck the anvil. Baylor barely noticed her reaction and kept at the work as though she wasn't there.

"So, can we talk now?" Laura asked after hesitating a few minutes. Not hearing a response from Baylor, she walked closer to him and repeated the question.

Baylor turned toward her, causing the skittish woman to jump back two feet. "Sure, let's talk."

Laura described the artwork she had in mind in minute detail. Baylor listened and didn't interrupt her during her entire recitation.

"Can you do it?" Laura finally asked, almost out of breath.

Baylor paused a long time before replying. Finally, he just nodded and returned to his work.

"When can you have it ready?" Laura asked him over her shoulder as she walked back to her car.

Baylor hammered several times, then stopped for a moment to say "Next Saturday." He put the piece back in the forge one last time.

"Okay, see you then."

Laura ran the rest of the way to her car. Baylor could hear her pull out on the road back to town.

That night, Baylor's sleep was disturbed several times by thoughts of Maddie and their time together. They met thanks to Maddie's brother and Baylor best friend, Joseph Walter Benson. J.W., as everyone called him, was to Baylor what silk was to burlap. As a young man, people would say that J.W. was as smooth as Scotch whiskey. It was J.W. who talked Baylor into taking his sister out on a double date with him when they were in high school and it was J.W. who pushed his large friend into popping the big question.

Until Baylor married Maddie, he and J.W. were inseparable. But as it happens when a man weds, friends become secondary, even a friend who also is a brother-in-law. It wasn't like they went their separate ways. Rather, Baylor assumed the role of a loving husband and J.W. continued to play the roving bachelor.

Baylor hadn't seen J.W. since Maddie's funeral. It was too painful for either man to even talk to the other, the memories of the woman they both loved too fresh in their memories. J.W. continued to pursue the pleasures of female companionship to dowse the pain while Baylor retreated within himself. Neither man sought out the other's friendship to try to overcome their mutual loss.

Throughout the long night, Baylor's thoughts continue to turn to Maddie and their all too brief time together. He loved her more than life itself, of that there was no doubt. The sun rose and set in her eyes and in her smile and a mere kind word from her in his direction would be all he would need to meet the day head on.

For brief moments, he could almost see Maddie standing next to his bed, staring down at his prone form. She didn't speak a word to him, but the look on her face showed every bit of her concern. Baylor called out to her, but the specter of his late wife never explained her presence. As the morning sun crept over the horizon, her image faded from his inner sight and he was finally able to get to sleep.

Baylor did not arrive at his workshop until nearly eleven the next morning. Maddie was foremost in his mind since he arose, even more so than the first year he was without her. He missed her so much and would do anything to bring her back, but he knew that she was gone forever. It was just something he would have to learn to live with, no matter how hard it was.

It took Baylor an hour to finish the job he was working on before starting on Laura's project. He checked his wrought iron supply and confirmed he had enough to make the piece she described to him, the largest he ever endeavored. He hauled several pieces from the bin to his work area, then sat down to sketch out the design.

Thirty minutes later, Baylor put the finishing touches on his rough drawing and held it at arm's length to visualize the final product. Satisfied with what he saw, he laid down the sketchpad and closely inspected the candidate pieces of metal he originally selected. He discarded two questionable slabs of iron and replaced them with better choices from the supply bin.

Baylor poured himself into the project, working well into the night to craft the work Laura wanted. When he finally crawled into bed exhausted but pleased with his work, it was close to three in the morning. He slept dreamlessly that night and the rest of the week, the physical effort allowing him to slumber deeper than any time since Maddie died.

Saturday morning arrived and Baylor was just putting the finishing touches on Laura's commission when he heard someone pull into the driveway. He was burnishing the last of the metal when Laura called his name.

"Hi, Baylor, is it ready?" she almost whispered, afraid to startle the man so deeply involved with his work. Buster dutifully ran over to greet their visitor.

Baylor didn't turn to respond, but simply nodded and kept rubbing.

"Hey there, Baylor," a man's voice called out. Baylor stiffened and stopped what he was doing for a moment.

"J.W.," he acknowledged, and then returned to the piece.

"She's beautiful, simply beautiful," Laura gushed, gliding across the garage to where Baylor stood. Before her rose a ten foot tall angel made of shaped wrought iron. Her white wings were spread as though she were about to take off. Over her head hung a halo of bright silver. Her face, though, was the most striking of all. If ever soulless metal could come to life, it could be seen in the golden visage of the angel that stood in their midst.

Baylor did not say a word, but the slight smile on his face showed his satisfaction. He waited for J.W. to say something.

"You remembered to rustproof her?" his brother-in-law asked simply.

"Yeah, I did. Do you have ropes? Baylor asked.

"Got 'em," J.W. replied and walked over to where Laura was standing. Baylor rolled over the flat cart and positioned it. He picked up the angel in one smooth motion and placed her on the conveyance. With J.W.'s help, he steered the loaded cart to the back of the pickup truck that was parked at the garage entrance. Laura climbed onto the truck bed and between the three of them, they wrangled the angel in place. After tying her down, they jumped out and closed the gate.

Laura was beaming. "She's so beautiful, Baylor. How much do we owe you?"

Baylor looked quizzically at Laura for a moment, then J.W.

"We're married," J.W. announced without hesitation. He held his wedding ring up for the big man to inspect. "We just had our one year anniversary."

Baylor opened his mouth to reply, then closed it without a word. Laura saw the downtrodden look on his face and spoke up.

"Baylor, we eloped. J.W. got me pregnant and we ran away to get married."

Baylor looked at her stomach and raised an eyebrow.

"She lost the baby," J.W. explained quietly. Laura glanced away, wiping her eyes.

Baylor nodded. "You don't owe me anything. Call it a belated wedding present."

Laura turned toward him, tears still glistening on her eyelashes, a huge grin on her face. She hugged Baylor happily and ran to the passenger side of the truck. Baylor could see her sobbing quietly as she sat waiting for her husband.

J.W. stuck out his hand and Baylor grasped it firmly. Neither man said a word, but thanks and appreciation were expressed in that single gesture.

Baylor watched the road long after the truck disappeared from sight. Finally, he shuffled back to his garage, Buster close at his heels.

As he cleaned up the workshop, he stopped to glance for the final time at drawing of the angel he crafted. This was the first time that Baylor could remember he was completely immersed in the creative process, right up to the time she was standing proudly in the back of the pickup truck. Now that it was gone, he almost felt bereft. His thoughts immediately turned to his sweet Maddie and for a moment, Baylor wept.

The next morning after church, Baylor made his weekly trek up to Mount Eli, a dozen white roses in hand. After arranging the bouquet, he sat down next to her to talk about the angel he made and how much it reminded him of her. He closed his eyes for a while and thought about his last day with Maddie.

It was an ordinary enough morning. They sat around the small table while they ate breakfast, planning their day. Baylor was busy creating small crafts for Christmas customers, so his thoughts kept drifting out to the garage. At one point, Maddie started to laugh, interrupting Baylor from his reverie.

"Baylor Thompson, are you there?" Maddie teased, refilling his coffee mug.

He smiled sheepishly. "Sorry, dear, you caught me. You know how it is around the holidays."

Maddie nodded, smiling. "I'm just teasing you, you big lug." She stood behind him, placing her arms around him and squeezing tightly. Neither one said a word, but none were needed.

"Okay, get going," Maddie finally said, cleaning up the kitchen table. "Don't forget your coffee."

"Thanks, darling."

He stooped down to kiss her and then headed to the door.

"I'll call you when lunch is ready," Maddie called out as he walked up the driveway.

He waved in response to her and strode to his workshop. Spotting him, Buster stopped digging in the yard and followed.

Hours passed and Baylor processed each piece quickly. During the holidays, the jobs were never large, but there were many of them. Each one was somewhat unique and required a lot of concentration.

It was two o'clock when he realized he hadn't heard Maddie call him for lunch yet. He wiped off his hands and face and ambled back to the house.

"Maddie?" he called when he didn't see her in the kitchen.

"Maddie? Where are you?"

He looked in each room and finally made his way to the master bedroom. There he saw her, sprawled out on the floor. He rushed to her side to check her pulse, but it was barely discernible.

The ambulance arrived twenty minutes later and the EMT immediately started applying CPR on the unconscious woman. Baylor's truck roared behind the speeding vehicle as they raced the twenty miles to the hospital. By the time they reached the ER, there was nothing they could do for her.

The sound of a flock of geese flying overhead stirred him from his thoughts and he opened his eyes. He looked around the cemetery and that's when he spotted her.

Baylor walked quickly down the side of the hill until he stood in front of his angel. It looked so beatific in the morning light, appearing to stand guard over all the town's dead. His eyes drifted down the length of his creation until he saw the tiny gravestone beneath her, engraved simply:

Madeline "Maddie" Laura Benson
Born and died, June 2005
Our Beloved Daughter

The big man stood before his creation and wept for the niece he never knew. He stared into the face of the angel, so calm and gentle, looking into the distance and immediately felt peace. After a moment, his eyes followed where the angel's gaze was focused and saw that it faced the very top of Mount Eli, where a dozen white roses could be seen in front of a pale white tombstone.

Baylor finally understood. He slowly walked back to his truck, prepared to start living again.

A Touch of Madness

Love is, first, a touch of madness,
A quaking desire filling the spirit,
With unimagined sensation that begins in the soul.

Love extends far beyond romance,
Simple intimacy or unrequited longing,
Its depths can never be imagined nor surpassed.

Love exceeds the bounds of language,
Mere words are diminished by its power,
A force that cannot be contained nor understood.

Love starts with the closeness of two,
There is no end, just more beginnings,
It is the unbroken circle, where you and I are joined.

Prized Possession

"All I asked is why not?"

Constance did not even look at her son this time before replying. "Because, my dear boy, I'm your mother and I said so."

In a heartbeat, Tyler was transformed into a seething mass of teenaged angst, his face turning bright crimson. Why did he have to beg every time he wanted the old lady to cough up some cash? Hell, it wasn't like she couldn't afford it!

"And before you explode and say something you'll regret again, let me remind you I've heard it all before, Tyler. I will not be moved on this point, no way, no how!" Constance closed the book she was reading with a snap.

Tyler stomped in front his mother to launch the first salvo in his latest tirade.

"Mother, you are such a b--"

"Tut, tut, my friend, I would watch both your language and your tone with me. Remember that I'm the one who gives you that generous allowance you burn through every week. I can very easily cut back to something more appropriate for a brat, er, I mean, a young man your age."

Constance stood up and walked to the nearby liquor cabinet. She poured two fingers of Royal Salute and returned to the sofa. Smiling humorlessly, she continued to observe Tyler's evolving fit of pique.

"Damn it, Mother!" Tyler screamed, kicking the ottoman and making it fly. The stool landed on the hearth, causing the sleeping Llasa Apso to jump out of the way before becoming part of the kindling.

"Enough, you ungrateful little monster! Get out of here this minute or I swear I will not only stop giving you any money, but I'll make it so you don't get a dime of it after I'm gone!"

Tyler stood defiantly before her, but did not utter a word.

"Good, I'm glad we have an understanding now." Constance smirked and took a long swallow of her drink. She knew exactly how to manage this ingrate, she thought to herself. Just like his father, damn him to hell.

The teenager stormed out of the room, glancing back only once. When he saw she wasn't looking, he took the chance of extending his middle finger in her direction.

"I saw that!" Constance advised and walked back to the liquor cabinet for a refresher. She chuckled as she took another sip.

Tyler bounded up the stairs to his bedroom, slamming the door behind him. In two quick motions, he had his stereo blaring and the door locked.

Guns n' Roses blasted from the quad speakers and soon Tyler was air guitaring to "Welcome to the Jungle," kicking any small object in his path to the other side of the room. Damn her, he thought angrily to himself, giving the fake guitar a mighty strum.

His phone rang. Tyler jumped on the bed and checked the caller ID before answering.

"Talk to me!" he shouted into the receiver.

"Tyler, dude! What's going on?"

"Jaybird, how's it hanging?" Tyler rolled off the bed and sat on the floor, his back against the door.

"Hey, what are you doing tonight?" Jay asked him. "Besides listening to tunes."

"Just mixing it up with the old lady, that's all," Tyler replied. "I can't get her to cave on that car."

"Sorry to hear that, dude. I mean, your mom's rich, isn't she?"

"You've seen our house, what do you think?" Tyler took off his boots and tossed them in the opposite corner, watching as each one left a black mark on the wall.

"Yeah, she is. Too bad she doesn't want to float you a loan on this one."

Tyler stood up and turned the volume up on the stereo. The sounds of "Smells Like Teen Spirit" filled the room.

"Nirvana! Alright" Jay cried.

"Loan? Who wants a loan? I want her to give me the money, bro."

"Sure, that's good, too. Whatever."

"Yeah, whatever."

"Anyway, do you want to go out tonight? I hear that C.W. is having a party at his house and anyone can crash it as long as they bring beer."

Tyler stood up and stood in front of his open closet. "Will Kerri be there?" he asked hopefully.

"She may be, dude, I don't know. We won't know unless we go."

Tyler paused for a moment. Kerri Morgan was this week's love of his life, especially when she wore that leather miniskirt last Monday.

"Sure, I'll go. What time can you pick me up?"

"Make it nine, okay? I gotta wait until my old man's in bed before I borrow some of his beer."

"We don't have any beer here," Tyler said. "My mother only drinks the hard stuff and believe me, she'd know if even a drop was missing."

Jay laughed. "No problem, bro, I gotcha covered. You can catch me on the next one."

"You da man, dawg," Tyler replied.

"Yeah, yeah, save that for your 'homies'!"

Tyler laughed. "See you at nine."

He hung up the phone and continued browsing through his closet for something decent to wear. Kerri was fine, probably too fine for him. He needed to have kick ass gear for this chick!

At 8:50, Tyler padded quietly down the long staircase to the study. He peeked in and saw his mother fast asleep in the big easy chair in front of the fireplace, the dog curled up in her lap. The room was bathed in the pleasant scent of burning wood mixed with expensive scotch.

Tyler watched his mother for a solid five minutes, but she didn't stir at all. Instead, he could vaguely hear her raspy snores, the Waterford crystal goblet she had been drinking from was now standing empty on the serving table next to her. He closed the door to the study and made his way to the front door.

"Dude!" Jay shouted as Tyler piled into his friend's BMW.

"Let's get this party *started*!" Tyler shouted at the top of his lungs. Jay peeled out and snaked quickly down the long driveway, merging into traffic with barely a pause.

It didn't take them more than twenty minutes to get to C.W. Dennison's house. C.W. was the class president and top jock at their school. Both Jay and Tyler knew C.W. from their grade school days, but now that they were in high school, the popular boy barely gave them a passing nod in the hallways.

Jay pulled his BMW in front of the large house, taking a moment to pull two sacks of beer out of the back seat before joining Tyler in the front yard.

"How are we going to do this, bud?" Tyler asked Jay, a little nervous about crashing a party of popular kids - and seeing Kerri, too.

"Let's just walk in and see if anyone stops us," Jay suggested. "Whatever you do, though, look like you belong. Confidence is key in this game, dude."

"Fine, I'm confident," Tyler muttered and followed Jay through the front door.

As soon as they entered the house, they were assaulted by the loudest music they ever heard in anyone's home. All around them they saw nothing but attractive boys and girls talking and dancing with each other. Almost everyone they saw was carrying a beer bottle or a wine cooler.

"Tammi, hey there!" Jay said, waving to a cute brunette standing next to coffee table in the living room. The girl raised her hand a reluctant greeting, then turned back to the two girls she was talking to.

"Smooth move," Tyler said under his breath, poking his friend in the ribs.

"Yeah, yeah, she wants me," Jay laughed. "Come on, let's drop this beer off somewhere."

After a couple of wrong turns and directions from one of the other guests, they found the kitchen. With the refrigerator already stuffed full of drinks, they put their donation on an open space on the kitchen counter, each taking a beer for himself before leaving to mingle.

"Dude, do you believe it? We crashed C.W.'s party and no one has even called us on it yet," Jay whispered to Tyler. Tyler grinned, but did not reply. His attention was focused on the sea of short skirts and primped hair in front of him.

Jay headed toward a crowd of kids they knew and Tyler followed him, half paying attention to two pretty girls that greeted them. Tonight, he only had eyes for Kerri, but that didn't mean he couldn't be friendly.

Three beers later, Tyler was amazingly friendly and already slurring his words, repeating everything he said at least twice. Without warning, he jumped on the nearby leather sofa and started dancing to "Fergalicious," pumping his fists in the air like a psychotic prizefighter.

"Dude, you better get done before C.W. finds out you're totally trashing his couch," Jay pleaded, looking around for the burly junior. Tyler was not to be reasoned with and danced with even more abandon when Prince's "Let's Go Crazy" blared from the Bose speakers hanging from every wall.

"Tyler, get down! Here comes C.W.!" Jay warned under his breath, but it was too late. C.W. spotted Tyler from across the room and strode purposefully to face him.

"C.W., my man, how are you?" Jay said, trying to distract the teen. C.W. ignored him and instead, aimed a steely gaze at Tyler. Tyler ignored him and continued dancing like a madman all over the expensive brown sofa.

"Hey! You! Get down on the floor! Now!" C.W. shouted up at Tyler, who continued to gyrate arhythmically up and down the leather cushions.

Unhappy that he was being ignored, C.W. pulled Tyler down to the floor by his belt. That didn't stop the drunk teen. He continued his out of control movements through the living room on his way to the kitchen. C.W. caught up with him and escorted him none to gently to the front door.

Turning to Jay, C.W. asked, "Are you okay to drive?" Jay just nodded.

"Fine, then take your jerk friend home. Some guys can't handle their beer and obviously, Tyler Lawson falls into that group."

The door slammed in Jay's face. He turned to find Tyler and saw him about to urinate on the rose bushes in front of the house. A gaggle of teenagers watched him and were visibly disappointed when Jay pulled Tyler away from the flowers before the show started.

"You totally messed up tonight, Tyler," Jay said, shaking his head as they walked to the BMW. "You're never going to hear the end of it at school on Monday."

Tyler stood before Jay's car, holding onto the vehicle's side to keep from falling over. He didn't answer, but was obviously upset.

"You're not going to puke in my car, are you?" Jay asked. "Because if you are, you can just walk home."

Tyler burped loudly. "Nah, I'm not going to puke. Let's just get going."

The teens got into the car and slowly pulled away from the front of the house. Tyler stared up at the house for a moment, hoping that he wouldn't see Kerri watching his graceless exit.

"Dude, you are so hammered!" Jay said, laughing hysterically. "I've never seen you dance before, but tonight, you were *en fuego*, my friend."

Tyler chuckled, and then burped loudly a second time. Jay burst out in another gale of laughter.

The boys didn't speak much the rest of the ride until they got to Tyler's house.

"Dude, do you think Kerri saw me acting like an idiot?" Tyler asked his friend.

"Tyler, listen to me. If she didn't see you out there, she's already heard about it from everybody else. No use hoping you can slide on this one, bud. But we both know memories are short and some day, this whole night will be forgotten."

"Yeah, but I might as well start forgetting Kerri Morgan now, I guess."

Jay looked over at Tyler. "Look, are you going to mope around the next month like the last time? If so, then let's cut to the chase and find you another girl to fall in love with. I don't think I can take another depressing month of Tyler Lawson dragging his butt through the school halls like a whipped dog."

Tyler looked up at the other teen, and then laughed out loud. Soon Jay joined in and patted his friend on the back.

"See you Monday, stud," Jay shouted out the car window and took off with a lurch down the street. Tyler waved and trudged to the house to face his mother. With any luck, she would still be out cold and he could sneak up to his room without her knowing.

Unfortunately, Tyler's luck wasn't about to improve. He opened the front door only to find Constance standing behind it, her hands on her hips.

"Tyler Vincent Lawson, where the hell have you been?"

"I'm tired, I'm going to bed," he mumbled as he tried to shoulder past her. She stepped in front of him to block his exit.

"I asked you, young man, where were you tonight?"

Instead of answering, Tyler burped in her face. A blast of semi-digested beer wafted in her direction, causing Constance to almost retch from the smell.

"Drinking? You're drinking now?" she screamed, waving her hand in front of her face to clear the air.

"Drinking? You're drinking now?" Tyler echoed, mimicking her voice, his hands also on his hips. "Look, Mother, you shouldn't be the one criticizing me about drinking. When I left tonight, you were half in the bag yourself!"

Constance stared at him, mouth agape. "How *dare* you, you insolent little brat! How *dare* you talk to your mother that way - or compare your teenage beer bashing with my adult and legal consumption of spirits!

Tyler stood sullenly, but didn't reply. Constance watched him as he swayed in place, shaking her head.

"You're pathetic, you know that, Tyler? You're as useless as your father was! At least when I met him, he was still good for something."

"Yeah, until you used him up and threw him aside," Tyler sneered.

Constance sputtered. "Get upstairs and go to bed *now*, young man! We'll discuss this further in the morning when you're sober!"

"And when you are, too," Tyler retorted and walked quickly past her to the stairwell. She watched him ascend the staircase, her face flushed in anger.

She weaved her way back to the study and quickly fixed herself a fresh drink. The bottle of Royal Salute was almost empty. Throwing all caution to the wind, she drank the remainder straight from the bottle, then picked up the full glass and walked back to her chair by the fire.

Tyler didn't even bother taking off his clothes before falling flat on his back in bed. He lay there for only few moments, the patterned ceiling spinning crazily in front of him. Too exhausted to get out of bed, he soon fell asleep.

§

Neither Constance nor Tyler got up until early afternoon. Tyler was the first to emerge from his room, his head pounding incessantly. He stumbled into the kitchen and pulled the big bottle of aspirin from the cupboard. Shaking four of the tablets into his hand, he reached into the refrigerator for a cold bottle of water to wash them down.

Constance stepped slowly into the kitchen, every footfall agonizingly painful from her toes to her hair. She ignored Tyler standing in front of her and instead, poured herself a large mugful of hot coffee.

After several noisy sips, she sat down at her usual place and began to browse the Wall Street Journal's weekend edition. Tyler watched her as she flipped pages.

"Good morning, Ms. Lawson," greeted the housekeeper sarcastically. "May I make you some breakfast now?"

"Just dry wheat toast for me, Maria, thank you," Constance replied. She took another sip of coffee and forced the hot liquid down her throat.

"Nothing for me, Maria," Tyler said to the maid, who just looked at him, wrinkling her nose in disgust. Constance took note of the exchange and chuckled.

"What?" Tyler demanded, standing in front of his mother.

"Oh, nothing, Tyler, not a single blessed thing," Constance said, still amused. "But if I were you, I would be treading lightly around me this morning. Your little escapade last night exceeded even your limits of misbehavior and you were already on my last good nerve when you left here, if you recall."

Tyler opened his mouth to argue, but seeing the warning look in Constance's eyes, he thought better of it and hurried out of the room. Constance chuckled again, shaking her aching head.

Tyler headed upstairs and limped into the shower. He turned on the water as hot as he could stand and stood under the stream, letting the steam clear his head. After thirty minutes, he almost felt human again and got out to dry himself.

"Tyler, get down here! Now!" called Constance. Tyler involuntarily shuddered at the sound of her voice, but dutifully finished getting dressed and went downstairs. His mother was waiting for him in the sitting room.

"Tyler, I think it's time we had a serious discussion about the future - *your* future," she began, patting the seat next to her. Tyler dropped on the cushion and crossed his arms in front of him, preparing for another long lecture.

"No, Tyler, I'm not going to berate you at length this time," Constance began, smirking. "I think the time for speeches is over, don't you? After all, you're going to turn eighteen in a few months and then you're legally free to leave here."

Tyler perked up as he heard her words and for the first time in a long time in her presence, he smiled broadly.

"Yes, yes, I thought you'd like the sound of that," his mother said, taking sip of coffee. "However, I think we need to talk about your future anyway."

"I'm listening," Tyler said jovially, already preparing to hear how much money his mother was going to give him to start him out.

"Here are your options as I see them, Tyler," Constance continued. "First, you could go to college, but frankly, both your grades and attitude have shown you really aren't college material. Over the years, I hired tutors for you, paid for expensive coaching classes and just about anything else I could do to put you on a level playing field with the other students in your class, but nothing has worked. Do you agree?"

Tyler thought a minute, trying to discern if this was a trick question. Finally, he nodded his assent.

"Good, I'm glad we see things the same way," Constance said, smiling. "Now, your second option would be some sort of junior college, or maybe even a trade school. Something that would enhance your natural skills. By the way, dear boy, what are your natural skills?"

The question flummoxed Tyler for more than a few minutes. I'm really good at making people laugh, he thought.

"I guess people think I'm pretty funny. I could work to be a comedian or something," he offered tentatively.

Constance laughed vigorously. "Yes, you do make people laugh, Tyler. Perhaps not for the reasons you think, of course, but you do make them laugh. You certainly make me laugh."

Tyler didn't know whether she was yanking his chain, but he wasn't too happy with her reaction.

"There, there, son, there's no reason to scrunch your face up like that, it's unbecoming," Constance chided gently. "No, it's certainly possible you could pursue a career in stand-up comedy or even acting. One thing you do have going for you is you have your father's personality and he was always the life of the party."

At the mention of his father, Tyler winced. He knew the man was an alcoholic and was only funny when he was falling over furniture in a drunken stupor. He may have been the life of the party, but he never was conscious long enough to enjoy the accolades.

Constance watched her son's face and could almost guess what he was thinking. Conjuring up his father's image was calculated on her part, but in her mind, all's fair in love, war and raising children.

"The third thing I can suggest is that you start a business. In what, I don't know. If you were going to start a business, Tyler, what would it be?"

Tyler looked at his mother in surprise, but didn't answer. A business? He never really even thought about a business before. Heck, what was he interested in that would make money anyway? Girls? Cars? Parties?

"Maybe I could be a party planner!" he said brightly. "Yeah, that would combine all of my interests and could make me some serious money!"

Constance paused. Just what the world needs is another party planner, she thought to herself wryly. She stood up and walked toward the study. Tyler followed her to her big mahogany desk.

"Let's just see about that idea," Constance said as she started typing on the computer keyboard. After a few Google hits, they found a site that displayed party planners throughout the US and Canada. In Los Angeles alone, there were almost 300 listings.

"Well, Tyler, there's your competition. You'll be starting out from square one while the rest of these people are already out there, making money - or maybe not. Any idea how you're going to stand above the crowd?"

This conversation was getting too complicated for Tyler, especially since he was still hung over from the night before.

Constance noted her son's sullen look. "Oh, I'm sorry, Tyler, did I say something to upset you?" Constance said, smiling. "I wasn't sure if you were ready for such a grown-up talk today, but I figured that since you're out drinking with your friends until all hours, you're ready to discuss things rationally like an adult does."

"Why are you doing this, Mother?" he mumbled without enthusiasm.

"Me? I'm just concerned about your future, Tyler. I had hoped you were equally concerned. I mean, you didn't think you were going to live here for the rest of your life, having my servants cater to your every whim, did you?"

A cold sneer was evident on the woman's face. Tyler had seen that look many times before, but it always was directed at his father. His poor, broken down father, God rest his soul. Tyler began to weep.

"Crying now? Is that a pathetic bid to get my sympathy, Tyler? Please, you can come up with something more creative than that, can't you?" Constance smirked and handed him a Kleenex. "Here, use this. I don't want you getting snot all over my desk."

Instead of taking the proffered tissue, Tyler wiped his nose on his shirtsleeve and stared angrily at his mother. Constance shrugged and put the box down.

"So, my almost grown-up son, what will you decide? I'm all atwitter thinking about the new life ahead of you."

Tyler stood up and headed toward the door.

"Hold on a minute, young man, not so fast. You're not getting away with your little party episode that easily. You're not to leave the house the rest of the weekend. No television, no telephone, no nothing. In fact, I'm going to have Henry pull those things out of your room just to make sure."

Tyler's face turned red, but he did not respond. Constance stood up and walked over to him.

"Since I'm going away next week - without you, as you know - we'll continue this conversation tomorrow night. In the meantime, please spend your alone time trying to get your homework done. And if you have the time, dear, think about your life. I look forward to some creative answers after Sunday dinner. You may leave now."

Tyler stormed out of the room and ran upstairs. He slammed his bedroom door behind him, knocking over several untouched books from the shelf. Burying his head in his pillow, he began to sob uncontrollably.

All I wanted was a car, he thought to himself. And now I have to decide what I want to do with my life in less than forty-eight hours.

"It's not *fair*!" he screamed at the top of his lungs. His voice echoed against the four walls. He heard a knock on his door.

"Who is it?" he sobbed.

"Master Tyler, sir, it's Henry, sir. I've been instructed to remove certain, er, entertainment items from your room. May I enter?" called the prim voice from the hallway.

Tyler wiped his eyes and opened the door. The manservant walked in, somewhat hesitantly.

"I'm sorry about this, sir," Henry said meekly, gathering up the video games and other portable devices in a box he brought with him. He unplugged the television, disconnected the stereo and removed the telephone from the wall and stacked them in the hallway. Henry returned and removed power cord from the computer, leaving the equipment in place.

"Is there anything I missed, sir?" Henry asked gently, standing before Tyler at relaxed attention.

Tyler didn't answer, but only shrugged his shoulders. Satisfied, Henry walked out of the room, closing the door behind him without another word.

§

The hours until Sunday evening were agonizing for Tyler. He spent the entire time in his bedroom, only coming out for meals that he ate alone. His homework occupied his attention for a couple of hours, but beyond that, he was bored out of his mind.

Finally, when he didn't think he could take the wait anymore, he heard his mother calling him on the intercom. He steeled himself before leaving and headed downstairs to face whatever was coming.

Henry walked Tyler to the study where he found Constance sitting demurely on the sofa, sipping a glass of brandy. She patted the seat next to her, but Tyler remained standing.

"Already defiant, are we?" she asked her son, smiling pleasantly.

"No, I've been sitting down all day," Tyler replied, crossing his arms over his chest.

"Fine, have it your way then," she agreed. "So, your future is on tonight's docket, Tyler. Let's hear what you've been thinking about."

Tyler took a deep breath before speaking. A lot was riding on this approach, a calculated gamble no matter how one looked at it.

"Well, Mother, I did spend quite a bit of time thinking about my future and everything we talked about yesterday morning. You're right, I'm not much of a student and I really don't think I am college material, at least right now."

Constance nodded. "Yes, go on."

"Well, about trade school," Tyler continued, "I don't have much that a trade school could work with. That much is true." He looked at his mother for any sign of acceptance, but saw nothing in her vacant eyes.

"So, I was mostly thinking about starting a business. I realized that being a party planner - or having any business - is an empty dream unless I get the right schooling. Not a college or anything - we both know that would be a failure. But some sort of school that would teach me the basics of running a small business."

"You mean a trade school that teaches business administration?" Constance offered.

"Yeah, something like that. I mean, I may not have the smarts other kids have, but one thing I have is a mother who would help me set up a business. That is, provided I applied myself to my studies and worked hard after school to learn the business world."

Tyler looked at his mother directly, hoping he hadn't overplayed his hand. If he had, Constance's face didn't show it.

"Is that all?" she asked him.

"Yes, that's pretty much it," Tyler managed to squeak out, shuffling his feet nervously.

Constance stood up and walked over to refill her glass.

"Well, Tyler, you exceeded my expectations. While I never expected you to present me a solid plan tonight, I also never thought you would give me a somewhat coherent approach to establishing yourself as you did. I give you a lot of credit for that."

Tyler examined her face for signs of sarcasm, but saw none. He began to relax.

"However, I'm afraid you may have assumed too much," she continued.

Tyler gulped nervously, but didn't reply.

"You see, you're right in saying that your mother would help set you up in business should you ever get far enough along for that to be a worthwhile investment."

Tyler nodded hopefully.

"But there is the matter of this business school you're aspiring to attend. How do you expect to pay for that?"

Tyler raised his eyebrows. "Wouldn't you --"

"No, not necessarily, my dear son. At least not right now, that is. Your high school record hasn't convinced me that paying for any kind of school for you right now is a good use of my money. You understand what I'm saying?"

"Yes, I guess so," Tyler replied without enthusiasm.

"Good, I'm glad we see eye to eye on this," Constance said pleasantly.

"So how am I going to get the money to go to business school?"

"By work, my dear, by honest work … with your hands, your head, your body. Whatever it takes, whatever you can do. You're going to scratch and earn every penny, scrimp and save until you're able to afford to put yourself through school."

Constance peered into her son's eyes. "You are going to bust your ass like your father busted his to get as far as he did … that is, until the booze finally killed him. Do you hear what I'm saying?"

Tyler nodded his head, but deep down, he was scared out of his mind. Constance easily picked up on that.

"Yes, I know you're scared, Tyler. We're all scared when we go out into that big world with little more than a dream to our name."

"You mean you're not going to even give me a little money to start out?" he asked her incredulously.

Constance smirked. "Oh, I'll give you a couple of thousand to make sure you have money for a security deposit and some basics to furnish your first apartment. But that's all, my friend."

Tyler looked at her disbelievingly. "What about a car? I need something to go to work in!"

"There's always the bus, Tyler. That's what working people do, they take the bus. I'm sure it will do you some good, learning the ins and outs of the Los Angeles bus system." Constance let out a little laugh and took a deep swallow of her brandy.

I can't believe this, Tyler thought to himself. A bus? Is she crazy?

"Damn it, Mother!" he shouted, taking her by surprise.

"Watch your language, young man," Constance warned, taking a step away from him.

"Look, it's bad enough you're kicking me out of the house and you're giving me a couple thousand dollars to start me out when you're worth millions, but to at least not let me buy a reliable car to get around in just isn't fair!" Tyler spat.

"Oh, cut the melodrama, Tyler," Constance said with a wave of her hand. "I'm not kicking you out, I'm merely encouraging you to start your adult life on your own instead of being under your mommy's protection. I'm just trying to toughen you up since you don't have a father to do that."

Tyler didn't respond. Instead he walked over to the fireplace and stared into the glowing embers.

"Another thing I guess I should tell you, Tyler," Constance said, walking back to the couch. "I recently changed my will."

"Your will?" Tyler echoed, not looking at her.

"Yes, my will. This will affect you, so you better pay attention."

Tyler walked back to the couch and sat down next to her.

"Good," she said. "Right now, my will stipulates that the house, furniture, all the artwork and sculptures and the majority of my investment and cash assets go to St. Jude's Hospital. You've heard of them, right?"

Tyler's face turned a ghostly white. He could barely nod his assent.

"Yes, St. Jude's," Constance repeated. "That doesn't mean I've forgotten you, though."

Tyler looked up hopefully.

"I've set up a trust for you should I die before you turn thirty-five," Constance continued. There is currently $50,000 in the trust, an amount I'll increase by $25,000 every five years."

"Wait," Tyler interrupted. "Are you saying that I won't see a dime of that until I turn thirty-five?"

"Tyler, you certainly catch on fast," Constance chuckled. "I guess when it comes to money, you and your father are quite a bit alike."

Tyler suddenly stood up. "Thirty-five? Are you crazy, old woman?" he screamed.

Constance looked up at him, quite amused. "Yes, I'm crazy, Tyler. If I really was fully sane, I'd bequeath you nothing - not one thin dime, in fact. However, my attorneys advise me that if I don't do something, you'd have grounds to challenge my will. Even though I'm sure my estate is unassailable, I don't want to put St. Jude's through a protracted lawsuit for money I want them to have."

"What does that mean?" Tyler demanded, angry and confused.

"It means this, my dear boy. You are getting the bare minimum my attorneys tell me will prevent you from offering one word of objection that a court would entertain. I made sure that thirty-five was a proper age, too, especially when in the will, I explain exactly why the trust will not be distributed until then."

Tyler looked at her with something akin to hatred. Constance could read this in his eyes and for a moment, she was fearful of her own son.

"One last thing, Tyler," Constance said, taking a sip of brandy. "If my death is not clearly a natural one, if there is any question whether I met my demise prematurely, the trust will be dissolved and whatever you were going to get will go to St. Jude's as well. That would leave you with nothing."

Tyler opened his mouth to object, and then realized it wouldn't make any difference. He began to leave the room.

"By the way, Tyler, I'm flying to West Palm Beach tomorrow. Henry has to visit his mother and none of the other servants want to take care of you. I can't say that I blame them, to be honest."

"What, you're going to leave me here all alone?" Tyler asked snidely.

"No, of course not," Constance said. "You're going to have to stay with your great-aunt Lucille."

"Aunt Lucille?" Tyler repeated. "She's, like, a hundred years old."

Constance laughed. "No, silly boy, she's only sixty-five. She lives alone, the poor thing, but she could use some help around the house. Help that a strapping boy of seventeen can provide."

Tyler looked dejected.

"Oh, chin up, Tyler, a little hard work won't kill you, trust me," Constance joked. "You better go upstairs to pack. Henry will be dropping you off there in about an hour."

Tyler trudged half-heartedly out of the room and up the stairs. Aunt Lucille, he thought to himself. This was going to be the worst week ever!

Promptly at nine o'clock, there was a knock at his bedroom door. Henry was standing before it, his driving hat perched jauntily on his balding head.

"Master Tyler, are you ready to depart?" he asked properly, looking into the room for the teen's suitcase.

"Yeah, I guess so, Henry," Tyler replied, dragging his duffle bag from the bed.

"Shall I take that, sir?" Henry asked him politely.

"No, it's okay, Henry, it's too heavy for you," Tyler said and followed the manservant down the stairs.

Constance stood by the front door as they approached.

"Do give Aunt Lucille my love, dear, won't you?" Constance asked, smiling slightly.

Tyler didn't answer, but instead, walked right by her and out the front door.

"Good-bye, Tyler, see you in a week," she called out to him, but if he heard her, he didn't give any indication.

Soon, the Bentley was pulling away from the front door and down Nottingham Drive. Constance closed the door, chuckling at her poor son's plight.

§

Aunt Lucille was very happy to see him. She led him to a tiny bedroom to the rear of the small house. The closet was empty and ready for him to hang his clothes, she explained.

"Thanks, Aunt Lucille," Tyler mumbled. "Oh, my mother wanted me to send her love."

"That's nice, dear. Your mother's always so sweet," Aunt Lucille beamed. It took all Tyler's willpower not to roll his eyes in response as he began to unpack his things.

"I'll leave you to get settled in, then," Aunt Lucille said to him. "When you're ready, come out and join me for a cup of tea."

Tyler finished unpacking and inspected the nearby bathroom. The vanity tiles were pink as were the walls and floor. Rose appliqués decorated the bathtub and to top it all off, rose scent wafted from a floral-shaped air freshener.

"You really like roses, don't you?" Tyler called down the hall, but heard no response. He walked into the living room and saw his aunt reading in a chair.

"Did you say something?" she asked, turning up her hearing aid.

"Never mind, it was nothing." Tyler looked around and saw the only place to sit was an afghan covered sofa. He eased into it and looked at her.

"Would you like some tea now?" she said. "It's getting kind of late, so I think I'll pass or I'll never sleep tonight."

Tyler shook his head. "Nah, not tonight for me either," he told her. He looked longingly at the blank television set.

"I'd offer to let you watch T.V., but it's been broken for a long time now and I never got around to getting it fixed," she explained. "You know, I really don't miss it. I spend my nights reading and that's all I need anymore."

"That's all?"

"Oh, I guess an occasional dish of ice cream. There's some in the freezer if you'd like," she said.

"Yes, ice cream would be great, thanks," Tyler answered, bounding from the sofa toward the kitchen.

"Would you like some, too?" he called to her.

"No thanks, I'm not very hungry tonight," she said. Tyler looked in the freezer until he saw the carton of vanilla. Better this than nothing, he thought as he scooped a serving from the container into a small bowl.

He walked into the living room, spoon already in his mouth.

"You like ice cream then?" Aunt Lucille asked him, looking pleased. Tyler nodded his head vigorously and sat back down on the sofa.

"Would you like a book to read, Tyler?"

Tyler shrugged his shoulders and swallowed a spoonful. "Sure, what you do you have?"

"Well, I have the Miss Marple stories. You've heard of Agatha Christie, right?" she asked him.

"Yeah, I guess so," Tyler said politely, but he really wasn't sure he had.

"Agatha Christie wrote wonderful mysteries and Miss Marple was the character in many of her books who solved them. Are you interested in trying one on for size?"

Tyler thought about it a moment. "No, I don't think so, Aunt Lucille. I'm a little tired tonight, so I'm going to head off to bed now. I hope you don't mind."

"Certainly not, dear, I understand. Good night, then," his aunt said to him, turning back to her book.

"Yeah, good night," Tyler responded, leaving the empty ice cream dish on the coffee table.

Despite how tired he was, Tyler did not fall asleep right away. His mother's harsh words kept ringing in his ears, over and over again. He always thought he was going to inherit everything from her and now he finds out she's going to give away almost all her assets to some charity.

Tyler tossed and turned all night long, his head full of vivid dreams of his living in a ramshackle apartment without even enough money for food. At six in the morning, he awoke with a start. For a moment, he was confused about where he was, and then remembered.

Aunt Lucille was already busy in the kitchen when he trudged out of the bedroom.

"Good morning, Tyler," she greeted him cheerfully. "I hope you were able to sleep okay last night."

"Morning," Tyler managed to say and sat down at the table. He rubbed his eyes until they turned red.

"Oh my, I'm afraid you didn't get much rest, did you?" Aunt Lucille asked him, concerned.

"No, I never sleep very well in a strange bed, at least at first," Tyler explained. "I'll be okay, though."

"Good, good," she said, pulling a hot frying pan from the stove. "I hope you like pancakes and sausage, because that's what's for breakfast."

Tyler nodded and watched her place the food in his dish. He began to eat, taking his time between bites.

"Now, is that any way for a teenage boy to eat?" she scolded him. "I thought all of you were just mouths on two legs!"

Tyler chuckled in spite of himself and dug in, mostly to please his aunt. She meant well and she was kind enough to take him in while his mother went gallivanting all over the state of Florida.

"That's more like it!" she observed approvingly. "You need a full stomach before you tackle those books at school today."

Tyler groaned inwardly at the word. How can I show my face there today, he wondered. Aunt Lucille noticed his hesitance.

"Something going on at school you want to talk about?"

"Oh, not really, Aunt Lucille. School just doesn't thrill me, that's all," Tyler replied.

"Well, you probably get that from our side of the family, I'm afraid," she said solemnly. "None of us were very good students. That's okay, though, not everyone has to go to college to be successful."

"Aunt Lucille?"

"Yes, dear?"

"What did Uncle Jim do for a living?" he asked her.

"My Jim? Oh, he was a great salesman, that man. He would buy and sell used things from all over the place," his aunt said, smiling at the memory of her late husband.

"Where would he find stuff to buy?"

"Oh, all kinds of places, I guess. Sometimes from junk stores and sometimes from estate sales. It all depended."

"Estate sales?"

"Yes. That's when somebody dies and the family wants to sell all that person's worldly goods ... at least the ones they don't want to keep for themselves, that is." Aunt Lucille helped herself to another sausage.

Tyler looked at her, somewhat perplexed. "Who would want to buy a dead person's old junk?"

Aunt Lucille laughed. "Well, Tyler, they say one man's trash is another man's treasure. Some people can find a lot of good in other people's old stuff. It doesn't have to be just old stuff that's sold at estate sales, you know. All kinds of possessions can be found at them."

Tyler thought a minute. "How would he find out about them?"

"From the newspapers mostly," she replied. "There's always a section in the newspaper that tells you where the estate sales are being held. These days, I'm sure people find out about them on the computer."

"Oh dear, look at the time!" Aunt Lucille said suddenly, looking at the clock over the stove. "Here we are lollygagging and you have to get ready for school. Finish your breakfast and get a move on."

After wolfing down the rest of breakfast, Tyler rushed out of the kitchen and down to his bathroom. He didn't have time to take a shower, so he washed his face and brushed his teeth as fast as he could.

"Tyler, you'd better hurry, dear!" his aunt called from the front door. Tyler raced out of the bedroom, putting on his jacket as he ran down the hall. He followed his aunt to her car and got into the passenger seat.

It took them over a half of an hour to get to school, just before the first bell rang. Tyler got out of the car, and then paused.

"Aunt Lucille, I'll get a ride back to your house after school with my friend Jay, okay?" he asked her.

"Okay, dear, just don't stay too late," she said. He nodded, closing the car door behind him. She slowly pulled away from the curb.

"Tyler! Dude!" Jay greeted him, slapping his friend on the back. "You decided to show your face here today?"

"Yeah, I guess," Tyler said, turning red in embarrassment.

"Hey, bud, don't sweat it. We all do stupid things. Besides, I bet no one even remembers what happened."

Tyler shrugged and walked to the school door with Jay a couple of steps behind him.

"Hey there, stud," Clovis Santone said in a mocking voice. "You really know how to hold your beer, don't you?"

Tyler ignored her and walked to his homeroom.

"Watch it or I'll have you arrested for a DDWI - dork dancing while intoxicated," teased Henry Meecham at the classroom door.

"Go to hell," Tyler muttered, shuffling to his seat. He avoided looking at Kerri, but he could tell she was staring at him along with everyone else. They watched as he sunk lower and lower in his chair.

"Class, come to order, please," Mr. Gambino announced. He walked to the whiteboard and began writing.

At the end of first period, Tyler grabbed Jay by the arm and led him outside.

"Dude, come on, I don't want to be late for the next class. Mrs. Tobias is giving us a pop quiz, I think," Jay said urgently.

"Never mind about that. I got something to ask you," Tyler whispered.

"What is it?" Jay said, looking suspiciously at his friend.

"How would you like it if I told you I have an idea to make some serious cash today?" Tyler looked at Jay to gauge his reaction.

"Cash? How much are we talking about?" Jay asked, obviously interested.

"Let's just say enough to fill your gas tank for the rest of the school year … plus a little extra," Tyler said with a grin.

"Okay, I'll bite. What's the deal?"

"Just meet me at my house at lunch. I'll tell you about it then."

The two went off in their separate directions, Jay to his class, Tyler to the school library.

At twelve-thirty on the nose, Jay pulled in front of Tyler's house and ran up to the door. Tyler was waiting for him as soon as he stepped on the welcome mat.

"So, what's this great idea, man?" Jay asked him. Tyler only waved him into the house. Together they walked into the study.

Jay looked all around in surprise. "What the h--?"

Tyler started laughing as he enjoyed the expression on his friend's face.

"Where is everything that was hanging on the walls?" Jay asked, his mouth agape.

"Oh, it's around," Tyler hinted, nodding toward the far corner. Standing against a wall were several picture frames all neatly stacked.

"Dude, what did you do?" Jay said, looking around the room again.

"I just did some tidying up, do you like it?" Tyler answered with a smirk.

"I don't get it," Jay said.

"It's simple, bud," Tyler said with a smile and began to tell his friend about the argument with his mother and her final pronouncement.

"That totally sucks, Tyler," Jay finally said.

"Well, not totally," Tyler responded. "You see, none of this stuff is going to be mine anyway, so I figured -"

The doorbell interrupted him. "Come on," Tyler said to Jay and the two walked quickly to the front door.

"Is this where the estate sale is?" asked the jean-clad woman standing on the front stoop. She poked her head and looked around.

"Yes, this is the place," Tyler said. "You're a little early, though. I haven't had a chance to put up any signs."

"What are you going to do, man?" Jay whispered to Tyler, but Tyler ignored him.

"If you could come back in an hour, I'll be ready to open," he said to the woman.

"Sure, no problem," she replied. "Is there some place I can grab lunch while I wait?"

Tyler directed to the nearest McDonald's, and then closed the door.

"An estate sale?" Jay yelled. "Are you insane? How do you think you're going to pull this off?"

"Calm down, dude," Tyler said, laughing. "I have it all under control, but I'll need your help to finish."

"Oh no, not me," Jay said shaking his head vehemently. "I'm not going to jail for something this stupid!"

"How about if I pay you for your help?" Tyler said, smiling sneakily. "How's ten percent of the take sound?"

"Well, not as good as twenty-five percent," Jay answered.

"Twenty-five percent? *Now* who's the insane one?"

"Okay, make it twenty percent and you have yourself a worker."

Tyler rolled his eyes. "Okay, fine, but you have to help me get the best price for all of this stuff. The more we make, the more you keep."

Jay looked around the adjoining rooms and saw the rest of the valuables were already lined up along the walls, ready for a sale.

"How do you think you're going to get enough people here to buy this stuff anyway?"

Tyler pretended to type on an imaginary keyboard. "Oh, how about posting this sale on every estate sale site in Southern California?"

Jay's bottom jaw dropped in response. "Tyler, you mean to tell me you're opening up this sale to anyone who wants to come here?"

"How else do you expect me to sell everything quickly?"

Jay didn't answer. "Okay, then tell me this … why?"

"Why? You mean, why am I selling all this?" Tyler asked, walking back into the study. Jay followed him.

"Yeah, Tyler, why?"

"Dude, I'm being screwed out of my rightful inheritance. This stuff should be mine, damn it, but my mother is trying to teach me a lesson. Now she's going to be the one to learn something!"

Tyler strode over to the computer and sat down. He looked up at Jay.

"So, are you going to help me or what?"

"Wait," Jay said, raising a hand. "What are you going to do with the money?"

"Buy that car, of course," Tyler said happily. "Then, I'm going to drive out of this town, maybe this whole state. I'll see the country, take odd jobs, and make my living on the road."

Jay looked incredulously at his friend. "Tyler, I got to tell you, I think you've totally lost it. Either that or you've been watching too many bad sitcoms."

Instead of answering, Tyler started typing on the keyboard. "Look, Jay, if you're going to help me, then I need you to start making an inventory of everything in this room. I already got the other downstairs rooms."

Jay hesitated, and then shrugged his shoulders. "Fine, have it your way." He walked over to the first group of paintings and started counting.

A little over an hour later, the doorbell rang again and the young woman who arrived earlier was back. Behind her stood a short line of people waiting to get in.

"Hello, everyone, thank you for coming to our estate sale," Tyler announced. "Just a couple of things to keep in mind. First, we're only letting five people in at a time." Jay stood behind him, scanning the assembled group.

A loud groan emanated from the crowd, but Tyler wasn't moved. "I'm sorry, folks, but there's only two of us here and this is a large house. To make sure no one sneaks in, we'll be locking the door after the fifth person comes in and will only be opening it when someone is ready to leave. Do you all understand?"

A smattering of yeses could be heard.

"Great, thanks," Tyler continued. "Now the other thing is this: no dickering, I repeat, no dickering! Everything is priced as marked by the signs. Also, if you bought it, no returns - and if you break it, it's yours for the set price. Are we clear?"

One or two yeses were heard after this last series of instructions.

Jay whispered in Tyler's ear again. "Come on, idiot, let's do this thing."

Tyler nodded. "Okay, the first five in line, please come in. Jay counted out the five visitors and closed the door in the face of the sixth.

"Hey, that was my husband," cried a blonde woman in annoyance.

"Do you want to go out and join him?" Tyler challenged and the woman withdrew nervously, shaking her head.

"Feel free to explore all the rooms on this floor," Tyler called out, "But please note that the stairs are roped off and there are signs on all the closed doors to keep out. Please mind the signs and we'll all be friends."

Jay and Tyler walked room to room as their customers examined the merchandise.

"Excuse me," called the blonde woman, holding three framed pictures. "How much for these?"

Tyler didn't answer her, but pointed to the sign above where the remainder of the pictures were stacked which said "All artworks, ten dollars each."

"Oh, okay," the woman said. "This one, too?" she asked, holding up a Picasso etching.

"Yes, all pictures are ten dollars," Tyler replied testily.

The woman shrugged and walked away, still holding the artwork.

"You're selling a Picasso for only ten bucks? You got to be out of your mind, dude!" Jay said.

"So what?" Tyler responded. "Who's Picasso anyway?"

Jay was about to answer when an elderly gentleman walked over to them.

"Excuse me, young man, but are you in charge here?" he said to Tyler.

"Yes, I am," Tyler said. "Do you need a price on that lamp you're holding?"

"No, well, yes, but that's not what I want right now," the elderly man said. "I didn't know that Constance had passed away."

"Er, yes, she did, last week," Tyler said nervously. "Did you know her?"

"Yes, or at least I did at one time," the man answered. "That's very sad to hear she's gone."

Tyler assumed a distressed look and patted him on the shoulder.

The man looked closely at Tyler. "Are you related to Constance?" he asked.

"Yes, I'm her, um, nephew," Tyler managed to spit out.

"Hmmmm, you don't look much like her," the man concluded.

Tyler quickly changed the subject. "So, that lamp's twenty dollars."

The older man reached into his pocket and pulled out his wallet. Jay walked the man to the exit.

"Are you coming in?" he asked a bearded man standing at the door.

"Yeah, my wife's in there," the stranger said and walked in, a loud chorus of disapproval from the crowd accompanying him. Jay closed the door quickly.

"Tyler, we have a mob outside and they're getting ugly," Jay whispered.

"Okay, help move the gawkers through. They're either buying or they're leaving," Tyler replied, leading his friend into the study.

"Folks, there are a large number of people outside waiting to get in. I need you to either purchase something now or leave to make room for others," Tyler called out. The buyers looked at him with disdain, but headed his way carrying items.

After each visitor had paid for his goods, Jay saw them outside and admitted another. The crowd seemed to grow with every look.

Soon, the two teens found their rhythm with their guests and easily moved them through the house to view the sale items. Tyler was pleased that most of them were also buying, sometimes six or more pieces at a time.

At four-fifteen, they sold the last of the lot and had to turn the rest of the buyers away.

"Sixteen hundred-fifty, seventeen hundred," Tyler counted aloud as Jay watched.

"Eighteen hundred and twenty dollars!" they shouted together.

"And that means almost four hundred for me!" Jay added, laughing.

Tyler promptly handed him exactly four hundred dollars in rumpled twenty dollar bills. "Keep the change."

"So, when are you going to buy the car?" Jay asked, pocketing his take. His excitement couldn't be disguised.

Tyler paused for a moment. It was probably too late to buy it tonight and he'd better get back to Aunt Lucille's house before she called the cops to find him.

"Tomorrow, could you pick me up in the morning for school, but drop me off at that used car place on the way instead?" Tyler asked.

"Sure, no problem. I'll stop by around seven?"

"Perfect. Let's go, my aunt is probably having a fit right now because I'm late."

Jay made record time driving back to Aunt Lucille's house.

"See you in the morning, bro," Tyler said. Jay gave him the thumbs up and took off.

Aunt Lucille was sitting in her favorite chair when he walked in. She looked up at him, and then turned back to her book.

"You're mother called, Tyler," she said matter-of-factly. "I told her you were with your friends. That's where you were, right?"

She stared at him intently, waiting for his reply. Tyler smiled meekly and nodded.

"Good," she said simply. "I bet you're hungry"

Tyler managed to grunt in agreement. His aunt stood up and walked to the kitchen. Tyler followed her.

"While I make dinner, why don't you wash up and do your homework?" she suggested, opening the refrigerator door. Tyler went off to do as she requested.

Thirty minutes later, Aunt Lucille called him out for dinner. Tyler shuffled into the kitchen and sat down.

"So, how was school today, dear?" his aunt inquired, taking a bite of lemon and garlic pasta.

"Oh, not too bad." Tyler took a tentative forkful of the penne and after measuring the taste, began to eat in earnest.

Aunt Lucille didn't respond right away. The two ate in silence for a few minutes.

"What did my mom say?" he asked casually.

"Oh, this and that, mostly about how warm and humid the weather is," Aunt Lucille said cheerfully. She raised one eyebrow when she looked at him.

"Did she ask about me?" He sounded hopeful

"Of course she did, dear. I told her you were adjusting to your little bedroom, but all was well."

Tyler looked up appreciatively. "Thanks, Aunt Lucille."

"Don't mention it, dear."

Tyler helped clear the table of the few dishes, and then went to his bedroom, telling his aunt he was going to do his homework. Instead, he doodled on his notepad, drawing several pictures of his dream car at different angles.

"Tyler, do you want any ice cream?" his aunt called to him.

"No, not tonight, Aunt Lucille. I'm tired and Jay's picking me up early for school."

"Okay, then, good night, dear."

"Good night," he replied.

Tyler was exhausted and fell asleep right away.

§

The next morning, Aunt Lucille knocked on his door several times before he got up to answer it.

"It's almost six-thirty, Tyler, and your friend will be here soon. I made a waffle for you. I hope that's okay."

"Thanks, Aunt Lucille. I'm going to get washed up and I'll be in shortly."

Tyler was just finishing his breakfast when the doorbell rang.

"I'll get it," Aunt Lucille told him. "You go brush your teeth."

Tyler ran to the bathroom and did what he was told. He rushed into the living room where Jay was talking to his aunt.

"Good-bye, Aunt Lucille," Tyler said, opening the front door.

"Wait, dear, you forgot your school books," she told him.

"Oh, yeah those," Tyler said. "One second, Jay."

He raced to the bedroom and picked up his backpack lying on the floor, then ran back.

"Let's go," Tyler said, leading Jay outside.

"Good-bye, dear. Have a good day," his aunt said.

"Thanks for everything, Aunt Lucille," Tyler replied gratefully. He and Jay jumped into the car and sped away.

Boys, Aunt Lucille chuckled to herself, shaking her head. She cleaned up the kitchen, and then headed into Tyler's room to straighten up. Picking up the sketchpad, she saw his car drawings. It went on for pages, the same car at many different angles. Lucille shrugged to herself and made the bed.

§

Jay stopped in front of the car dealer. He looked over at Tyler who was almost straining to get out.

"Dude, are you sure you want to do this?"

"Absolutely!" Tyler said.

"What about clothes and food? I mean, what about gas?"

"Leave that to me, bud. I'll be fine," Tyler assured him, opening the car door. "Look, I don't know how long I'm going to have cell service before my mother cuts me off, but I'll try to call you in a couple of days."

"Sure, I guess." Jay sounded distant.

"What?"

"Well, man, you're my best friend. I don't want you get hurt or anything."

"Come on, Jay, I'll be okay. I'm smart, I'm healthy. I can work for my food. Hell, I don't need much in the way of clothes."

Jay looked at him, but still wasn't sure.

"Later," Tyler said, extended his hand. Jay shook it and Tyler left.

He watched Jay merge into traffic and waited until he was out of sight.

It's too early for the dealer to open, he thought to himself. He scanned the surrounding neighborhood, but the only place that looked open was a diner across the street.

The bell over the door rang as he entered and the few customers that were in there looked up at him, then turned their attention back to their breakfast. He sat at the counter and ordered a cup of coffee.

"Cream, hon?" the waitress asked him. He shook his head and picked up the mug. His hands shook a little.

"Anything wrong?" she asked him, looking a little concerned.

"Oh, nothing's wrong, thanks," he replied.

"School out today?" she pried.

"Yeah, teacher's conference," he muttered and took a sip of the hot coffee.

Satisfied, the waitress walked away. Tyler looked around for something to read and spotted the morning paper. He picked out the classified ads and browsed the car sales.

The 2001 Ford Mustang he had his eye on was still for sale. Relieved, he scanned the rest of the section, but barely paid attention to what he read.

After several cups of coffee and two pieces of rhubarb pie, Tyler looked out the diner window to see activity going on at the car dealership. He paid his check and hurried across the street.

"Ramon," Tyler called out to the strapping young man opening the front gate.

"You again, Tyler?" Ramon said, laughing. "How many times do you want to look at this car, dude?"

"Today's the day, Ramon," Tyler replied, cash in hand. "Twelve hundred dollars for everything, tags included, right?"

"Yeah, that's what we agreed on," Ramon said, a big smile now on his face. "Shall we go in and do the paperwork? Or do you want to look at the car one more time?"

"Let's just get it done," Tyler said.

Ramon just shrugged and led him to the office. The inside of the dealership was a hubbub of activity, with dealers, managers and mechanics all going about their daily chores before they opened.

It took close to two hours, but finally Ramon was ready to turn over the keys to Tyler.

"Look, Tyler, remember that this is a used car, so don't think it's going to run as perfectly as one from the new car lot, okay?"

Tyler barely heard him, he was so anxious to get on the road.

"Yeah, I know. Thanks, Ramon."

Tyler handed him the keys and shook his hand.

"Good luck with her," he called to Tyler, but the teen was already in the car with the stereo blaring and couldn't hear him. Ramon watched the Mustang pull out of the lot.

Tyler got on the first I-110 exit he could find and soon was on the I-10 heading east. By his calculations, he would be in Las Vegas just before the rush hour traffic tied up the roads as long as he didn't stop for anything more than gas.

He was just driving past San Bernardino when his cell phone rang. He looked at the caller ID and saw it was his mother. At first, Tyler was going to ignore it, but something told him he had better answer.

"Hello?" he answered, trying to sound casual even with his heart pounding in his chest.

"Tyler? It's your mother," Constance said. "Can you hear me?"

"Yes, Mother," he said, remaining patient.

"Hello, dear," she continued. "I'm sorry for calling you at school like this and all."

"That's okay, Mother, it's my free period," he lied, glancing at the clock. He pushed harder on the accelerator.

"Well, Tyler, I've had a couple of days to think," Constance continued. "And do you know what?"

Tyler didn't answer.

"I think that I overreacted," his mother admitted. "I forgot what it is to be a teenager and I'm sure it's even harder these days."

"So what does that mean?" he asked her.

"Well, what it means first, silly boy, is that I'm coming home early," Constance said. "Then, I'm going to see my lawyer first thing in the morning."

"And then what?" Tyler asked, gulping loudly.

"Then I'm going to change my will again."

Tyler hesitated. She wasn't leaving him anything as it was. How could it be worse?

"I'm still going to will a sizable donation to St. Jude's Hospital, but the lion's share of my estate is going to go to you."

"Everything?"

"Mostly everything, yes," Constance agreed. "You know all of those paintings in the house? You probably aren't aware that many of them are worth a lot of money."

Tyler winced.

"Yes, between the Picassos and the Dalis, I'd say my, or should I say, our collection is worth close to one hundred thousand dollars."

"Um, Mother, I don't know what to say," Tyler finally managed to spit out.

"There's nothing to say, dear," Constance burbled. "Between the art and all the furnishings, you'll stand to inherit over a million dollars in furnishings alone!"

Tyler pulled the car off the side of the road, slamming on the brakes before going into the weeds.

"Well, Tyler, do you have anything to say? Tyler? My goodness, at the very least you could say thank you or something!"

"Um, sorry, Mother, one of my, er, teachers just saw me and said hello. Um, that's great news, I'm glad to hear it."

"I would imagine you would be! Anyway, I'm almost at the airport, so I'll see you in a couple of hours. Bye!"

Tyler stared at the dead cell phone for several minutes. He started up the car again and rolled down his window. The cell phone flew out of his hand in a spinning hook shot over the edge of the embankment. He merged carefully into traffic. Only three hours to Vegas.

Guise of the Past

Faith bends, but does not break,
Its strength braces us.
Weathered, and yet brighter when burnished,
Not unscathed for its trials,
But remains fearless because of them.

Hope rises, then falls,
And is ultimately reborn.
Wiser, but more cautious for the memory,
A bit worse for the wear,
But willing to stand tall once more.

Love guides, yet is sometimes lost,
Trust keeps it true.
Weary, and yet stronger in the end,
Beaten up, but not beaten,
As long as faith and hope endure.

The Cage Door Swings

"Skin me, Brer Fox," says Brer Rabbit. "Snatch out my eyeballs, tear out my ears by the roots," says he, "But please, Brer Fox, PLEASE don't fling me into that briar patch!" – Georgia folk tale

"I literally could have died!"

Literally again, Lori thought to herself as she watched the giggly group of teenage girls huddled at the popular table. If that Heather doesn't stop abusing the English language, I'm going to beat her with my Merriam Webster!

"What are you staring at with that pimply face of yours?" Heather demanded, staring at her with derision.

"Nothing, really. I was just literally wondering if you 'literally' had any brains in your illiterate head, that's all," Lori smiled sweetly. She closed her world history textbook and stood up to leave.

"Oh, no you don't," Marcie, the biggest of the four girls, said, walking over to her. "You don't diss one of my friends without answering to me!"

Lori, a mere five foot, three inch waif, looked microscopic standing next to the almost six-foot Marcie. She moved as close as possible to the bigger girl and put her hand on her shoulder.

"Marcie, I know you have a thing for me, well, for all girls, really. But please, I don't roll that way. Buh-bye, now!" Lori waved brightly to the four of them and wandered off trying to look as casual as possible.

"Did you hear that b-" Marcie began, pointing to the Lori's retreating figure.

"Hold on now, Ms. Tyler," Mrs. Dennis interrupted, looking particularly matronly in her dowdy Sears muumuu. The teacher's three hundred pound frame was more daunting to the four girls than any wisp of a teen wiseass like Lori Guinness. "What ever happened to being lady-like, girls?"

"But Mrs. Dennis, she-" Marcie protested, but stopped at the sight of the teacher's outstretched palm. Besides being the eleventh grade math teacher, Mrs. Dennis was also the regular cafeteria monitor. When she raised her hand for silence, everyone knew to sit down and keep quiet.

"Girls, I won't warn you again. Fighting is unbecoming of respectable young ladies, first of all, and more importantly, it's against school rules. Can't you all just get along with each other and stop all this useless bickering?"

The four teens didn't respond. Marcie walked back over and sat down next to her friends, her anger and frustration quite evident.

"That's better," Mrs. Dennis told them and rushed off to intercede elsewhere.

"I hate Mrs. Dennis," Marcie growled under her breath. "And if I get that Lori Guinness chick alone for five minutes, I'll make her eat her dictionary."

The other girls tittered at this and Marcie eventually joined in. Soon the conversation returned to boys and all talk of getting even with Lori flew out of their minds.

Meanwhile, Lori was also laughing about her most recent encounter with the "Giggle Gang," as she referred to Heather and her friends.

They must be the stupidest girls in this school, she thought to herself. She was still laughing when she entered the library.

"Shhh!" hushed Miss Clemson, the school librarian. Lori tiptoed to the nearest study carrel and took her seat.

She was halfway through her math homework when she could almost feel brooding eyes boring holes into the back of her head.

"What is it, Marcie?" Lori asked without looking behind her.

"How did you know it was me?" Marcie whispered gruffly.

"I could tell your snort anywhere." Lori giggled at her insult and tried to ignore her visitor.

"You know what your problem is, Guinness?"

"No, but I'm sure you're going to tell me anyway."

"Let me lay it out for you, piss-ant. No one has shown you what happens when you smart off like you did back in the cafeteria. And you know something? I'm the one that's going to take care of that."

Lori turned around and calmly faced her tormentor. "And just where are you planning to do that, Marcie? Here in the library? I think not."

Marcie stared blankly at her.

"Good, I'm glad you're listening. So, here's the deal. You're going to turn around and leave the library, then go back to your little playmates and tell them that you scared the skinny little girl so much you had her peeing in her pants."

"And then what?" Marcie wasn't particularly bright and today was one of her better days.

"And then, my ape-like nemesis, you're going to forget we had this conversation and not bother me again. Why is that? Because you really don't want to get me angry."

"Why not?" Marcie decided to err on the side of caution and took a step backward. Lori observed this, but said nothing.

"You don't need to ask why, just listen to me and everyone will be happy, Marcie. Got it?"

Lori watched Marcie's face as the bigger girl processed the information. It took a few moments for it to sink in. The big girl turned and walked away without another word. Nearby students watched the confrontation and its conclusion in silence.

For her part, Lori quickly forgot Marcie was even there. She knew the simple girl wouldn't be bothering her for a while. It was always this way and had been since all of them shared a classroom beginning in second grade.

The sixth period bell shrieked, causing Lori to start. I hope college isn't this stressful, she mused, gathering up her books for the next class.

World history didn't thrill her much, but Lori tried to pay attention. History in general was her least favorite subject, mainly because it already happened; it wasn't going to change no matter how well you learned it. Computers were her main interest. With enough effort, you could make them do almost anything. She proved that to herself many times.

While class dragged on, she extracted the latest printout of her semester computer project from her notebook. One particularly nettlesome bug was driving her crazy, but she knew if she read through the code enough times, it would pop up at her. It always did.

By the time eighth period arrived, Lori was sure she had figured out the cause of her error. She went into the computer lab and sat down at her assigned PC and typed in her login information. Instead of giving her access to the Windows desktop, an error flashed indicating her account had been flagged.

"Again?" Lori muttered aloud and left her workstation to find the technical support intern. She could see him talking confidentially to the computer studies teacher. They both looked up when they saw her approach.

"Yes, Lori?" Mr. Ingalls inquired. Gerald, the intern, just looked on innocuously.

"Mr. Ingalls, I think my login was hacked again," she began, watching both of their expressions. If they knew about this ahead of time, neither one gave any indication.

"Oh, I'm sorry to hear that, Lori," Mr. Ingalls replied. He turned to Gerald. "Did you know about this?"

"No, Mr. Ingalls, this is the first I heard of it."

Lori could detect a slight grin on his gerbil-like face, but she didn't acknowledge it.

"Lori, I'll have Gerald look into this problem right now. He'll let you know what he finds, okay? Go back to your workstation and study for now." Mr. Ingalls flashed his trademark condescending grimace and turned away from her.

Lori sat back down at her place and looked around to see her fellow students busy with their final projects.

"What wrong, Lori?" McElroy asked her, his pudgy body pouring over the tiny swivel chair. Lori liked Mac, as his friends called him. No one called him Wilbur, his name his slightly addled parents gave him to honor his great uncle, a war veteran.

"I've been hacked again, Mac," Lori confided, looking forlornly at the login error message.

"How many times is it this semester? Three?" Mac reached into a nearby bag of corn chips and munched loudly. He saw Lori watching him and offered her some, but she shook her head.

"This is the fourth, actually. It's driving me nuts this time, Mac! I'm so close to completing this project. Only one more bug, just one more."

Mac laughed aloud, snorting noisily. "Lori, all you ever say is 'just one more bug.' You're going to be saying that until you move to Massachusetts."

"It's still not a done deal that I'm going to MIT, Mac, but thanks for the positive vibes."

The two were interrupted by Gerald. His resemblance to a member of the rodent family was legend among the computer students. Even his nose twitched whenever he was trying to figure out something.

"Lori, I think we fixed the problem. Why don't you try to log in again?"

"Whatever you say, Gerbil, er, I mean, Gerald." Lori never showed the intern even a modicum of respect. He only got the job because his mother was the assistant principal.

Lori tried her login again and this time it worked. She looked at Gerald expectantly for an explanation, but wasn't surprised at all to find none was forthcoming.

She pulled out her notes and hurried to correct the bug she found. The program only took a few minutes to compile. Lori ran the executable and pointed it to her test file for processing. She watched as her program began to display its analysis of her input on the LCD monitor.

"Yes!" Lori shouted triumphantly. All heads turned her way in a half-curious, half-annoyed sort of way, but she was too much in the moment to notice.

"What?" Mac asked her, his hand still reaching in the seemingly bottomless bag of corn chips.

"It ran error-free for the first time, Mac!" Lori said happily. "I have a working semantic analyzer for a programming language that I developed myself. This is excellent!"

Now I have something that will really impress those recruiters at MIT, she thought to herself. Up until now, she wasn't sure she was going to wow them enough to accept her into their freshman program this fall. The fact that she was moved ahead a grade in high school didn't really cause them to raise an eyebrow. They had a twelve year-old from the Ukraine starting in September.

Mr. Ingalls suddenly appearing in front of her interrupted her reverie. His condescending grimace was particularly menacing at the moment.

"Lori, is there a good reason for disrupting our class?" The other students watched, relieved it wasn't them being called to task by the computer teacher.

"Yes, in fact there is, Mr. Ingalls. I finally got my semantic analyzer to execute without a single error. The source file I had it process was so complex that it would show up any bugs in a second, but it ran through perfectly."

Mr. Ingalls nodded grimly, a slight smile threatening to show. "Most impressive indeed, Lori. And if I recall, part of this independent study project was that you create your own computer language."

"Yes, that's right, Mr. Ingalls." Lori showed him the input file and pointed to the screen to show how the analyzer handled each line of code flawlessly. Mr. Ingalls scanned all of her data and nodded curtly.

"Well done, Lori, well done. Congratulations!"

Mr. Ingalls turned to the class, still rapt with the drama unfolding before them. "Students, Ms. Guinness has successfully completed her independent study project. Let's all give her a round of applause, shall we?"

Lori glowed a bright red as she acknowledged the sea of hands clapping for her. For the first time since she met him, Mr. Ingalls was actually grinning. Look out MIT, she thought to herself, smiling at the accolades.

After the applause died down, Mr. Ingalls handed back her printout and returned to his desk. The other students continued to work on their projects with even more enthusiasm. Even Mac, who usually had one hand busy fondling some sort of edible, was now fully engaged in his own work. There was nothing like the smell of competition to motivate a computer student!

The bell rang shortly thereafter and Lori walked outside with Mac.

"So, Ms. Genius, what are you going to do in computer class now? There's a month left until graduation."

"Oh, I don't know. There are some more refinements I could make to speed it up a bit, I guess."

Mac laughed. "Not me. If I was in your shoes, I'd just coast for the rest of the semester. Heck, you have a sure 'A' now, why spend any more time on that same project?"

Lori thought a minute. "Maybe you're right, Mac. I mean, I do have projects in other classes that will be keeping me busy right up to finals."

"Finals! You had to say that word, didn't you?" Mac slapped his hand on his forehead and groaned. Lori looked at him and couldn't help but laugh.

"What's so funny, Guinness?"

Lori looked behind her. There stood Heather and the other Giggle Gang. She rolled her eyes at Mac, who made a hasty retreat from the pending conflict.

"I see your boyfriend had to run, Lori," Caitlin Densmore said in that sing-song voice every schoolchild on every schoolyard on earth has heard at least once.

"He's not my boyfriend," Lori mumbled and headed to her locker. The Giggle Gang followed her, Marcie lumbering behind them.

Heather grabbed Lori by the shoulder. "We still have to talk about your smartass comments in the cafeteria today, Guinness. I've told you before I don't take back talk from a puny little runt like you."

Lori knew better than get into a physical altercation with Heather or any of the other girls on school property, especially Marcie. But for the time being, Marcie was still being docile. Good thing Lori had her under control. Information in the right hands is a valuable thing.

"Look, Heather, I don't have time to have a discussion with you. I have to head to my judo lesson now and besides, don't you girls have cheerleading practice or something?"

"Judo? You don't take judo lessons," Brittany exclaimed. "I've known you all my life, Lori Guinness. We've lived on the same block since before kindergarten. I've never seen you take any lessons of any kind."

Lori laughed. "I'm glad you monitor all my activities, Brittany, maybe you'll be my biographer one day."

Brittany took a step toward Lori, but Heather held her back.

"Judo, huh? Why don't you show us one move?" Heather said. "In fact, why don't you try something on Marcie? I'm sure she won't mind."

Marcie just looked on, but said nothing. Lori glanced around, but none of the few friends she had were in sight. She'd have to talk her way out of this one yet again.

"Look, not here, Heather. I don't want to get in trouble so close to graduation."

"Okay, fine. We can go to the gym, then. I know that they have the mats laid out for the gymnasts and they're not practicing today."

Lori felt like a cornered rat, but nodded. "Sounds good. Give me fifteen minutes to change into my gym clothes."

The four girls walked off in opposite direction. Lori walked quickly to her locker and got her jacket. Instead of heading to the gym, she rushed to the side exit and out to Maple Avenue. She was about to cross over to Grove when she heard them.

"Running away, chicken? What about that fancy judo?" she heard Heather call down the street.

"I have to go to my class," Lori yelled as she continued down Grove. She moved as quickly as she could without seeming to be running for her life. However, her heart visibly pounding in her chest would be the first thing that gave her away had they been close to her.

Lori was almost out of breath when she opened her front door. Her mother was sitting in the living room, watching television. A bowl of popcorn sat on the coffee table and she reached in distractedly to get another handful.

"Hi, honey, how was school?" Mary Guinness asked her daughter. She was a typical middle-aged woman, a bit heavy around the middle, her hair slightly gray and in need of an updated look.

"Oh, okay, I guess." Lori walked quickly to her bedroom

"You better hurry, you don't want to be late again," her mother called to her.

Lori quickly changed her clothes and grabbed her backpack, then raced back to the living room.

"I'm ready," she announced to her mother.

They drove in silence, Lori lost in her thoughts about her program and the apparent slam dunk of her getting into MIT now that it was finished. How many high school students invented their own sophisticated computer language and successfully wrote an optimized semantic analyzer to process it?

"Anything happen at school today I need to know about?" her mother asked her pleasantly, interrupting her reverie.

"Actually, yes. I finally got my analyzer to work all the way through," Lori replied, somewhat embarrassed.

"That's great, honey!" her mother exclaimed. "We should celebrate."

Lori shook her head. "Not tonight, Mom. I still have a lot of homework to get through when I get home."

"Are you sure, Lori?"

"Yeah. Maybe this weekend, okay?"

"Okay, dear, this weekend. We'll go to your favorite restaurant and then afterwards, we'll drive over to that Italian ice place we both like and get dessert."

"That would be nice, Mom, thanks."

Mother and daughter sat in silence for the rest of the drive, both daydreaming about Lori's future. Since Lori's dad left them when the girl was three, the two developed a stronger bond than they might have otherwise. Both were excited about Lori's expected admission to one of the top engineering universities in the country, but Mary was sad because she would be all alone come September.

Mary pulled into the strip mall and slid the SUV into an available parking spot.

"Lori, now listen to me. No more arguments with the other kids, okay? You have to start learning how to get along with others. I can't be there with you when you're trying to make friends in college, you know?"

"I know, Mom. You tell me this every week."

Mary looked at her daughter with a mixture of love and sadness. "You're so much like me when I was your age. The only thing that's different is I didn't have your brain. That's going to make all the difference for you, you got that?"

Lori nodded. She waved as her mother pulled out of the parking lot.

"Hey, Lori! Are you coming?" called a man's voice from the open door.

"Yeah, I'm coming," she answered.

§

"How was it tonight, honey?" Mary asked her as they waited for their turn at the drive-through.

"Okay, I guess," Lori said, looking out the window.

Mary paused for a moment. She's so introspective, just like I was at her age, she mused. She pulled up to the window and handed the cashier her credit card.

On the way home, Lori munched on some fries without saying much. Mary allowed her daughter her space, knowing she needed thinking time. She sipped on her soda and negotiated her way through evening traffic.

"Mom?"

"Yes, Lori?"

"When you were a girl, did other kids pick on you?"

"Of course, honey, all the time. I told you about that time in the girl's gym. You remember, right?" Mary started giggling thinking about it.

"I don't know why I'm laughing, it was pretty traumatic when it happened."

Lori tried to suppress a smile, but started giggling along with her mother. "How long were you on detention?"

Mary wiped a tear from her eye. "Oh my, I haven't laughed like that in ages."

Lori looked at her expectantly.

"Detention? Oh, I guess I had to stay after school a couple hours every afternoon for a month."

Lori unwrapped her chicken sandwich. "What did Grandma say?"

"Grandma? Oh, she really didn't say much. I didn't make too big a deal of the whole thing at the time."

"You didn't tell her, did you?!"

Mary tried to look serious, but quickly gave up. "No," she replied meekly, and then laughed out loud.

"Oh my God, Mom! Did you ever let her know?"

Mary shook her head vigorously, and then looked sternly at her daughter. "And you aren't going to tell her either, got it, Miss Smarty-pants?"

Lori nodded solemnly and put one finger over her mouth.

Mary and Lori rode in silence, both lost in their own thoughts. When they got home, it was almost six o'clock. Lori immediately ran to her room to do her homework.

It was almost nine-thirty when Lori emerged from her bedroom.

"All done?" her mother called to her from the kitchen. Lori walked in and sat down next to her.

"Yep." Lori paused a moment. "Um, Mom?"

"Yes, dear?"

"Can I ask you a question?"

"Sure, Lori, of course. Something on your mind?"

"Yes, I guess so. It's those girls at school I told you about."

Mary nodded. "You mean Heather and her friends? What about them?"

Lori told her about the argument in the cafeteria and the showdown in the hallway later.

"Lori, why did you have to say anything to instigate a fight with that girl?" Mary looked at Lori and shook her head. "You know you shouldn't say anything at all if you can't say something nice, right?"

Lori looked at her hands, but didn't reply. Mary put her arm around her.

"I can imagine how difficult it is for you, Lori, being as smart as you are, especially when compared to those other girls. They just don't understand you. That's why college is going to be so much better for you, I think."

Lori nodded and sighed deeply. "What if all the other freshmen ignore me because I'm younger than them?

Mary smiled. "Lori, don't worry about that. You're going to MIT. There will probably be kids even younger than you and maybe in the advanced classes. It's not going to be like high school, you know? You're going to have to work hard to keep up with the other kids."

"I know, Mom. In some ways, I really can't wait for that. But the next few weeks until graduation are going to be agony … especially since I finished my project for the semester."

Mary got up and hugged her daughter. "Don't worry, my darling daughter, we'll get through it together. But do me a favor, okay? Can you try to avoid getting into any fights before graduation?"

Lori nodded.

"That's my girl. Now, what do you say to a nice bowl of ice cream?"

"I say 'Hello there, ice cream!'" The two laughed at the old family joke.

§

The next morning, Lori arrived at school just before the first bell rang. She didn't want to be hanging around the halls in case Heather and the other girls decided to meet her before first period.

Just as Lori was walking into Mrs. Hennessey's class, she turned to see Marcie glaring at her from her locker.

"Hey, Guinness!" the big girl shouted. "We have to talk."

"Not now, Marcie, I have to go to calculus now." Lori stepped into classroom before the other girl got too close.

Lori took her seat and watched the door. Within moments, she could see Marcie peering in.

"What is she doing?" whispered Mac, his pudgy hands unwrapping a chocolate bar.

"Not much of anything, it seems," Lori replied and turned her attention to the teacher.

Before she knew it, the bell rang. Mac waited for her while she packed her books. They walked together, Mac leading the way.

"Guinness!" shouted Heather across the hall.

"Sorry, I gotta run to my next class," Lori called out as she hurried along, Mac struggling to keep up.

"Lori!" Mac panted. "Where are you going? French class is the other way."

"No time to talk, Mac. I'll catch up with you later."

The heavy boy stopped and tried to catch his breath. He could see Lori turn the corner and head toward the auditorium. He only hoped she could find a place to hide. Those girls are mean!

"Hey, fat ass, where did she go?" Marcie was almost on top of him, her tall, wide frame preventing him from leaving.

"To class," Mac managed to sputter and tried to pass the human roadblock before him.

"Which way?" Heather demanded. Brittany and Caitlin were flanking her, as always.

"Yeah, which way?" Marcie echoed, intimidating the overweight boy.

"Um, that way," Mac pointed, his stubby finger aiming the opposite way from where he last saw Lori.

"Come on, girls," Heather shouted and the four girls headed where Mac was still pointing.

"Oh, Lori, I hope you're paying attention," he prayed aloud.

§

Lori was indeed doing just that. She peeked in Piano Room #3 and seeing it was empty, she quickly walked in. After locking the door and putting the piano bench in front of it for good measure, she turned off the light and waited. She thought about calling her mother on her cell phone, but figured she was too busy with her job to come and save her again. Besides, it was about time she started handling these kinds of problems herself.

To pass the time, Lori pulled out a penlight and started working on a particularly difficult Sudoku puzzle. She was concentrating so hard that she jumped when she heard someone test the doorknob.

"Who's in there?" demanded the muffled voice. Lori held her breath and tried to will the intruder away.

"Is there a student in there? Answer me!"

Lori could discern it was a voice of an adult. She reluctantly turned on the light and opened the door.

"Who are you?" asked the woman, her hands poised on her hips. Lori knew that this was Ms. Cole, the music teacher, but the teacher obviously didn't know her.

"Um, Ms. Cole, I'm Lori Guinness. Do you remember when you had me in ninth grade chorale?"

"Guinness? Hmmmm, I vaguely remember a Guinness. Weren't you taller back then?" Ms. Cole asked, somewhat mystified.

"No, you must be thinking of someone else," Lori said, suppressing a smile. How many high school students actually shrank?

"Yes, I guess I must," Ms. Cole admitted. "But that doesn't explain why you've locked yourself in this room with the lights off. Were you doing drugs or something?"

Lori couldn't help but let out a short laugh, but quickly stopped when she saw Ms. Cole's cold stare.

"No, Ms. Cole, I wasn't taking drugs. I'm hiding from some people that keep picking on me."

"Who are these 'people,' Lori?"

"Oh, just some girls, that's all. Look, I don't want to cause any trouble. I'm going to graduate in a month and I don't want to get into a fight or anything that would get in the way of going to college in the fall."

Ms. Cole peered into her eyes until she was convinced Lori was telling the truth.

"Okay, Lori, I believe you. Let me tell you this, though. You can't hide here all day. Where are you supposed to be right now?"

"French class," Lori said with a sigh. "It's not my strongest subject, either. I didn't have any choice but to ditch today, I swear!" She gave Ms. Cole her most pitiful look until she could see the teacher start to crack.

"Well, I guess you can stay here until the next bell. But then you have to leave. All of these piano practice rooms are reserved from mid-morning until the end of the day."

"Thanks, Ms. Cole! You're really doing me a big favor!"

"My pleasure, Lori. After all, I was young once, too, and I wasn't exactly the class favorite, either." Ms. Cole smiled warmly, then walked down the hall. Lori quickly locked the door again and turned off the light.

After the bell rang, Lori stuck her head out of the room and scanned the hallway for any signs of the Giggle Gang.

Confirming she was safe, she scurried out to blend into the sea of other students rushing to their next classes.

Luckily, the gym teacher was out with the flu, so with class canceled, Lori was able to make it to the library early without being discovered by Heather and her cronies. She chose a study carrel in a hidden corner of the rear wing.

Lori spent half of the time going over her world history assignment and the other half looking out for the Giggle Gang. At one point, she thought she could hear Brittany's voice talking to another girl, but neither one came into view.

The fourth period bell rang and Lori left the library to go to the cafeteria. She had every intention of quickly buying a sandwich and finding a private place to eat, but the long line foiled her plan. Maybe she could fade into the crowd.

"Guinness! We want to talk to you!" Marcie suddenly roared, appearing in front of her almost as though she ascended from Hades itself.

Lori steeled herself for the onslaught, but held her ground.

"Look, Marcie, I'm hungry. I'm sure you can understand that, right?" Lori made a point of inspecting the larger girl's ample girth.

"What are you looking at?" Marcie demanded. She looked over at Heather, who gestured for her to hurry up.

"Come on, Guinness, it's time we all had a nice chat," Marcie threatened and took Lori forcibly by the elbow, leading her to where the other girls stood.

"You ducked out on us yesterday, Lori," Heather accused, her arms crossed nonchalantly in front of her. "I thought you were going to show us all your judo moves."

Her friends giggled mockingly. Marcie stood behind Lori to prevent her from running away.

"What, do you want to cause a scene here, Heather?" Lori took a menacing step toward the other girl, but Marcie held her by her shoulder.

Heather continued, "Come on, Marcie, let's take Lori to the gym. Nobody's there now, so she can show us her skills without being bothered."

With Marcie pushing Lori forward, the five of them walked out of the cafeteria.

As Lori was led to the gym, she scanned the hallway hoping to see a friendly face or even an unfriendly teacher to whom she could go for help. Unfortunately, her luck ran out this time. She groaned audibly.

"What's wrong, Lori, are you scared?" mocked Brittany. The other girls laughed derisively.

Lori didn't answer, but trudged as slowly as possible, hoping to delay the inevitable.

"Come on, Lori, stop wasting time," Marcie muttered and almost picked her up bodily to move her faster.

Heather opened the gym door and peered in. "It's empty," she announced and the five girls filed inside.

"Caitlin, block the door with something," Heather ordered. Caitlin grabbed a nearby broomstick and slid it through the double door handles.

"There are some mats already laid out for us. How convenient," Heather said. Marcie pushed Lori over to where Heather was now standing.

"Okay, Lori, let's see what you're made of," Heather said. Brittany and Caitlin stood on opposite sides of the mat to prevent Lori from escaping.

"Marcie, she's all yours," Heather said matter-of-factly and stood back to watch the show.

"Judo, huh?" Marcie taunted. She stood solidly on the mat and faced Lori.

Lori gulped. "Okay, Marcie, we'll fight. I mean, I tried to tell you the other day you didn't want to give me any trouble, but it seems you won't listen."

The other girls laughed uproariously at the thought that puny little Lori Guinness was going to even lay a hand on big Marcie Briton.

"I guess you don't remember when we were in second grade, do you, Marcie?" Lori asked her, planting both feet squarely on the mat. Marcie looked lost in thought.

"I didn't think so." With that, Lori grabbed Marcie by the upper arms and pulled her over her extended leg. The big girl was felled by a perfectly executed leg wheel.

"That's called an *ashi guruma*," Lori instructed, looking down at her opponent.

After a moment, Marcie got up on one knee and shook her head.

"I'll remind you about second grade," Lori continued, standing at ease. "You were new in school and tried to pick a fight with me. Don't you remember?"

Marcie stood up, slightly unsteady on her feet. She was breathing heavily already.

Lori grabbed Marcie again and this time threw her backwards over her right leg. Marcie lay sprawled on the mat, the back of her head breaking her fall. The collision echoed across the gym. Heather and the other girls took a step back.

"That was the *kosoto gate*, in case you were curious. Yes, you thought because you were ten times my size, you were going to beat me up and show everyone how tough you were," Lori said, waiting for Marcie to rise again. She gestured to the bigger girl. "Come on, Marcie, show me what you got!"

Suddenly, Marcie sprung up and aimed for Lori's midsection with her huge head. Lori easily grabbed her by the back of her jeans and with her backwards momentum, flipped Marcie over her body and slammed her, back first, into the mat.

"Meet my friend, the *hikikomi gaeshi*," Lori said, standing over her foe. "You know, Marcie, I thought you learned your lesson that day. That was nine years ago and now I'm a third dan black belt. Perhaps I scrambled your brains worse than I thought."

Heather trembled. "What are you going to do to us?" The other girls echoed her fears.

Lori sneered at them. "You three? You aren't even worth a drop of my sweat. But this one here," Lori gestured to Marcie who remained motionless below her, "well, she's almost indestructible. I can do this all day if she wants."

Marcie only vigorously shook her head in response. "I give," she croaked.

"I'm sorry, say that again," Lori insisted. "I want to hear you shout it loud enough so these other bimbos can hear it in their sleep tonight."

Marcie complied. The three girls cowered at their friend's bellowing.

"Very good, Marcie. Now, ladies, will I be hearing any more from you for the rest of the semester?"

"N-n-n-o-o, Lori," Heather stammered. Caitlin and Brittany only shook their heads in response.

"Fine, just fine. You can go now. And don't forget to take 'Bruiser' here with you."

The three girls struggled to pick Marcie off of the mat and drag her with them to the exit. Lori waited until they were long gone before picking up her backpack and leaving herself.

In eighth period, she sat next to Mac as always, who just looked at her curiously. Lori pretended not to notice, but eventually succumbed to his stares.

"What, Mac?" she asked wryly.

"Oh, nothing, I guess," Mac said. He reached into his nearby bag of Doritos and stuffed a handful into his mouth.

"Did you have something to ask me?"

Mac washed down his chips with a Coke. He wiped his mouth with the back of his hand, leaving red streaks from the food coloring that coated the chips.

"Lori, did you really beat up Marcie?" Mac finally asked her nervously.

She shrugged. "What do you believe, Mac?"

"Well, I saw those girls lead Marcie to the nurse's office earlier. She wasn't looking too good."

"I'm sure she'll be alright, Mac. She may have fallen a few times, that's all."

Mac opened his mouth to reply, but instead, grabbed more chips. Lori watched him and smiled.

"I'm glad *we* are friends, Lori," he finally said, trying to suppress a giggle. Lori started chuckling, too, and before long, the other students stared at both of them laughing out of control.

After the last bell rang, Lori raced to her locker to get her books for the weekend. When she stepped outside the front exit, she saw her SUV at the curb, her mother waving to her from the open car window.

"Hi, Mom, what's going on?" Lori asked as she buckled herself in.

"Oh, I decided to take the afternoon off and spend it with my almost-graduated daughter. What do you say we go out tonight somewhere special?"

"That sounds great, Mom."

Mary pulled away and exited the parking lot.

"So, how was school today?"

Lori smiled. "Never better, Mom."

The Value of Imperfection

Perfection is nearly
Impossible to achieve, no matter
How hard one strives.
Driven to an ideal,
Unattainable.

Perfection is always
So illusory, so vague, a mirage.
A distant ghost
Out of reach,
Beyond.

And when it appears
Perfection is within your grasp
Your outstretched hand
Is left empty,
Wanting.

Holding only a
Faded memory, a love that's lost.
A hope deceased,
Desire denied,
Gone.

Flaws lend color
To an otherwise drab palate.
They provide character
For any landscape or
Soul.

Imperfect hands
Twisted with their tired sinew
Build the inspired art.
Rises above all,
Renewed.

Imperfect minds
Strive to see what cannot
Be understood, if
All is known and
Complete.

Injured hearts
Beat stronger for the pain
No matter the loss,
Its bitter depths
Impel.

Macdougal Street

"Dance with me, Rosie."

"What did you say?"

"I said 'Dance with me,' *mi amor.*" Lucien moved to grab his wife, but she wriggled out of his grasp.

"Oh, come on, Rosie. Just one dance? *Una danza*?"

"No! Get away from me!" Rosalinda said, arms crossed defiantly over her ample chest. "You know how I hate when you get like this, Popi."

Lucien sat down on the pockmarked cement floor with his knees tucked under him, his graying head hidden in his hands.

"My Rosie loves another," he crooned softly, rocking back and forth like a small child.

Rosalinda watched her husband and suppressed a giggle. Lucien heard her and looked up.

"Dance with me?" he asked hopefully. Rosalinda couldn't hold it in any longer and soon she was out of breath with laughter.

"Lucien, you know I love you," she said after composing herself. "But Popi, you drink too much and whenever you do that, you want me to dance with you. Why's that?"

Lucien finally smiled, happy to make his Rosie laugh. "I don't know, *cara*, I just do. Wine makes my feet loose, I guess."

"Yeah, well, you better watch yourself, Lucien. You know what the doctor over at the free clinic said. Your liver ain't so good."

"Maybe I have an onion imbalance?" Lucien offered with a smirk.

Rosalinda threw a nearby pillow at his head, but missed him by a foot. "Same bad joke every time, Popi. I'm not kidding here. If your liver goes, you could die. Then where would I be?"

Lucien looked out of the eight foot tall window, the one that faced Washington Square Park. "Rosie, would you dance at my funeral?"

Rosalinda stormed into the kitchen. "I don't know why I ever bother trying to talk sense into your stupid head, Lucien. You understand you're slowly killing yourself, right?"

Lucien struggled to his feet. He stood hunched over for a moment, trying to maintain his balance.

"All of us are dying a little at a time, *mia esposa*. Maybe I'm just helping the process along a bit, who knows?"

Rosalinda walked back into the living room carrying a glass of ice water.

"Here, drink this," she commanded. "You can start washing that *mierda* out of your system. From now on, I'm putting you on a healthy diet and you're not going to drink any more wine. And this time, Lucien, you're not going to have your friend Orlando sneak you cigars and Muscatel."

"Now hold on there, Rosie." Lucien reached out for the glass she held out for him. "Orlando is innocent of any crimes. If anyone has to be blamed, let it fall on my head."

"Orlando's trouble, that's all I know. Ask Sissy, she'll tell you."

"Sissy's a whore," Lucien spat. "She left Orlando at the altar."

"Popi! Sissy's my best friend, you know? She only left his sorry brown ass because he was all over the Village, acting all crazy like he was God's gift or something."

"Orlando is a gentleman and he's my friend, Rosie. I don't want to hear any more aspersions cast in his direction."

Rosalinda stared him, mouth agape. "What is it with you and your big words? You only do that to make me feel stupid."

Lucien staggered over to the table where his typewriter laid in wait. He poured himself into the rickety chair and stared at the empty page already in position.

"What are you going to write, Lucien?" Rosie looked out the window, feigning indifference.

Lucien didn't reply. With a heavy sigh, he pecked out a couple of letters and then brought his face close to the platen to read what he wrote.

"Stupid man, where are your glasses? You know you can't see shit without them. *Dios mio*, you're so vain."

Lucien cleared his throat, then began writing again. Soon he found a rhythm and his typing became more confident.

"See, my love?" Lucien called out after one of many carriage returns. "I don't need glasses to write. Glasses are for the weak."

Rosalinda didn't answer. She walked into the kitchen and ran the water in the sink. Soon she had forgotten her drunken husband, losing herself in washing the mountain of dishes threatening to tumble from the counter.

An hour later, Lucien was still banging on the old Remington. Every once in a while, he would glance at the growing pile of completed pages and smile.

"Popi, I'm getting hungry. Are you ready to stop?"

Lucien didn't immediately respond and finished another page.

"Lucien! Did you hear me?" Rosalinda glared at him, her hands on her hips.

Lucien finally looked up and saw her standing in front of him. "Rosie, haven't I told you I can't be interrupted when the Muse visits?"

"To hell with your muse, I'm hungry!" Rosalinda pouted like a petulant child, waiting for him to comply.

"Damnit, Rosie!" Lucien shouted, slamming his fist on the table. "If you're hungry, go ahead and get something to eat! I'm almost done with this script and I can't stop for anything, even food."

Rosalinda started to cry, glancing at Lucien to see if he noticed. Lucien began typing again, jaw clenched in defiance.

"Fine! I'll go get something to eat without you. See if I care!" Rosalinda flung open the door and slammed it behind her.

Lucien sidled to the window and looked down at the sidewalk. In a moment, Rosalinda strode into view, heading north on Macdougal Street. She must be going to Panchito's, he thought. Maybe she'll bring me back some *arroz con pollo.*

He sat back down in front of the Remington and reread the last line of dialog. Soon his fingers were flying effortlessly across the keyboard. The air was punctuated with staccato blasts as page after page slid through the gray typewriter. Lucien wrote like a man possessed, each word perfectly selected for the mood he was trying to create. Action begot intrigue, punchy dialog led to further sparkling repartee.

An hour later, Lucien typed the final scene, adding "FADE OUT" with a flourish. He pulled the page out of the typewriter with a satisfying zip, placing it at the bottom of the large stack now facing him.

To celebrate, he walked over to the cabinet to pull out a bottle of the good wine. Beaujolais Nouveau, a perfect accompaniment, he thought to himself. Not standing on ceremony, he popped the cork and poured himself an oversized glass.

"Here's to a sure winner, Lucien," he said aloud, raising the glass in a toast. After a long swallow, he walked over to the window to wait for Rosalinda.

It was past dark when she finally did return. Lucien had fallen asleep sitting in the chair next to the window, his forehead creased by the wooden frame during his slumber.

"Popi?" Rosalinda called into the unlit room. "Popi, are you asleep?"

She turned on the overhead light and saw him stirring uncomfortably against the wall. His wine glass sat on the window sill, propped up against the dirty pane.

Lucien shaded his eyes from the bright light and looked blindly in her direction.

"Rosie, is that you? What time is it?"

"Yeah, it's me, Lucien. It's almost ten, I guess." Rosalinda walked over to the couch and plopped down.

"Where were you, *cara*? Were you out breaking my heart?" Lucien walked over and sat down next to her.

"Popi, no, I wasn't with a man or anything. You know I don't do that. I was with one of my friends." She purposely looked away from him.

Lucien blinked several times to clear the sleep from his eyes. "Who, Rosie? You can tell me. Was it Hector?"

"No, it wasn't Hector, Popi. It's Friday night and you know Hector, he's with the pretty boys, dancing over at Splash."

"Who was it then, Rosie? Who could keep *mia esposa's* attention for so long?

"It was Sissy, okay? Lucien, I went to spend time with my friend Sissy. Just because you hate her doesn't mean I can't hang with her, you know?"

Lucien laughed. "That's right, *cara*, you can be friends with whomever you want. Don't worry, I won't say anything to Orlando. Besides, he's having more fun playing than he ever had with her. Don't tell her that, though! I don't want to hurt your friend's feelings."

He laughed again, watching Rosalinda's face for a reaction. She didn't disappoint him.

"Popi, why are you so mean to me? Don't I love you so much? Here, you want to write and do I make you go out to eat with me? No! Do I come home early and disturb you when you're in the middle of a great idea? No! So why do you try to make me feel bad?"

Rosalinda started to cry, hiding her face from her husband. Lucien watched her a long time before he spoke.

"There, there, Rosie, there, there. I'm sorry, I didn't mean to make you cry. You know how I get when I'm tired."

Rosalinda wiped her eyes with her sleeve, but didn't answer.

"Come on, *cara*, forgive a stupid old fool. Please?" Lucien put his arm around her and gave her a gentle squeeze. He felt her body finally sagging into his arms.

"Okay, Popi, I forgive you. But don't say any more mean things about Sissy, okay? She and Orlando are better apart than together. I know that you think that."

Lucien kissed her on the forehead. "You're right, *mia esposa*, you're right, I'm wrong. They're better off apart and I shouldn't be saying bad things about your friend. Never again, I promise." He made the sign of the cross to show her he was sincere.

Rosalinda hugged him tightly. "I knew you loved me, Popi, thank you."

"I finished it, Rosie," Lucien said after a moment.

"Your script? You're done?"

"Yep, it's done. I still have to edit it, of course, maybe several times until it shines like your eyes. Then I can sell it and we can move out of this tiny place. Wouldn't you like to live someplace nicer, maybe on the Upper West Side?"

Rosalinda let go of him.

"What, *cara*? Isn't that what you want?"

"Leave the West Village, Popi? Where all our friends are? I've lived here ever since I came over from Cuba and I don't know anywhere else."

Lucien looked at his hands in his lap. Worried she may have upset him, Rosalinda kissed him on the cheek and laughed.

"I'm sorry, Lucien, there's no reason to even talk about this right now. First you have to finish editing and selling your story. Are you going to take it to Doc Fields first?"

Henry Fields was once an English professor at New York University, but a scandal involving a female student caused him to quit in the prime of his career. These days, Doc Fields (as the neighborhood called him) worked as a night watchman at the Bank of America building. Lucien liked to give Doc Fields his manuscripts before trying to sell them. The older man always had wonderful suggestions for him.

"I sure will, *mia esposa*. Doc Fields knows how to fix stories. Maybe I'll be able to sell this one and make him happy again."

Rosalinda nodded with a smile. "That's my Popi. I know this is going to be the one. You've been so inspired lately!"

"The Muse, she gives when she wants to give, Rosie. I wish I could make her come out whenever I want to, but she has her own schedule. We writers are only here to serve her at her whim."

"Well, she should be with you all the time, Lucien. You are the best writer in the West Village. Everyone says so. Even Sissy says you are."

Lucien laughed. "If everyone feels that way, then I'm sure to sell this script, *cara*. Now, I'm thirsty and need something to eat, too. How about we run over to Monte's? I would love a bowl of their spaghetti and a carafe of Chianti."

"Okay, Popi. Let me freshen up and we'll go out and celebrate. I'll only be a second."

Rosalinda hurried to the bathroom and closed the door. Lucien made his way to the kitchen sink and washed his face with a generous amount of dishwashing liquid. He dried himself off with a dishtowel, then walked over to the framed Van Gogh print next to the door and combed his hair in the glass's reflection.

"I'm ready, Popi, let's go."

Lucien held open the door for her, locking it before following his wife down the stairs.

It was a perfect spring night in the Village, the first nice one since a series of rainstorms drenched the city and kept the residents indoors. As they walked up Macdougal Street, they saw the neighborhood kids enjoying the dry weather, kicking a muddy soccer ball back and forth across the damp street. Cars were forced to wait until the ball made it to the curb before proceeding, the driver hoping that the next kid wouldn't pass it back until he drove past.

"Lucien!"

The couple looked up and saw Orlando Onefre walking in their direction. He carried a brown bag in one hand and his trademark silver-tipped cane in the other. Instead of his regular New York Yankees cap, he wore a brown beret that was too small for his head.

Lucien shook Orlando's hand vigorously, slapping him on the back.

"Orlando, look at you! You must be out on the town tonight," Lucian joked, pointing at the silly looking beret. He looked at Rosalinda, but her attention was focused on some unseen object across the street.

Orlando glanced at Lucien's wife and shrugged as if to ask "What's her problem?" Lucien only rolled his eyes in response.

"My friend, I'm in a particularly good mood tonight," Orlando said, watching Rosalinda's face for a reaction. If he expected to see one, he was disappointed. The dark haired woman stood with her arms crossed in front of her, a stoic look marring her normally soft features.

Lucien watched the two of them for a moment. "What happened to make you so happy, Orlando?"

Orlando leaned heavily on his cane, his body angled toward Lucien. "I am the luckiest man in the world, Lucien. Carmen finally said she would be mine for life. We're going to get married!"

"Bravo!" Lucien shouted with a broad smile, pumping the younger man's hand. "Isn't that wonderful, Rosie? True love has triumphed again."

Rosalinda only shrugged in response and continued staring across the street.

"Don't pay attention to her, Orlando, she's happy for you, I'm sure. She doesn't always show her true feelings, you know? I think it's from living in Castro's Cuba for all those years. It isn't healthy to express yourself too much, eh?"

Orlando laughed. "*Sí, mi amigo.* At least my Puerto Rico flies the flag of America."

Lucien chuckled. "So tell me, my friend, when is the happy day?"

"We think just before Christmas, Lucien. Carmen still has to tell her family in Corozal. They have to make arrangements to fly over here."

Orlando looked down where the tip of his cane rested on the uneven sidewalk. "Lucien, I have a favor to ask you. Would you do the honor of being my best man?"

Lucien smiled broadly and looked over at Rosalinda. She turned to glare at Orlando and began to say something, but the warning in Lucien's eyes staved off her tantrum. The two men watched as she regained her composure.

"Orlando, I would be honored to be your best man. I only hope that I am deserving of such a privilege."

Orlando hugged Lucien in response. "*Gracias, mi amigo, gracias*! I can't wait to tell Carmen. I'll talk to you later!"

Lucien smiled as he watched his friend fly up the street as though he didn't have a care in the world. "Isn't love grand, *mi amor*?"

Rosalinda didn't respond, but Lucien could now see she was sobbing silently.

"Rosie, my dear wife! Why are you crying so? I know you don't like Orlando, but you must be happy for him and his dear Carmen. You are a woman of love and your romantic heart must feel the joy he has because his darling has agreed to join him in holy matrimony."

"Oh, Lucien," Rosalinda cried. "My poor, sweet Sissy will be heartbroken. Can't you see that?"

Instead of arguing with his wife, Lucien proceeded up Macdougal Street. "If we hurry, we'll be able to get to Monte's while the pasta is still fresh."

He was almost a block ahead of Rosalinda before he turned around to see whether she followed him. From a distance he could observe her standing where he left her. He waited several minutes before he gave up and continued walking to the restaurant.

Lucien stumbled home well after midnight. He felt his way around the darkened living room until he finally found the bedroom door, but when he turned the knob, it wouldn't budge. Locked out, Lucien made his way back to the couch and collapsed like an empty wineskin on the brown cushions. He was asleep in seconds.

§

Morning arrived too early for Lucien. He gingerly lifted his head and surveyed the surrounding room. Nothing looked out of place. The door to the bedroom was still closed. Maybe a good night's sleep had improved his beloved's mood, he thought.

Lucien pulled himself up from the old couch and tested his balance before walking. Assured he was going to stay upright, he shuffled to the bedroom door and knocked.

"Rosie, my darling, it's time to wake up!" he crooned, his ear to the door to hear any sound of her stirring. "I have a wonderful idea. Let's stroll over to the Caffe Reggio and have a nice espresso and cannoli like we used to do when we first moved to Macdougal Street. What do you say?"

He strained to hear some word, but Rosalinda didn't respond. He knocked louder.

"Cara, please! Come on, you still can't be mad at me! I know a nice breakfast will make you feel better. Let me in, okay?"

Growing impatient, Lucien turned the knob and was surprised to find the door opened easily. The bed was neatly made, but there was no sign of Rosalinda. He rushed to the bathroom and was relieved to see her makeup bag still in its usual place.

Lucien walked back to the kitchen. He found a note and in Rosalinda's carefully printed block letters next to the telephone, she wrote:

Dear Lucien,

I'm going to stay with Sissy for the day. She's a wreck since I told her about that louse Orlando getting married. Don't try to call me.

I'll see you later.

Rosie.

He crumpled the brown scratch paper and threw it on the counter. Realizing he was on his own for the day, Lucien decided he would make his rounds throughout the neighborhood. He took a hot shower to clear out the cobwebs and took special pains to dress appropriately, remembering to don his favorite houndstooth jacket and silk fedora. Thus comported, he headed out the door, new manuscript in hand.

No sooner did Lucien's feet touch Macdougal Street than he saw Hector Sufuentes heading in his direction.

"*Jefe, qué tal?*" the broad-chested man greeted him, extending a friendly hand.

"Hector, what brings you here?" Lucien replied affably. Hector was not one to be overly friendly without reason.

"I'm here to see my girlfriend. Is she home?"

Lucien grimaced. "My wife isn't home, if that's what you want to know."

"Oh, Lucien, you're so cute. You know you don't have anything to be jealous about. As much as I love my darling Rosalinda, my heart belongs to one of my gentlemen friends."

"So I've heard, Hector. For me, it doesn't matter who you dance with. My Rosie's heart belongs to me. I can't help but feel a stab deep inside me when she spends time with another man."

Hector's eyes twinkled playfully. "If I only could meet a man like you, Lucien, my dancing days would be over." He looked forlornly up at their window.

"I don't know when she's going to be home, Hector. I'll let her know you were looking for her."

"You're a dear, Lucien, in spite of your machismo. *Gracias*."

Lucien watched Hector cross the street and disappear into an alleyway. He then strode along the sidewalk until he reached Bleecker Street. The brownstone where Doc Fields lived was on the corner.

"Lucien!" the bearded man shouted as he let him in.

"Hello, Doc, my old friend. Did I find you at a bad time?"

"Oh no, not at all. I was just reading a few Shakespearean sonnets. I'm writing a book critiquing them, you know?"

Lucien smiled. Doc Fields had been writing this book ever since he left the university. Since that time, Lucien had written six screenplays and a book of poetry of his own.

"What do you have there, Lucien? A new baby has been born?" Doc Fields eyes crinkled, a feature that nicely complemented his trademark toothy smile. He always referred to new works in terms of babies: their birth, their care and feeding and sometimes, their early demise.

"Yes, she is newly born and waiting for others to admire her. As always, I'd like you to be her godfather."

Doc Fields laughed. "It would be my honor, sir. Please have a seat and I'll get us something to wet our whistle."

Lucien rested on the small sofa and waited. He could hear cabinet doors opening and glasses clinking, sounds that always lifted his spirits.

"You're smiling, Lucien? That must mean you have a good one there." Doc Fields sat a serving tray down on the coffee table. He took his place next to his friend and began to fill the wine glasses.

"Yes, I think this may be the one that will put us on the map, Doc." Lucien took his glass from the tray.

Doc Fields stood and held his glass aloft. "First, let's toast the new baby, Lucien."

Lucien stood and faced him, holding his own glass up as well.

"A new child has been brought into this world. May she grow big and strong, but most importantly, may she make her papa a whole lot of money. Cheers!"

The two men touched glasses and took generous sips of wine, then sat back down.

"Okay, let's see what we have," Doc Fields said, lowering his reading glasses. Lucien sat back and watched the other man's face as he read.

Doc Fields skimmed the manuscript quickly, occasionally letting out a chuckle or an enthusiastic "oh" when he came across a particularly good passage. Lucien looked on patiently and took and occasional sip as he waited for his friend's verdict.

Finally, Doc Fields reached the last page and placed the script on the coffee table in front of him. Lucien squirmed as he waited for the verdict.

His friend saw him fidgeting and laughed. "I guess you want to know what I think?"

Lucien clenched his fists. "Are you fond of torturing promising writers, professor?"

Doc Fields chuckled. "Not usually. But when I read something of such fine handiwork, I admit a touch of jealousy runs through me and tickles a cruel streak."

"You really like it?" Lucien's face was alit with pleasure.

"No," the professor said, taking off his glasses. "I love it, absolutely adore it. Lucien, you have a real winner here."

Lucien stood up in excitement. "I knew I got it right this time, Doc!"

"This calls for a drink, by God!" Doc Fields shouted, picking up the bottle and pouring generously for both of them.

The two friends drained their glasses in unison and sat back down.

"Now, I do see some editing work that needs to be done, Lucien. I hope you'll let me help you there."

"Of course, Doc, that's why I brought this to you. You've helped me so many times before and each time, I learn so much from your suggestions. And remember my promise, right?"

Doc Fields smiled shyly. "Of course, but I told you that I don't want money if you sell something."

"Come on, old friend. I wouldn't be able to enjoy any success unless I had paid you back for all you've done for me. Don't forget the editing credit, too!"

"Yes, the editing credit would be valuable to me. It will help when I try to sell my critique on the sonnets. That would be my fondest wish, to once again be a published author."

Lucien watched the tears well up in his friend's eyes and he turned away embarrassed. Doc Fields was a good man, the best of his kind. He didn't deserve to lose his job over a coed who seduced the kindly professor to raise her grade.

"Come now, Lucien, my sadness is gone. Let's drink one more glass and then I can get to work on these edits."

They quickly emptied the bottle and Lucien stood up to take his leave.

"Thank you, Doc, you know how much I appreciate this."

"Please, Lucien, the pleasure is all mine. I promise to have this back to you before I go to work tomorrow night."

"Until then, old friend." Lucien shook the professor's hand and ambled out the door.

By the time Lucien reached Macdougal Street, it was close to two in the afternoon. He walked by Orlando's apartment building and saw his friend's window open. A little diversion on a pleasant spring day would be nice, he thought, as he bounded up the stairs to the landing.

Lucien pressed the button to Orlando's apartment several times, but there was no answer. He walked back out to the street.

"Orlando, are you home?" he called up to the window. From his vantage point, Lucien couldn't see anyone inside. "Orlando!" he shouted again, but his friend didn't appear.

Giving up, Lucien walked along the street until he came to the Ale House. Inside, he could see some of the regulars deep in the middle of a bridge match.

"Lucien!" cried out Augusto, one of his frequent bridge partners. "You're just in time! I'm just waiting for a chance to get in on the next match. What'll you have? I'm buying."

Lucien shook Augusto's hand gratefully. "I am a bit parched, my friend. An ale would hit the spot perfectly right now."

"You got it! Hey, Carlos, how about bringing a couple of ales over here?" Augusto called out, waving to the bartender. Carlos filled two mugs and set them on the bar.

"What do I look like, a waitress? Come get 'em yourself!" Carlos snarled, turning his back on the game in progress.

"Bastard," Augusto said under his breath. Lucien laughed and walked with his friend to collect their drinks.

"How's Rosalinda, Lucien?" Augusto asked him after taking a long gulp of ale.

Lucien lifted his glass in a salute. "Thank God, she is well. She is my life, you know?"

"I know it well," Augusto nodded solemnly. "I can see the love look you give her whenever you two are together. How many years has it been, Lucien?"

"We've been in wedded bliss for almost ten years, Augusto. I am truly the luckiest man in the West Village."

Augusto took a deep swallow of ale and smiled. "You always say that, Lucien. That's why I love having you as my bridge partner. You bring all that luck to the cards."

Lucien laughed, following Augusto back to the bridge table and sat next to him to wait for their turn.

They didn't have to wait long. The match ended with a grand slam which excited all the onlookers, including Lucien. It was a long time since they saw such a dramatic finish to a match.

"Ready, partner?" Augusto asked him, taking his place at the table. Lucien nodded and sat facing opposite him. Their east and west opponents took their seats. Augusto picked up the cards and started to shuffle.

"Let's play some bridge!" Lucien announced and the first hand was dealt.

An hour later, Augusto and Lucien were down four hundred points with what was clearly going to be the final game. Their opponents smirked across the table from each other, something Lucien noted with a grimace.

"Don't count us out yet, Jorge," Lucien warned the east player, a young man only recently a visitor to the Ale House. "Augusto and I have come from behind in these situations before."

"That was back in the old days, Pop," Jorge teased good-naturedly. "It's time to give way to us young bucks now."

"How's this, young buck?" Augusto taunted, overtrumping his opponent. He led with a higher trump and collected the remaining trumps from the others. Lucien, in the dummy's chair, sat back and proudly watched his partner.

Jorge groaned. "Damn, I didn't expect to lose that other hand. I hope your cards are better than you let on, partner."

Stefano looked up and grinned back at Jorge. "Come on, *amigo*, you know I always keep my weapons hidden until I need them." He laid down an ace of spades to take the hand. Then he followed with a king of spades and was able to take one of dummy's diamond honors in the process. Augusto started looking nervous.

"Don't worry, partner, you've got plenty of firepower left on the table," Lucien reassured his friend, pointing to the high cards in the other suits. "Remember that game last summer?"

"No table talk!" Jorge growled through gritted teeth. "I'm trying to think here."

Lucien laughed. "You young people are so easily distracted. While you're thinking, I'm going to get something to drink. Augusto?"

"Of course, my friend. I'll take one of their finest drafts."

Lucien threaded his way through the honeycomb of chairs and tables and ordered the drinks. While he waited, he looked out of the front window of the Ale House hoping to spy Rosalinda walking home, but did not see her.

"Here you go, partner," Lucien said as he handed the ale to Augusto. "How are we doing?"

"I think we have them, Lucien, but we'll see." Augusto took two large gulps and placed the mug on the table. "There!"

He laid down a low diamond, hoping he counted right. The dummy was void in diamonds, but if his memory was correct, the other diamonds were lower than his.

"Damn it!" Jorge cried, dropping the two of diamonds on the table. Stefano didn't say a word, but laid the three of diamonds in front of him.

"I knew it!" Augusto cried out, picking up the hand and placing it in the pile in front of him. "What about this!" To everyone's surprise, he laid down the four of diamonds and won the hand easily.

Lucien watched as Augusto masterfully took the remainder of the hands, making their contract and winning the match on bonus points. "Yes!" Augusto shouted, standing over their vanquished foes. Lucien raised his glass in salute to his partner.

"Well played, Augusto," Jorge admitted. He held out his hand to the victors.

"*Gracias, gracias*," Augusto replied happily. "Lucien, let's buy these young men a drink. They played very well."

Lucien nodded and led the other three to the bar. Carlos poured the ales and Augusto handed them out to the others.

After they finished their drinks, Lucien placed his glass on the bar with a slam. "Okay, Augusto, it's time for me to head home. Rosie will be waiting for me. Thanks for the game, gentlemen."

"Give her my love, Lucien," Augusto replied, slapping his friend on the back. He watched him walk out the door. "There goes the most loyal of men," Augusto proclaimed.

It only took ten minutes for Lucien to return to the apartment. When he opened the door, he hoped to see the smiling face of his dear Rosie greeting him. Instead, there was no sign of her even being home since he left.

Lucien opened the cupboard door and pulled out a near empty bottle of Chianti. He poured the contents into a water tumbler and discarded the spent container. Glass in one hand and a box of pretzels in the other, he walked over to the old brown couch and sat down heavily.

Soon, Lucien was asleep, his hand still in the pretzel box. He dreamed he was playing bridge, but this time Rosie was his partner. Every time he bid, she bid higher and he would go higher still. Back and forth, the bidding went, everyone watching them and waiting for it to end. "Rosie," he said to her in his dream, "do you know what you're doing?" She didn't reply, but just shook her head and smiled sadly.

The sound of the apartment door opening woke him with a start. He watched as Rosalinda quietly entered, closing the door behind her and locking it without a sound. She tiptoed across the living room to the bedroom.

"Rosie? Are you okay?"

Rosalinda jumped at the sound of Lucien's voice, but maintained her composure.

"Y-y-yes, Lucien. Everything's fine. We'll talk in the morning, okay? I'm really tired."

Lucien thought wife didn't sound like her normal self, but he couldn't put his finger on what it exactly was.

"Fine, *cara*. I'll come with you."

He stood up and walked over to where she stood. A sour odor emanated from her.

"Rosie, where were you today?"

"Popi, I told you I'll tell you all about it in the morning. Let's just go to bed now, okay?"

Lucien put his hand on the small of her back and felt she was trembling. He opened his mouth to ask her another question and thought better of it. "Sure, my darling, let's go to bed. Tomorrow, everything will be clearer."

He put his arm around her shoulders and led her to the bedroom.

The next morning, Lucien woke up and found Rosalinda had already left the bed. He dressed quickly and walked into the living room. There his wife sat, staring out the window, a mug of coffee in her delicate brown hands.

"Good morning, *cara*."

Rosalinda looked over at him and smiled.

Lucien poured himself a mug coffee and sat down in front of her.

"Are you feeling better today?" he asked her as he took a sip.

"Yes, Popi. I'm sorry I was gone all day yesterday, but I had to look after Sissy, you know? She's my best friend."

Lucien looked into his wife's eyes and for the first time since they met, he knew she wasn't telling him the truth. He chose not to press further.

"What were you looking at?" he asked her, pointing to the window.

"Oh nothing, I guess. Just the birds, I don't know."

"Are you hungry, darling? We could go get some pastries."

Rosalinda shook her head. "No, you go ahead, Popi. I think I'm just going to stay in today. Yesterday took a lot out of me."

"Are you sure everything's okay, *cara*?"

"Yes, go ahead, Lucien. I'll be fine."

Lucien shrugged and walked to the front door. "Should I bring you back anything?"

"No thank you, Lucien."

Lucien hurried along Macdougal Street, determined to make it a quick breakfast. He didn't think he should leave Rosalinda alone for very long.

As he passed Orlando's apartment, he looked up at the still wide open window. On a whim, he bounded up the steps of the apartment building and tried the buzzer. Again, there was no answer, but just as he was turning away, one of Orlando's fellow tenants exited the building. Lucien stepped into the foyer and began climbing the four flights to Orlando's floor.

He knocked on his friend's door several times, but there was no answer. He was about to give up when one of Orlando's neighbors stepped into the hallway.

"Excuse me, aren't you a friend of Mr. Onofre?" the neighbor asked him. She was a short, Latin woman, dressed in hospital scrubs and white shoes.

"Yes, I am," Lucien replied. "Have you see Orlando today?"

"No, sir, I haven't. I usually see him around at the mailboxes or hear him go into in his apartment. It's been a couple of days since I saw him. That was since the argument, I mean."

"Argument?" Lucien asked, walking to the neighbor's door.

"Yes, I heard him yelling at someone and then she started yelling at him. The two of them fought, oh, how they fought!"

Lucien paused. "Did you see who this woman was?"

"No, I'm afraid I didn't. I thought I recognized her voice, but it's really hard to be certain. These walls are paper thin, but they still block some of the sound."

"Did you hear what they were arguing about?"

The woman closed her eyes, deep in thought. "Well, not completely. A lot of it sounded like accusations, I guess. I thought I heard her say something about his hands or something."

Lucien grew impatient. "Anything else? Come on, anything?"

"No, nothing else, really. I'm sorry, I just thought since you looked familiar, you were a friend of his and knew what was going on."

Lucien looked down the hall and nodded. "Yes, I appreciate that, thank you. I wish I knew what happened myself, but I don't know what I should do next."

"Maybe if you ask the super, he could let you in. It wouldn't hurt to give him fifty bucks to make him cooperate, you know? Remember, you didn't hear that from me, okay?"

Lucien smiled. "Thank you for you help. I promise this conversation is just between us."

"Good-bye and good luck finding your friend," the woman said as she walked down the hall to the exit. Lucien watched the door close behind her before moving.

He walked down to the other end of the hallway until he saw a door with a mailbox nailed to the side. It took several loud raps until someone answered.

"What is it?" an old man asked gruffly. "If you're here about the rent increase, don't complain to me. I just manage the joint. You can send a nasty letter to the owner, if you want."

"No, I'm not here about the rent increase. I'm trying to find out what happened to my friend in 4B. You know, Orlando Onofre?"

The super stepped into the hallway. "What, are you a cop or something? I don't want any trouble in my building."

Lucien shook his head. "No, I'm not a cop. Orlando is a friend of mine and he's been missing for the last couple of days. I want to know if he's alright."

"Did you knock?"

"Yes, of course I knocked," Lucien replied, exasperated. "I want to get into that apartment. Can you let me in?"

The old man shook his head. "Nope, unless you have a warrant or you can prove you're a relative of his or something, I can't let you in."

Lucien thought for a moment. "How about you go in and check and I wait outside?"

The super sneered. "I don't think so. The last time I did that, I walked in on a woman who just got out of the shower. She wasn't very happy I saw her in her altogether."

"I promise you, I'll take full responsibility. If I have to get the cops to do it, I will. Wouldn't you rather avoid the unpleasantness of the authorities coming into your apartment building?"

The old man paused for a moment. "Yeah, I guess you make a good point. Come on."

He led Lucien back down the hall to Orlando's apartment. "Wait here."

A moment later, Lucien heard the strangled cry of the super. "Murder! Murder!" the old man shouted, rushing out the door. "Murder!" He ran down the hallway back to his apartment. Lucien stepped inside.

Orlando was lying face up on the floor, a kitchen knife sticking out of his stomach. The carpet around him was soaked in fresh blood. His friend's eyes were still staring at the ceiling above him, his mouth frozen open in a rictus of shock.

Lucien rushed out of the apartment, fighting the urge to vomit. Outside the door, he started gasping until the nausea passed. Then he walked quickly to the stairwell and down the steps to the street.

He returned to his apartment in moments. Lucien flung open the door and saw Rosalinda still looking out the window where he left her. He slammed it shut, startling her.

"Rosie?"

She turned slowly to look at him, a sad, faraway look in her eyes. "Yes, Lucien?"

"What did you do?"

Rosalinda immediately started sobbing, her body shaking with each inhaled breath. "Oh, Lucien!" she cried pitifully.

Lucien walked over to his wife and enfolded her into his arms. She wept for several minutes on his shoulder, alternating between shuddering and moaning. He soothed her by stroking her long, black hair. "There, there, *cara*, whatever it is, we'll handle it."

Rosalinda pulled away from him and stood erect with her hands clasped in front of her. "Lucien, he ... he ..."

"He what, Rosie? Tell me what happened!"

She took a deep breath first, then began. "I went over to Sissy's yesterday. She was so sad about Orlando! I was with her for three hours, Lucien, and she didn't stop crying once!" She paused.

"Go on."

Rosalinda took another deep breath and continued. "Well, I finally couldn't take it anymore! I decided to go over and confront that louse right in the face!"

She stopped to blow her nose, then went on.

"Orlando was home, drunk on cheap wine as always. I told him how he broke Sissy's heart, but he kept saying that she broke his heart by leaving him at the altar. Do you know why she didn't show up that day, Lucien? Do you?"

Lucien remained silent.

"Because he was sleeping with anything with a skirt, Lucien! That's why she left him at the altar. He disrespected her too many times and then when he invited that skank, Carlita, to their wedding, the same whore that he was with the night, she decided enough was enough. And I told Orlando that, too."

"What did he say?"

"He denied it, of course. At first, anyway. But eventually, he admitted that he was playing all over town and making my girl look like a fool."

Lucien sat down and gestured for her to continue.

"Then, he tried to be all nice to me. He kept saying that you and him were best friends, *hermanos*, and that it wasn't right for him and me to be hating each other so much. He went to hug me and I pushed him away."

"He tried to hug you?"

"Yeah, Popi, but I wouldn't let him. Then he got all crazy like he wasn't going to let me out of there until he hugged me. Here I am, in this crazy drunk man's apartment and he's chasing me around the place! I tried to get out the door, Lucien, I tried! You got to believe me, Popi!"

Lucien rubbed his closed eyes. "Then what?"

"Then what? Well, I finally ran into the kitchen, but that bastard chased me in there and cornered me. I grabbed the first thing I saw to protect myself, this long kitchen knife. I kept stabbing it toward him, but all he did was laugh and kept trying to grab my wrist. I finally had enough and I kneed him, Lucien!"

Lucien nodded.

"I then ran out into the living room again, but that asshole could barely walk out the kitchen door to come after me. I almost made it to the front door, but he grabbed me by the throat and started choking me. So, I took the knife and stabbed him in the stomach. I didn't even look back to see what happened to him, I just ran out of there."

"He's dead, Rosie."

"Dead? I killed him?"

"Yes, I saw him dead with that knife in his belly."

"Are you sure, Popi? I couldn't have stabbed him that bad."

They were interrupted by a loud knock on the door. "Police! Open this door!"

Rosalinda immediately began to sob hysterically. "Oh no, Lucien, what am I going to do?"

Lucien smiled. "Don't worry, *cara*, Popi will take care of everything." He walked over to the door and opened it.

"Come in, officers, I think I know why you're here. I'm ready to go with you now."

Saints In Solitude

Deep azure, silvery white-capped,
Floating jewels so clear.
Blinded by memory, faded
Dreams drift to sullen fear.

Call to arms, bring out forgotten
Cries of moments lost.
To past glories we have shouted
And tallied up the cost.

Lift heroes in on feted bier,
Standing toe to toe.
Watch over all our cares unwound,
Salute the friends we know.

Salt wind and under billowed sail,
Seas beyond the sun,
Wait, your pearly spires are raised
Under the skies undone.

Sounds of broken glass defy,
The quiet morning calm.
Open minds closed by time, submerged
In silent molten palm.

Lament no more, be strong of heart,
Time will not pass us by.
One day this all will fade to black,
Today we must not die.

Will the sound of scriptures echo,
Across the holy glen?
They must wait for mankind's folly
If it's not now, then when?

We count ourselves among the gods
No mere men are we
To lift our words to skies above
And soar beyond the sea.

Terminus

Thomas paused with his wrinkled hand on the door of the flat, gray building, briefly resisting the wind's uninvited invitation to enter. The sidewalk shook with each thunderclap echoing overhead, causing him to hold onto the door frame for balance. After another almost blinding flash of lightning, he hobbled inside.

Thomas stood in the entryway and stared at the huge glass windows that rose from the parquet floor all the way to the twenty foot high ceiling. He could make out intricate figures etched in gold on the walls, mythological figures spanning all of history.

"Quite impressive, isn't it?"

Thomas looked around to see who was speaking to him. He noted a man about his age, sitting on one of the oaken bancs, arms crossed over his chest.

"I said 'Quite impressive, isn't it?'," the man repeated, a big grin plastered to his face. Thomas could see he was missing his lower plate.

"Yeah, it is," Thomas finally answered, scanning the room for emphasis. "And it's so big, too."

The man nodded. "It has to be. From what I've heard, this place fills up pretty fast during the day." He paused for a moment. "I see you're an early bird like me."

"Yes, I guess I am. I thought it better to be early than miss my bus." Thomas looked down on the floor where he planted his cane.

"Good thinking. I'm Ernest Freeman, by the way. What's your name, friend?"

"Thomas Benson. Nice to meet you, Ernest."

The two men shook hands. Thomas took a seat next to Ernest and leaned back with a relieved sigh.

"Tough day?" Ernest asked him.

Thomas nodded. He tried to remember how his day started, but it all seemed to be a blur. Travel always did that to him.

"Yeah, quite a day. I'm glad to be sitting down for a while."

Ernest stretched his legs out with his hands behind his head. Thomas did the same. Both men started laughing.

"Are you from around here?" Ernest asked him.

Thomas nodded. "Yep, just over there . . . Oneida."

"Oneida? I've never been. What's it like?"

"Oh, not much of a town, really. What about yourself?"

Ernest looked at the door at another traveler trudging her way toward them. "Well, I'm from nowhere now."

"Excuse me, gentlemen, am I in the right place?" the elderly woman asked. She held a white piece of paper in her hand.

Thomas began to stand up.

"No, please don't bother with the formalities," the woman admonished with a gesture of her hand. Thomas sat back down again with a groan.

"My name is Nettie," the woman said, taking a seat beside Ernest. "I presume we're going to the same place?"

"You bet!" Ernest chortled, waving his own white piece of paper. "My name is Ernest, by the way. And this is Thomas."

"Is that a ticket?" Thomas asked, a bit franticly. "When does the ticket office open so I can get mine?"

"Ticket office?" Nettie repeated. "I got my ticket before I came."

Ernest nodded, waving his ticket again.

Thomas looked all around. "No ticket office that I can see."

"When does the bus arrive?" Nettie wondered aloud.

Thomas stood, propping himself up on his cane. "I don't know about that, but I better find out about getting a ticket before it's too late."

"How do you know what ticket to get? You don't even know where you're going," Ernest pointed out.

"You don't?" Nettie asked, her eyes widening.

Thomas shrugged.

"Who are you going to visit, Ernest?" Nettie asked him, smiling.

"Oh, family and friends. I have so many of them who live up north. It's been a long time since I've seen them."

"A family reunion?" Thomas wanted to know.

"I guess you could say that, yes. How about you, Nettie?" Ernest rested with his hands behind his head again.

"Same for me. I haven't seen my son in a long time. He's been anxious to see me, I know."

Thomas looked at her. "Why doesn't he come to visit you? You're his mother, after all."

Nettie giggled. "Oh, he *has* visited me many times throughout the years, ever since he moved north. But now it's my turn to visit him. And I'm going to surprise him this time and tell him I'm staying for good."

"He probably already suspects that, Nettie," Ernest said with a smile.

While the other two talked, Thomas watched as a little girl approached them. She couldn't have been any older than seven or eight, with pretty blue eyes and curly yellow hair. The girl sobbed, eyes darting all around the huge bus station.

"Are you okay, sweetheart?" Thomas called out.

"I want my mommy," the child screamed, crying even harder.

"Come here, dear," Nettie said to her. The girl wiped her eyes and walked toward the three adults. Thomas could see she had a ticket in her hand, too.

"Are you traveling alone?" Nettie asked, stroking the child's head.

"Yes," the girl whispered. "I thought my mommy was going to come with me, but she couldn't. She told me I had to be a big girl and take the bus by myself."

Ernest smiled broadly. "Are you heading north, sweetheart?"

The girl looked at her ticket, then nodded. Nettie clapped her approval.

"We're going north, too," Ernest confirmed. "At least Nettie and I are. Thomas isn't sure which bus he's taking."

"You're not?" the child asked, mouth agape. "What does your ticket say?"

Thomas shook his head. "I don't have one. Yet. I'm hoping to get one soon."

Nettie interrupted. "Sweetheart, do you want to sit next to me on the trip?"

The girl squealed and snuggled in next to Nettie. The woman put her arm around the little girl and hugged her.

Their conversation was interrupted by a large group of travelers that walked in. All of them were shouting or slapping each other on the back. A few appeared to have just been reunited after a long separation.

"They're *loud*!" the little girl said, putting her hands over her ears.

Nettie patted her on the head as she watched the revelers.

"Are they going to be on the northbound bus?" Thomas asked.

"We'll see, but I hope not," Ernest said, his perpetual smile disappearing.

They watched as the group started chanting, raising brown bottles in the air after each word was shouted.

"Is that beer?" Nettie asked.

"What are they shouting?" Thomas wanted to know.

Ernest squinted at the group a long time. "Yes, it's beer, I believe. And it sounds like they're shouting about some sports team, but I can't make out the name."

Soon, the group flopped down on an empty bench several rows behind them. The walls echoed with their cacophony. Several of the woman reclining against the shoulders of the men, settling in for a long wait.

"They must be headed south," Ernest concluded, visibly relaxing somewhat.

"Good!" the little girl exclaimed, leaning close to Nettie again.

Their moods considerably brightened, Ernest, Nettie and the little girl sat back in silence. Unappeased, Thomas stood up again, tapping his cane nervously on the floor.

"Maybe I should go talk to them?" he asked his companions.

Ernest looked quizzically at him. "Are they your kind of people, Thomas?" Nettie and the little girl watched Thomas' face.

"No, I guess not," Thomas muttered. He opened his mouth to say something else when the door to the depot opened again. This time, a priest and a nun walked in, tightly clenching their tickets. More than once, they stopped to read their destination on the white paper, then pressed forward until they were in front of the rowdy bench. They sat down at the end of the row and looked ahead, silent as statues.

"Interesting," Ernest observed to Nettie. The woman shot Ernest a warning look, glancing down at the little girl for emphasis. Ernest nodded and looked back at the clergy.

Thomas spoke up first. "They don't look very happy."

"Nope," Nettie said simply, patting the little girl on the head.

Thomas prepared himself to walk over to talk to the latest arrivals when the door to the station opened again. This time, pairs of men and women entered, all of them dressed in fancy evening wear. They looked around the huge complex and stifled bored yawns until they spotted the loud collection of travelers further down the aisle. They walked quickly toward them and before long, were drinking bottles of beer with the rowdy group.

"I wonder who *they* are," Thomas asked aloud. Before he could continue, a well-dressed man entered alone. Without warning, he started orating to those inside the station, gesticulating stiffly to an unheeding audience.

"What's he doing?" Nettie asked, staring at the man.

"We call that speechifying where I come from," Ernest informed her, snickering loudly.

Nettie stared at the man silently for several minutes. "Is he a politician?' He's doing a lot of talking, but he's not saying anything."

"Must be," Ernest said with a chuckle. "I'm guessing he doesn't belong on our bus."

As soon as Ernest finished that statement, the nattily dressed man strode over to where the southbound bus passengers had collected and sat down.

"Waaaaaa!"

"What was that?" the little girl asked, looking around.

Thomas peered at an object at the opposite end of their row. "Sounds like a baby!"

"Waaaaa! Waaaaaa!"

Nettie and the little girl headed in the direction of the mewling infant. They walked back carrying a bassinet.

Thomas stared in amazement. "What's a baby doing here by itself?"

"I don't know, but he has a ticket," Nettie answered, pointing to the white piece of paper attached by a string to the infant's little wrist. The baby stopped crying once he was in the midst of the others.

"Where's he heading?" Thomas wanted to know.

Ernest shook his head. "Why would you have to ask?"

Nettie clucked her disapproval, but the little girl giggled hysterically.

"I wonder where his parents are," Thomas said, blushing.

Nettie smiled. "I don't think his parents could come with him on this trip. They probably miss him terribly."

"I know I would if he were mine," Ernest agreed.

Thomas slammed his cane on the floor. The little girl jumped and hid behind Nettie. "Who would be so irresponsible as to leave a little baby alone in a bus depot?" he demanded. He shouted so loud, the passengers waiting for the southbound bus stood up to see what the noise was all about.

"Hey, quiet down there in the cheap seats," shouted one of the young men. His friends high-fived him for his cleverness, followed by whoops of glee. The group started to chant again, while the two clergy and the politician looked on.

Thomas walked away from his companions toward the furthest side of the terminus. As he neared the giant windows, he noticed a group of men and women around his age or even older, all huddled under blankets and snoring. Large versions of bus tickets were pinned to their fronts.

"Who are those folks?" Thomas asked Ernest when he returned.

Nettie was the first to answer. "I bet those people are on our bus."

"Most of them are, Nettie," Ernest corrected. "That one guy over there doesn't seem to have a ticket."

Thomas looked over and confirmed that was true. "He's in the same circumstances I am," he muttered.

Ernest laughed, nodding vigorously. The little girl decided she had enough of all this adult talk and lay down on the bench. At her head rested the bassinet with the baby fast asleep inside it.

After a while, Thomas sat down to puzzle his predicament. Mostly everyone here has a ticket but me, he thought.

Ernest spoke up. "You didn't know you were supposed to bring a ticket with you, Thomas. I'm sure the bus driver will understand."

"I don't know about that, Ernest," Nettie warned. "They made it pretty clear when I stood in line for mine."

An announcement over the public address system interrupted their conversation.

"Northbound bus passengers, northbound bus! The northbound bus will be departing in fifteen minutes. I repeat, the northbound bus will be departing in fifteen minutes. Please make sure you have your tickets with you when you line up to board."

Nettie woke up the little girl. She rubbed eyes and stretched, then reached out to take Nettie's hand. Ernest stood and picked up the bassinet. Thomas watched them walk to an arched doorway with the word "Northbound" over it in simple block lettering.

"Hey, wait!" Thomas called out, panicking. He started limping after the others, but they didn't slow down for him. He stopped after a few steps, wheezing loudly. His four companions continued outside and into a white bus parked just outside the door. A few minutes after they boarded, the bus drove away.

Dejected, Thomas sat down on the bench again to rest. He was almost asleep when he heard a young couple giggling next to him.

"Hey, where are you headed?" a bearded youth asked him, his skin sallow and parched. He had his arm around the waist of a waif of a teen girl. She appeared to be half awake and hung onto his shoulders to keep herself from falling.

Thomas shrugged. "Nowhere, I guess."

"Nowhere?" the young man said with a loud laugh. "What's your ticket say?

"I have no ticket," Thomas said, looking down at his empty hands. The girl hiccupped loudly and slipped to the ground. Her boyfriend picked her up again and sat her next to Thomas. She fell over and landed on Thomas's shoulder. He could smell her sour breath and turned his head away from her.

"She's had too much to drink," the youth apologized, looking down at her blonde tresses. "We're headed south. Maybe you should come with us."

Thomas shook his head so hard that the girl stirred from her resting place. Her boyfriend propped her back up again.

"I'm going to wait until I get a proper ticket," Thomas averred, thrusting his chin out defiantly.

"Sure thing, Pops, whatever you want. It's your bus ride. I was just being sociable."

The young man picked up his girlfriend and started dragging her away.

"Have a good trip, man," the youth said. He shook the girl several times until she started walking on her own, leaning heavily on his arm for support. Thomas watched as the couple rejoined the others. Their friends slapped them on the back and handed them beer bottles to celebrate their return.

I don't want to go on *that* bus, Thomas thought to himself. He looked at the sleeping people against the wall. Maybe I can borrow a ticket?

Casually, Thomas shuffled over to the sleeping passengers and took an empty seat next to them. Their snoring was painfully loud, but Thomas ignored that for the moment. He looked at the ticket of the man closest to him.

"Direction: northbound. Travel date: August 1, 2021."

"2021?" Thomas shouted. The southbound travelers looked over at him for a moment, then continued their celebration.

Thomas pondered this new development. Here it is, 2007, and this guy isn't even leaving until 2021. He's going to sleep here for fourteen years?

Sighing loudly, Thomas arose and walked back over to his seat. No need to borrow their tickets, he mused. They're going to be here a while and I need to get moving.

The public address system blared again.

"Attention, southbound passengers, attention! Your bus has now arrived and is outside the appropriately marked door. Please make sure you have your tickets with you before you board! As a reminder, please deposit your bottles in the trash receptacle as you exit. This is for southbound passengers only!"

Thomas watched as the rowdy group cheered and headed toward their exit. Eventually, the clergy people shuffled along behind them. The politician brought up the rear, his ticket flapping jauntily in his hand.

The southbound bus pulled up to the door. This one was also white, but the years hadn't been kind to it. Graffiti marred the entire outside of the vehicle. Someone even scrawled red paint across the windows. Once the passengers finished boarding, it pulled away from the depot.

Thomas had enough for a while. He closed his eyes again and soon fell asleep. In his dream, he chased after a white bus, but the faster he went, the faster the bus drove. He ran as hard as he could, but he could never catch up. He thought he saw the driver waving at him, but then he realized it was actually Ernest urging him to go faster.

"Sir!"

Thomas struggled to wake himself.

"Sir, why are you here?"

Thomas opened his eyes and was surprised to see a man in uniform shaking him awake. He wore a green cap that said "Depot Master" on the front.

"What's wrong? Why can't I sleep here?"

The man looked at him oddly. "Don't you have a ticket?"

"No, sir, I never got one. I thought I could buy one somewhere in the building." Thomas stood, his cane wobbling as he picked himself up.

"Oh no, we don't sell tickets here," the man explained, leading Thomas to the exit. "But one thing I do know for certain is you can't stay."

"What should I do?" Thomas managed to ask.

The man shrugged. "If it were me, I'd go back home and figure it all out first before coming back. Buses leave once a day, every day, at the same time."

Thomas took one more look behind him. He glanced up at the ceiling, mouth wide open.

"I never noticed that!" he said in awe. The ceiling was painted sky blue with clouds randomly placed along its expanse. Sunlight appeared to shine through the clouds, lighting up the entire surface.

The depot master looked up. "Yeah, that's quite lovely, isn't it?"

"Yes, it certainly is," Thomas agreed.

The depot master opened the door, but Thomas hesitated.

"Hey, wait! How will I know which bus to take?"

"How would *I* know your destination, friend? You'll have to work that out yourself."

Thomas shook the man's hand. "Okay, thanks. Hope to see you soon."

Thomas squinted from blinding sunlight that flooded the parking lot.

§

"Clear!"

"Doctor, I'm getting a pulse! Blood pressure is coming up!"

"Normal sinus rhythm, doctor!"

"Blood pressure, 120 over 80!"

Thomas carefully opened his eyes and found a crowd moving frantically around him. A bright examination light almost blinded him. He tried to raise his hand to cover his eyes, but found someone had tied down his wrist.

"What's going on here?" Thomas mumbled. He felt hands removing a tube lodged in his throat.

"Hey, you decided to come back!" a man in a blue mask said, looking down at him. "We were wondering what took you so long to make up your mind."

Paper, Pen & Ink

A poet's words may paint the picture
the world wants to love.
Or they may unfasten a timeless belief
that has held us captive.

Wander down the pages, scan the lines,
believe they have no sway.
Cover both eyes with myopic hands and think
the verse has no meaning.

Listen! That is your heart beating in rhythm
to the pulsing symphony.
Shed no tears, this is no eulogy for the damned,
echoing your ancient fears.
Believe with every sense, this is a new life,
born from tenuous epiphany.
It jolts you into this immediate existence,
exhaling a higher purpose.

Trace the faint drama, sing a plaintive rhyme and
bleed black on the canvas.
Test each sinew, the endless stream of thought pours
from every blistered cell.

A new door opens, with a fresh dawn breaking
through grisly, awestruck clouds.
Turn the page, the book of your soul lays bare and
offers nothing, but gives all.

Wandering

"I wander thro' each charter'd street,
Near where the charter'd Thames does flow,
And mark in every face I meet
Marks of weakness, marks of woe."

- William Blake

Nobody hitchhikes anymore. I don't make that observation casually, but I derived it after careful contemplation of the human condition. The day of the American nomad has faded far behind us, along with our innocence and overall sense of adventure. Blame it on hard core cynicism, bred from watching too many of our heroes turn out to be schmucks. Or maybe we're seeing a reaction to the long adagio of guerrilla politics that plays nightly on the TV news.

Nope, the days of thumbing rides has gone the way of the corner store, I guess. I'm one of a dying breed of wanderers, a poet in walking shoes looking for a town with my name on it. There's nothing like the thrill of seeing that car pull over to let you in. Who will this one be? A beautiful woman escaping the clutches of an abusive boyfriend? A college boy hitting the road after a long semester of boozing and babes? Or maybe, just maybe, this traveler will turn out to be someone that will teach me the bigger truths.

That's not to say I don't learn something from every driver, I do. It isn't always abstract or even engaging, but it's knowledge and knowledge remains the itinerant's only treasure.

I remember this one time on a long stretch outside of Abilene, a nervous looking middle-aged woman pulled over to give me a ride. The fact that she even stopped surprised me because she didn't appear to be the type to talk to strangers, let alone invite an unknown man into her car on a deserted road just as dusk approached. This woman, Sadie, well, she didn't talk much at first. Eventually, she admitted she was married to the same man for almost twenty-five years and just that morning, she woke up, got in her car and drove south.

You may not think I learned much from Sadie, but I did. She taught me that it's never too late. That's all; it's never too late. I've kept that lesson close to my heart ever since, because when you travel around without any plan or destination, you need to know you can always settle down if you want.

Sure, I've come close to putting down stakes a couple of times. I remember the last one most clearly. It was back in 1997, probably late summer, and I was passing through Kansas. An old farmer driving a red Ford pickup truck dropped me off on Route 169 just outside this nondescript little town. It must've been close to noon when I walked past the sign that stood proudly at the city limits announcing "Welcome to Prairie Village, Home of George Brett."

I ambled into the first diner I saw and took a seat at the counter.

"Coffee, hon?" the waitress predictably asked, a steaming pot at the ready. I could see her looking at my backpack and already calculating how much of a tip I was going to give her.

"Yeah, I could use some. Black is fine." I pushed the cup in her direction. She filled it to the brim and carelessly dripped the overflow into the saucer. I'm sure she saw the mess, but didn't offer to sop it up and walked off to spill her wares on her next victim.

The menu looked like someone used it to fend off an egg attack from a band of marauding Cub Scouts. I used a sheet from a discarded newspaper to wipe off the debris so I could read the breakfast selections.

"What'll you have, hon?" My favorite waitress came back, her glass coffee pot still occupying her trigger hand.

"Give me a number two, please. Eggs, over easy. Whole wheat toast, dry," I replied, returning the menu to the dull chrome holder next to me.

"You got it, hon."

You have to love small town diners. For the most part, they're not much different than their predecessors from a hundred years ago. I bet waitresses were calling customers "hon" back then, too.

I didn't have to wait long for the waitress to deliver my bacon and eggs. Much to my surprise, the eggs were perfectly done and the bacon strips had a satisfying crisp to them. I felt pretty hungry that day and ate every crumb I could see, wiping up the remainder of the yolk with the last corner of toast with a practiced swipe.

After my second refill of java, I called it quits. I left a generous tip and took off to check out the town.

At the center of Prairie Village is Austin Harmon Park and that's where I headed first. I've found that to get a full measure of a town, all you need to do is look at how well they maintain their public facilities. A community with good parks usually means they have a strong school system. Families, kids . . . all signs of a stable society. Places that are full of nomads like me are poorly kept up.

Austin Harmon Park was a stunner, I give you that. On that day in Prairie Village, the town was preparing for its Founders Day celebration. Workers from the Blue Moose Bar and Grill, clad in their establishment's T-shirts and hats, were busy setting up a twenty foot replica of the legendary Blue Moose. According to local lore, sightings of the large mammal were routinely been reported to the authorities ever since the original families settled there.

At first, no one paid attention to the gangly, slightly sooty stranger that sat on the park bench, watching the Blue Moosers (as I called them in my mind) festooning the park entrance with bunting and the largest collection of sunflowers I ever saw in one place. After a while, though, I saw a big, beefy sort of fellow casually heading in my direction. He carried himself like he the leader of the work crew.

"Hi, stranger!" he boomed, his voice echoing through the cottonwoods. Several of his crew watched the exchange as they worked.

"Hello," I smiled, shaking the man's extended hand. I waited patiently for the pitch.

"Just passing through?"

"Yep, heading over to Los Angeles to see my brother." I had no brother, at least none that I knew of. My mother may have spawned more after I ran away fifteen years before.

The boss looked around the perimeter of the park for a while. "What do you drive?"

I anticipated that question. It's a generally accepted rule that a man isn't a real man unless he owns a gas-powered vehicle. Motorcycles are fine, mopeds and mini bikes don't count, but a sturdy riding lawn mower will pass most of the time.

"Broke down in North Carolina. Been on the Greyhound line since Asheville." I sat back and watched his reaction.

"I used to live in North Carolina." Of course, you did. Here it comes.

"Yeah, I grew up in Greensboro. You know the area?"

A test, as I expected. "No, I can't say that I do. I was only passing through the state when my engine seized on my way. A '71 Mustang convertible. When they towed it to the shop, the mechanic put it on the lift and showed me where I cracked the frame. Dead engine and damaged carcass. I sold 'er in for scrap metal."

That's how you converse with the locals in a strange town, at least with the men. Talk cars with them. Everyone can relate and you can form bonds immediately.

Boss man let out a whistle and shook his head. "A 'stang to the garbage pile, eh? That must've hurt."

Someone turned on the sound system. The strains of Santo and Johnny's "Sleepwalk" filled the morning air with sweetly sad steel guitar. The big man sat down next to me.

"Yeah, but I guess I should be glad it happened when I wasn't out on an empty stretch of highway," I told him.

He chuckled. "My name's Grady, what's yours?"

"You can call me Duley, everyone does. You're the straw boss here?"

"Who me?" Grady was one of those guys who laughed with his entire body. He wasn't a small man, that's for sure, so there was a lot of him to shake. "Yeah, I guess you could call me that. I'm the bartender over at the Blue Moose. You know it?"

I shook my head. "No, but I do now. I guess I passed through town at the right time."

"Hey, Grady! We need your help over here!" We both turned to look at a diminutive fellow perched up on the ladder, straining with all his might to hang one end of a welcome banner on the wooden pole raised for that purpose. How did the little man get to be the lucky one for that job?

Grady stood up. "Look, I gotta go help these guys. Are you planning to stay through the weekend for the celebration? There'll be lots of food and drink, not to mention live music if you like to dance."

Now, I normally made it a policy to not eat two meals in the same town if I can absolutely avoid it. On rare occasions, bad weather would force me to stay put for a while and then I'd have a second meal before I finally shoved off.

Grady saw me pause. "Well, look, if you decide to stay, Duley, the festivities start at seven tonight and shut down at midnight after the fireworks display. Tomorrow will be a farmer's market and art sale that will go until nine o'clock at night."

I smiled at the memory of fireworks. It had been a long time since I sat under a dark sky alit with pyrotechnics. The idea tempted me.

"Thanks, Grady, I'll think about it."

I watched him saunter off to replace the short guy. Grady had no trouble hanging the banner proclaiming the town's fifty-sixth year in existence. Pictures of the town mascot, the infamous Blue Moose, were carefully drawn on either end of the banner.

The celebration wouldn't begin for several more hours. I leaned strongly toward moving on again, but something about Grady's friendly nature and the general tempo of the town appealed to me. For the first time in a long while, I could see myself settling down and frankly, the thought scared the hell out of me.

I grabbed my backpack and walked back down Delmar Street and turned up W. 77th Place. The cottonwoods grew lush there, too. The way the sunlight poured through the branches and lit up the pavement made me think of my days as a child, riding my bike back and forth past our tenement.

I passed a guy standing on a ladder, dressed in well-used coveralls. He was painting the front of a furniture store and from the looks of it, he had quite a bit more to do before the day got too hot to work.

I proceeded less than two hundred yards past him when I heard him call out to me.

"Excuse me! Sir?" I turned back to look at him. He gestured for me to walk over there. Always the curious sort, I complied.

"Yes?" I asked him, looking up the length of the ladder. He had a pleasant enough face, his forehead creased in frustration.

"Hey, are you looking for work?"

Now there was nothing about my appearance that suggested I was in the market for a paying gig, but it seemed that no matter where I went, people assumed I wanted odd jobs. I guess I should've been thankful because I always ended up with enough money to move around without forcing me to panhandle.

"Maybe," I replied. "It depends what it is."

The guy chuckled. "Yeah, I'd answer the same way if I were you. Did you ever paint before?"

Now, I once called painting my full time occupation, that is, before building construction tanked and I lost my job. I tried to hang onto my house after that, but in the end, I lost it all.

"A little," I offered. "Not very good at it, though."

"What's there to be good at? Put some paint on the roller, roll it on. Repeat. Simple, right?"

I liked this guy. Straight, direct and knew what he wanted. That was me at one time.

He saw me hesitate and added, "Look, I'll pay you twenty bucks an hour and you can have all the pops you want. I'll even throw in lunch."

The guy was desperate, I guess. From the size of the front of the building, he was looking at eight hours worth of work at an amateur pace. I could get it done in six, including the clean-up. He watched me as I sized up the job.

"Well? You interested?"

"Sure, why not?" I answered. "Where can I put my pack?"

"Go around to the side door and stow it inside there. You'll see a pair of coveralls laying over the chair there. Put that on, if you want. The painter's cap, too."

I returned in a few minutes, uniformed once again like a professional painter. I didn't exactly have nostalgic feelings about it, I had to say.

"What's your name?" the ladder guy asked me as he descended.

"Duley."

"Pleased to make your acquaintance, Duley. I'm Jake Perlmutter. This is my furniture store." He had big, meaty hands like my grandfather's and squeezed mine just as hard as the old man used to.

"Look, Duley, I have a business to run and I can't be out here painting, too. I'll check on you in an hour and see how you're coming along."

I started climbing up the ladder, but then paused. "What about those pops?"

Jake chuckled. "You don't miss a trick, do ya? I'll have one of my guys bring a cooler out here full of 'em. Will that do ya?"

"That'll work, thanks."

I climbed to the top of the ladder where the painting gear awaited me. Lime green, I thought to myself, a bit disgusted with the paint color choice. Oh well, it's his store, he must have his reasons.

True to his word, Jake came out about an hour later to see how I was making out.

"Whoa, you sure move fast! Did you ever paint buildings before?"

"A little," I called down. "Back in my younger days."

Jake laughed so hard he almost choked. "Younger days? How the hell old are you, anyway?"

"Older than I look, but not as old as I feel." That was my pat answer, one that usually deflected any follow-ups.

"Gotcha," Jake replied, flashing me the thumbs up signal. "Need anything before I go back in?"

I checked the cooler I brought up with me and shook my head. Jake gave me the thumbs up again and went back inside.

Around twelve-thirty, one of Jake's workers, a guy about my age by the name of Andrew, called up to me.

"Jake wants to know if you're hungry for lunch yet." I could see his lime green baseball cap clear as day from where I was standing. Hell of a company color, I thought.

"Yeah, I'll be down in a sec." I wiped the excess paint off the roller with the stir stick and headed down.

Jake met me at the door and handed me a brown bag.

"I hope you like roast beef," he said, leading me to the break room. "The Blue Moose makes a great sandwich. Gotcha potato salad and pickles, too."

I thanked him and grabbed a seat.

"Mind if I join ya?" Jake asked, sitting down across from me.

"You're the boss."

He laughed at that and nodded.

"How long are you in town for, Duley?"

I took a bite of the sandwich and shrugged. "Oh, I don't know. I really don't expect I'll be here much past six tonight."

Jake eyed me carefully. "Will you have the painting done by then?"

I nodded. "The base coat will be done. You'll have to find somebody else to do the second coat."

He cleared his throat before he continued. "Look, Duley, there's something about you I like. I can't place my finger on it. Hell, I never met you before in my life. But from the little bit I saw, I can tell you know your way around a paint brush. There's a lot of work for a good painter in this town."

I kept eating, patiently hearing him out.

"Anyway," Jake continued, "this is a nice town, Duley. A town where a man can plant roots, ya know?"

Of course, I understood. That's one reason I always kept moving. Roots are too easy to catch. I just nodded and hoped my subconscious ignored all of that.

"I'm not from here myself," Jake admitted. He rubbed his huge hands together, over and over again. I could see the fluorescent overhead lights highlighting the clumps of silver in his thinning mane. "I moved out here from Los Angeles nineteen years ago. Back then, I served as a high-powered executive at an ad agency you may have heard of."

He told me the name of the place and I nodded, impressed.

"The only thing that helped me relieve the stress was woodworking. I picked up the hobby from my father. During a particularly rough patch, I was creating one piece of furniture after another. It got to the point where I didn't have any place to store 'em all!"

I didn't even know I had finished my sandwich, his story had so engaged me. Jake walked over to the refrigerator and pulled out two pops. He handed me one and opened up the other. After taking a long gulp, he continued.

"It was my wife who had the idea of selling the pieces I made. She started out with a yard sale one weekend and we were both surprised that we sold everything in a couple of hours. I believe the thought implanted itself when I pocketed the cash from the final sale of the day."

I smiled. "To ditch it all and make furniture for a living?"

"Damn right! I walked in the office that Monday, called an emergency meeting with my senior managers and announced my resignation. A month later, we moved to Prairie Village."

I could see the fire in the man's eyes as though he was reliving that memory all over again. "Why Prairie Village, Jake?"

Jake shrugged and finished the rest of his pop. "Why not? Winters are fairly mild here and summers aren't unbearable. Housing is cheap, especially compared to the west coast. All in all, it seemed like a fine decision to me. I'm glad my wife agreed at the time or who knows what institution I'd be locked in now."

I stood up and carried my trash to the waste bin. "Well, I better get back to the painting if I'm going to remain on schedule."

Jake walked me to the door. "Hey, Duley, I hope I didn't bore you with my tale of escape. In some ways, you're a lot like me . . . looking for answers and a way to make your mark on this world. And do that on your own terms too. Do me a favor and think about what I said, okay?"

"Sure, Jake, I'll think about it. Talk to you later."

Honestly, after that sales pitch, I couldn't wait to get back to painting. I found peace sitting in my artificial aerie once again and soon became lost in my work.

I was about to take a break around midday when I heard a little boy's voice calling to me.

"Mister! Hey, mister!"

"Hold on, I'll be right down," I called down to him as I made my descent. He waited for me at the base of the ladder.

'What's your name, young man?" I asked cheerfully, taking a pop out of the refilled cooler one of Jake's people left for me.

"Rory," the boy said, staring at the cooler.

"You thirsty? Help yourself!"

I barely got the words out before he stuck his hand in the plastic container, fishing out a cold drink. He managed to open the top by himself and took a huge mouthful, his cheeks filling up with all the cola he could fit.

"Do you live around here, Rory?" I asked him, sitting cross-legged on the sidewalk. Rory did the same thing facing me.

"No, my grandpa works here." Rory had an impish grin and I smiled back by reflex.

"What's your grandpa's name?"

"His grandpa's name is Jake," Jake answered for the boy as he walked out to the sidewalk. "I see you met my grandson."

"Yeah, Grandpa! He gave me a pop and everything!" Rory's smile extended ear to ear, causing both Jake and me to laugh.

"He's not keeping you from your work, is he?" Jake asked me.

"Who, him?" I pointed at Rory, who busied himself drawing something indiscernible in the dirt. "No way, he's working me a like a dog."

We both looked over at the boy to see if he was paying attention, but he was too engrossed in whatever little game he just invented for himself.

"How's the job coming?" Jake asking me, looking up at the wide expanse of building's façade.

"Real good, Jake. I should have the entire front done by six o'clock like I thought."

"Grandpa, look what I made!"

Jake walked over and saw the artificial world his grandson created out of dirt, stones and a couple of leaves.

"You're going to be an architect some day, right?" Jake told him, rubbing the boy's sun-bleached mop of hair.

"Yep, Grandpa," Rory dutifully replied, continuing to build up his little dirt town. He turned a stick into a trench digger, complete with sound effects.

"Ever think of starting a family, Duley?" Jake looked up from his grandson's project to gauge my reaction to the question.

I shook my head. "No, I can't say that I have, Jake. I'm not really a family kind of guy. I have too much of a traveling bone in me."

"Too bad. Having kids of your own, it's a challenge. But watching them grow up and then raising their own is the reward for all your hard work. After we left Los Angeles, our daughter got lonesome for us, so she moved out here, too. Met a local fella, got married. Rory came along nine months to the day later. How old are you, Rory?"

The boy held up four fingers on one hand a one bent one on the other. Jake and I smiled at each other. Oh, to be the age where we're counting half years!

I looked up at the front of the building and then stood. "Time to get back to work, chief."

Without missing a beat, Rory piped up, "Yes, you're on a schedule."

Both Jake and I looked at each other and burst out laughing. Rory ignored us and continued erecting his burgeoning play city.

I climbed the ladder and started painting. After an hour, I noticed Rory had left, probably off inventing another new world somewhere else. If you ever feel the need to envy someone, watch a child. As long as that brand of innocence exists somewhere, the world will remain an amazingly beautiful place.

The sun had drifted below the tree line by the time I finished the paint job. I gathered up all the supplies and organized them on the sidewalk, then took down the ladder and laid it along the side of the building. I headed into the store to collect my wages.

"Five forty-five? You're done?" Jake said when he saw me.

"Yes, sir! The entire front is painted as I promised. It will need a second coat, though. I would wait a good twenty-four hours before you start."

Jake reached into his pocket for his wallet. He opened it up, flipped through a few bills, then shook his head.

"Look, Duley, I'll have to get some cash at the ATM to pay you. Where are you staying? I can run it over to you in an hour."

Normally, I would be more than a little suspicious that I was about to be taken, but I had come to trust this man implicitly.

"Well, I guess you can find me at the park, Jake. I'm not checked in anywhere."

"Are you planning to be at the Founders Day celebration?"

"At least until you pay me, I will be," I said with a wry smile. I started to think he was subtly manipulating me, but I didn't feel angry about it.

"Fine, I'll see you over there around seven."

I removed the coveralls and hat, then picked up my backpack and jacket still sitting where I left them.

The work crew had completely transformed the park from where I first saw it in the morning. There were bunches of blue and silver balloons tied to the tallest trees. I saw several large picnic tables lined up with folding chairs neatly tucked underneath them. Workers had strategically placed huge overhead lights around the tables in order to provide illumination for dining. Someone had set up three large grills which were already lit and being monitored by a single barbecue chef, a huge man donned in a blue apron. I wandered over to talk to him.

"What's on the menu today?" I joked.

The man looked at me and grinned. "You must not be from around here, son. The traditional Founders Day meal consists of hamburgers, hot dogs, steaks, roasted corn on the cob, potato salad, and fried pickles. For dessert, there's homemade ice cream and apple pie."

My stomach started to growl at the sound of all that food.

"How much will it cost me?"

The man sized me up for moment, but not in a threatening way.

"For non-residents, it's twenty dollars for a full meal with dessert. It's free if you live here, though."

"Sounds like a good deal in either case. You're the only cook?"

"Nope, my helpers will be here shortly."

I watched him trim the fire for a while.

"Are you somehow affiliated with the Blue Moose?" I finally asked.

The man laughed. "Hell yeah, you think I'd be working on a holiday otherwise? I'm the head chef over there, too. Name is Big Chris."

"I'm Duley. Nice to meet you."

He nodded and moved over to the second grill.

"We usually eat around eight, Duley. Don't forget to buy your meal ticket at the front. My wife, Vivian, is running that show tonight."

"Thanks, Chris"

"Big Chris," he corrected me with a smirk.

"Sorry, Big Chris. I'm looking forward to your cooking."

"Bring your appetite, Duley. There will be lots of it."

I headed over to the entrance to the park. From a distance, I could just make out a red-headed woman sitting at a card table.

"Hello," I said politely when I arrived.

"Hi, there!" she greeted me, a broad smile on her pleasant face. She had the tallest bouffant I ever saw. The woman couldn't be called tiny herself. I guess she had to be big to be married to Big Chris.

"You're Vivian?"

"Why, yes! How did you know that?" Vivian replied graciously.

"Big Chris told me to look for you to get my meal ticket," I said, reaching into my pocket.

"You're not from around here, right?"

"Nope, I'm paying cash money." I handed her a ten and ten ones. That left me with exactly one whole dollar. I certainly hoped Jake wasn't going to stiff me or I'd be sunk.

Vivian took the wad of bills and placed it carefully in the small tin lockbox in front of her. She handed me a small ticket in exchange.

"Give this to the table monitor when you're ready to eat. You'll be handed a paper plate. Then you can stand in line to get your food. Don't lose that ticket!"

I shook my head. "No way will I do that, Vivian. I told Big Chris I'm looking forward to trying his cooking. He's a man that doesn't take too kindly to being let down."

Vivian chuckled. "Nope, you're right. But despite his size, he's a teddy bear. And he's the best cook in this county, though I think I'm a bit partial. Anyways, enjoy yourself, er -- "

"The name's Duley. And I'm just passing through."

"Nice to meet you, Duley. Have fun tonight! Don't forget to stay for the fireworks show!"

"Thanks, Vivian. I wouldn't miss it."

After a long day of work in the hot sun, I was beat. Since the park was still empty, I decided to take a nap on a park bench. I found one a bit out of the way and settled myself in for a short snooze.

I remember dreaming about being at a carnival when I was a little kid. It appeared to be the county fair, I guess, one I used to go to when I was still in grade school. My mom held my hand as we wandered through the maze of tents and booths that dotted the fairgrounds. In my dream, I dragged her to get to the Ferris wheel, a ride I remember both thrilled and scared the hell out of me.

My mom seemed to be like a dead weight as I tried to pull her forward through the crowd. I finally looked back to see why she was moving so slowly and instead of it being my mother, I realized I was being dragged the opposite way by a huge black bear with red eyes. I could see saliva dripping from his bared fangs and the worn spots on his furry legs and back. It all seemed so vivid!

"Duley? Duley!"

I opened my eyes with a start and saw Jake's smiling facing looking down at me.

"What's going on?" I asked, still a bit confused.

Jake laughed. "I think you were dreaming, son. And from the looks of it, I don't think it was a particularly pleasant one, either."

I rubbed my eyes, then stretched. "What time is it?"

"Time to eat! Did you get your meal ticket?"

I reached into my pocket and displayed it for his inspection.

Jake handed me a wad of cash. "Here's the money I owe you. Feel free to count it if you'd like."

I shoved the cash in my pocket and stood up.

"Well, come on then, we're wasting time here talking," Jake said, me toward the eating area.

"By the way, Duley, I hope you don't mind sitting next to Rory while we eat. He's quite taken with you."

"Sure, no problem. I like the little guy."

I handed my ticket to the table monitor and received my plate just as Vivian promised. The food line moved quickly and in a few minutes, Jake and I were sitting down with the rest of his family, enjoying fresh grilled delicacies. Rory sat to my right, chomping on a hot dog that measured probably as long as his forearm.

"Good?" I asked the boy after a moment's rest from my meal.

Rory just smiled and nodded, but the hot dog never left his mouth. I couldn't help but chuckle.

"Duley, this is my wife, Patty," Jake said, pointing to the attractive woman sitting across from him. "To her right are our daughter, Lisa, and her husband, Bobby."

I nodded to them and resumed cutting into my steak.

"Duley here did an excellent job painting the store today," Jake announced. "Just like a pro."

Patty spoke up. "Have you ever painted professionally before, Duley?"

They caught me. "Yes, I have. I worked as a house painter for five years a long time ago. I finally got tired of working with so many drips."

I paused, waiting for the groans from the bad joke I just made. They didn't disappoint me.

"Any plans to stay longer, Duley?" Bobby asked me. I could see everyone's eyes watching for my reaction.

"I don't think so, Bobby. I don't like to stay in one place very long."

"Too bad," Jake said. "I have that entire building yet to paint a second time. I bet a professional like yourself could do a great job. The money would be useful, too."

I smiled. "Jake, you're really trying to sell me on Prairie Village, aren't you? Heck, you don't even know me. How do you know I'd be an asset to your community?"

That's when Jake got serious on me. "Look, Duley, I wasn't successful in business by being wrong-headed about people. I'm proud of the fact that I can spend five minutes with a man and understand him at his core. No one can change my opinion of him once I've made up my mind."

"You can say that again," Lisa interjected. All the adults laughed.

A little red-headed girl ran over to our table. She couldn't have been older than six or seven.

"Hey, Rory, you wanna go play?" she shouted.

"Rory, honey, did you get enough to eat?" Lisa asked her son. Rory put the remainder of his hot dog down on his plate and nodded.

"Okay, son, you can go play with Jilly," Bobby said. The boy ran off with his friend toward the center of the park.

"Jilly belongs to Vivian and Big Chris," Jake explained, pointing to the couple standing near the grill.

"She has her mother's hair," I observed. "Cute, too."

"So like I was saying, Duley, there's a lot this town has to offer to a good man like yourself. Maybe you should stay a few days, finish painting both coats on my store and then we can talk about it some more." Jake looked at me quite sincerely. What could I say?

"I promise I'll think seriously about it, Jake," I finally answered.

"Good! That's all I ask. Now, is anyone ready for seconds?"

Tried as I might, I couldn't eat another morsel of food. Besides I was saving room for dessert.

"I think I'll take a walk, Jake. I need to exercise a bit of this dinner off of me."

"Okay, partner," Jake said affably. "The apple pie and ice cream won't be brought out until nine-thirty or so."

I excused myself from the table and headed toward the center of the park. The smell of the cottonwoods and pine trees filled the night air. I began to admit this little town's charm was seducing me.

There were couples also walking down the park's well-lit pathways. A few joggers passed me along the way, their running shoes crunching pebbles as they progressed. Everyone I met greeted me as though I belonged there. How could I not be taken with the place?

That's when I heard the scream.

"Help! Help me!"

I looked around to see where the voice was coming from.

"Help me! He fell in the water!"

I could barely make out a small figure standing near a pond about a couple hundred yards away. I ran in that direction.

"I'm coming!" I shouted, sprinting as fast as I could.

The figure I saw belonged to Jilly.

"It's Rory!" she sobbed, pointing in the water. "He went after a frog and fell in. I don't know where he is."

She cried hysterically.

"Jilly, go run and tell Rory's mommy and daddy what's happened! Hurry!"

I watched her run back toward the eating area, then turned back to the pond.

There was no sign of Rory or anything else moving in that water. I feared the worst, but I was determined to do what I could.

After stripping down to my shorts, I waded into the cold water and searched for the blond boy. As luck would have it, the moon was full and with the large overhead lights around the pond, I could see into the shallow, murky waters. But once I dived deeper, I was almost swimming blind.

I broke the surface and took several deep breaths. I held the last one and dived deep again.

When I was a kid, I known as the strongest swimmer in my neighborhood, thanks to my mother's insistence I get swimming lessons at seven. Every summer, I could be found at the public swimming hole from morning until dusk almost every day, so much so I earned the nickname "Otter."

The pond water felt much colder the deeper I dived, but thanks to my day in the sun, it didn't affect me much. I swam in a zigzag pattern, reaching my arms out as far as I could to feel where Rory may be.

I rose again, this time coughing the excess water from my nose. The other adults hadn't arrived yet. I couldn't give up!

Several deep breaths later, I dived even deeper into the water. I veered to my left and felt something oddly familiar graze my leg. I turned in that direction and swam hard.

Moments later, I held my hand under Rory's chin. I pulled him up to me and squeezed him hard as I kicked us up to the surface. I concentrated so much on getting us out of there that I didn't feel the pop in my chest.

Rory's parents and grandparents were there to meet us at the water's edge. A number of the other townspeople also surrounded the pond. Two policemen helped carry Rory to the shore where paramedics waited to treat him. I could hear Lisa sobbing loudly as they loaded the boy into the ambulance. It sped away, sirens shrieking. The crowd followed the bouncing vehicle across the park.

"You're bleeding, mister." I looked up and saw Jilly staring at my face. I touched my mouth and examined my fingers. She was right. Then I took a deep breath and felt like my lungs were on fire.

"More blood," Jilly said calmly. "Lots of it. I better get my mommy."

I saw her running as fast as her little legs could carry her. Once she was out of sight, I lay flat on my back and tried to breathe slowly. Every time I inhaled or exhaled, it felt like a knife was tearing a jagged hole into my chest. I remember thinking that I never was injured even once since I took to hitchhiking.

Despite my attempts to stay alert, I felt myself drifting off. I didn't see a bright light or choirs of angels, but I do recall that one moment I felt terrible pain, the next moment it was gone. And so was I.

Yep, that's the time I almost settled down in one perfect spot. I still pass through Prairie Village from time to time. It's a lovely town, probably one of the nicest ones in the entire universe. The people who live there are some of the nicest you'll ever meet. Too bad I couldn't stay. I really think I could've called it home. But I'm a traveling man and I know I'll keep wandering until I find a better place. Until then, my thumb will be out waiting for the next ride.

Going my way?

Descend Now, Venus

Orate, intone in one voice frantic;
Pontificate, advise on sin pedantic;
Gravitate, attract one's inner light;
Levitate, soar high in windless flight.

Pinnacle, elevate to heights supreme;
Pentacle, descend to depths extreme;
Rational, opine aloud with soulless face;
Emotional, inspire anew with mirthful grace.

Clamoring, assault the walls with discordant ire;
Enamoring, adore at last with unquenched desire;
Stammering, loss of heart, of word and pen;
Hammering, ceaseless sound is heard again.

Clarify, open channels long denied;
Deify, raise your voices, gods abide;
Mortify, praise the humanity in all;
Sanctify, lift our spirit, hear our call.

The Deepest Cut

Hello, my given name is Tony, and I'm a barber. I know that sounds like an announcement at a twelve step meeting, but unlike drinking, cutting hair ain't addicting. What I *will* tell you is that barbering can be bad for your health nonetheless.

Before you ask, yes, I know the name "Tony" for a barber sounds like it came right out of Central Casting. Wanted: one Italian guy by the name of Tony to play a barber in some Scorsese movie. I swear my name is Tony - Anthony DeSilvio is what I was born as, though only my mother and my parish priest ever called me Anthony.

I learned to be a barber thanks to Uncle Sam. When I was sixteen, I got into some trouble with these kids in my neighborhood. Before you start thinking I was framed or something, let me say for the record that I was hardly innocent of the crimes we got caught for. The judge, a guy as old as my grandfather, told me I had two choices: go to the juvenile delinquent detention center for a year or join the service. My mother told me I had no choice, so into the Navy I went. Learn a good trade and see the world, she told me. So, I became an apprentice barber on the USS Franklin, the best damn aircraft carrier in the fleet. Once I got out of the service, it was time for me to make my living, so it was only natural for me become a professional barber.

Everybody knows barbers got stories. We're like bartenders that way. You spend time up close and personal with some guy's nose hairs, you learn things. It's not like you have to ask or nothing, they just tell you. I'll let you in on a little secret . . . not all of the stories we barbers hear are worth telling. How many times can you hear the one about some guy running around with his secretary, making a monkey out of everybody, starting with his wife? Those ain't the ones worth repeating, I tell you. Not that I judge anyone, believe me. I just listen. And learn.

Getting back to those stories I started talking about, guys sitting in my chair tell me things. Sometimes they're things I don't want to know about. That's where I begin this personal confessional. Please stop me if you've heard it before.

Back then, I had a thriving business. Two chairs, two barbers, plenty of customers. Walk-ins, regulars, I had 'em all. We had 'em all, I should say. Joe, my partner, was the other half of the duo. Frick to my Frack, as I used to tell new customers. We weren't brothers, but we looked alike. That made for all sorts of jokes at each other's expense. Our clientele ate it right up and business boomed.

This was before the days of hair stylists and all those fancy haircuts you see now. No such thing as a blow dryer in a barbershop, at least not in ours. Nope, you had about a dozen standard haircuts to choose from . . . the flat top, the Ivy League, like those. Most guys came in to get the "usual," which was shorthand for a little off the top and sides, not too short.

I remember the first time I cut Jackie Delvecchio's hair. It was a Wednesday afternoon, usually a slow time for us. I was sitting in the chair, reading the ball scores. Joe was playing Solitaire; always with the cards, that guy. Delvecchio comes walking in with a pair of tough guys flanking him. The three of 'em looked like they owned the joint. Dressed to the nines with fedoras to beat the band. This was 1955, by the way ... guys were still wearing hats, though the fad was coming to an end.

Delvecchio walked over to me and asked if I was the boss. I looked over at Joe who was staring at his cards like he was catatonic or something. We both knew who Delvecchio was. You had to be living in a cave not to know this guy was a real Boss.

"One of 'em," I said to Delvecchio. "You need a haircut?"

His goons laughed and the taller one said, "Yeah, this is a barbershop, ain't it?"

I stood up and brushed off the seat for Delvecchio, then waved my hand over it like I was introducing the newest model out from Detroit. After I took his hat, I covered him with the sheet and raised his chair. The tough guys sat down and started browsing the skin mags we kept around when there were no women or kids there.

"What'll it be?" I asked Delvecchio. "Shave and a haircut?"

"Two bits!" one of the goons sang and the other one laughed himself silly.

"Pipe down, you two," Delvecchio ordered and both buried their heads in their reading material. I didn't hear from either one of 'em the rest of the time.

"Just a little off the top and sides will be fine," Delvecchio instructed me and I got right to it. Out of the corner of my eye I saw Joe looking a bit fidgety like he was going to do something stupid like run out to get a cop. I shook my head once to wave him off. Luckily, he calmed down and went back to his cards. Smart boy, my partner.

I got to cutting Delvecchio's hair, deciding to hold off on the small talk until I got a measure of him. Delvecchio wasn't very chatty either, so the only sound you heard were the snips of my scissors and the occasional flip of Joe's cards. Quiet as church, you might say.

The boss must've been happy with my work because he gave me a two dollar tip for a seventy-five cent haircut. Not too bad, eh? I could see Joe burning up from where I was standing. Makes me laugh today just to think about it.

I saw Delvecchio a couple of weeks later, again in the middle of the week. This time, his two goons waited outside. I could see them keeping watch over the shop from a dark sedan parked across the street.

"The usual?" I asked Delvecchio after I prepped him.

"Yeah, but give me a shave, too."

I handed him a newspaper and got to work. Fifteen minutes later, a freshly minted mob boss got up and gave me a three dollar tip and a slap on my back. Joe wasn't there that day or he would've been fit to be tied.

That's how I became Jackie "The Neck" Delvecchio's number one barber. Every two weeks he showed up for either a haircut or the whole works. Every time, he'd give me a fat tip. It was getting to the point where I was starting to depend on that extra cash every month.

After a while, Delvecchio started opening up to me like so many guys do. It started slow at first. You know, how the Dodgers were doing, local politics, stuff like that. Turns out he was a regular art connoisseur, at least compared to me. I don't know from stick figures, but Jackie knew his art. And he spent a lot of money on it, too. You got to envy a guy for having culture even if he is a crook. And The Neck was a crook, if nothing else.

I remember one day I was sitting in the shop, taking a break after a nonstop Saturday full of customers when I saw his mug plastered on page one of the Daily News. Seemed he got himself into a little trouble with the Feds and they were bringing him in on suspicion of murder. The guy he supposedly killed was this bookie in Brooklyn who wasn't cutting Jackie in on any of his action. As it turned out, they caught the real killer a week later and the next thing I knew, here comes Delvecchio into my shop ready for his usual. I could see a purple mouse still healing under his eye, but he didn't say anything about it. The cops could do what they wanted to keep crime in check back then, I guess.

A few months later, Delvecchio did get around to telling me about his time in the slammer, however short it was. Sure, the cops roughed him up, but he wasn't complaining. They had their job to do just like he had his. They weren't that hard on him anyway. At least he didn't end up with any broken bones! We both had a good laugh over that.

Sometimes I wouldn't see Jackie for a month or more, but then he'd show up on a Wednesday like he never was gone at all. Turned out he would be out of town on "business" … usually Vegas or Chicago. A few times, he'd come back from Miami, browner than a berry and more relaxed than ever. I wish I could see Miami, just once. It must be something.

Over time, Delvecchio started talking to me about his business "situations." At first, he didn't give me much in the way of details, but gradually, he started naming names, places and things. I learned more about the underworld from that guy in the fifteen minutes I spent with him twice a month, than I ever could reading those dime store novels.

More than once, Jackie warned me that one thing the mob didn't ignore were rats. I think he meant to scare me into keeping quiet about his stories, but he didn't need to do that as much as he did. One time was enough for old Tony here. Besides, who was I going to tell?

It was around this time that I met Tommy Minotti. That's right, that Tommy Minotti. He had the very charming nickname of "Kneecap" because of what he'd do to you if you were on his bad side. Blam! A .38 slug in the leg, usually right in the patella. That's the correct name for "kneecap," as I discovered one day ... but that's another story.

Minotti came into my shop one day wanting a haircut. I recognized him right away. You couldn't mistake that guy for anyone else. Six foot, four inches of the most foul-mouthed mobster you ever saw. Take your most hideous nightmare, multiply it by ten, and that was Tommy Minotti.

I was already with a customer, so Kneecap went over and sat in Joe's chair. My partner didn't know who it was right away, so he started treating him like a regular guy. That is, until Minotti took off his hat and showed off his huge head of hair. This was the guy's trademark, for God's sake, and here's poor Joe having to cut it perfect or he would end up losing the will to kneel!

Joe looked at me for help like I could do anything. I just shrugged and kept cutting hair. While I had one eye on my customer, I had the other one watching Joe (and a third one looking out the window for any trouble). Things could get dicey in a hurry in such a predicament.

I finished my customer in a few minutes, then glanced over at how Joe was doing and could see he wasn't getting very far. Minotti could see that, too, and started to look antsy. That's when I stepped in.

"Hey, Joe, I forgot to tell you your wife called a little while ago. She needs you at home, I think. Something about the plumbing."

Joe looked at me like I grew an extra pair of arms or something. "Hey, you know I ain't got no-"

"You better run over there fast, pal! No telling what kind of mess she's bailing out right now." I had to interrupt the mug before he made us both look bad.

Joe still sat there like a mope. God, he could be dumb sometimes!

"Go now!" I ordered him and helped push him to the back exit. Joe grumbled something about me being nuts and left.

Minotti eyed me like a snake eyeing a mouse sandwich. I tried not to squirm too much.

"Oh, sorry about that, Mr. Minotti. I'll take care of you in no time. A little off the top and sides?"

Turned out he wasn't one of those "gimme the usual" kinds of guys. He had a laundry list of things I should do or not do to make his famous mane pretty. Guys like that make me nervous as hell, but what was I going to do? Exactly what he asked for.

It took me about thirty minutes to get Kneecap looking presentable enough to meet his standards. When I was done, I handed him a mirror to check out the back. After several minutes of deliberate consideration, he nodded his approval. My kneecaps were saved!

Minotti didn't tip as good as Delvecchio and I did twice the work on him. I wasn't going to look a gift horse in the mouth, though. Two bucks was two bucks and it always came in handy. I had an expensive horse habit that needed an infusion of cash every now and then.

I didn't see Kneecap again for about three weeks. This time, he went right to my chair instead of to Joe's. Joe didn't look unhappy about that, either, I can tell you that!

Back then, I had a good memory for haircuts, so I didn't need any instructions to fix Minotti's hair the way he liked it. I think that impressed him because he gave me a three dollar tip that time. I did good! Even Joe smiled after he saw the mobster hand over the cash.

So, it became a regular ping pong match. I had Delvecchio every other week and Minotti every third week. Both of them were my biggest tippers and I became their only barber. Another thing they both had in common … they liked to talk about their "work."

Minotti warmed up to me faster than Delvecchio. By the fourth haircut, he was telling me things that hadn't even been in the papers yet. Hijacked milk trucks, bootleg cigarettes and the occasional murder over at the docks … all in a day's work for a mob boss. Like Delvecchio, he gave me a warning about being a rat and like I told his counterpart, there's no one I need to talk to about any of this.

A year went by and my two high profile customers were still making their regular visits, but they both were more sullen than they were when I first met them. It wasn't until this one July day that I started to understand what was happening. I was taking my lunch break in the shop and turned to the first page of the Daily News and what did I see? A mob war had broken out right on the streets of Brooklyn! The entire newspaper was filled with pictures of crooks with holes in them the size of Buicks, blood oozing from their mouths like streams from Red River Valley.

Thereafter, the rags were filled with news of mob reprisals, hits and other shenanigans. The cops were going crazy trying to keep a lid on everything, but it was too late. The door was open and Hell in all its fury was breaking loose. Who knew how it would all end?

Delvecchio kept coming into the shop despite all the crazy business going on. Tommy, on the other hand, went underground. I didn't see him for a couple of months and for a while, I thought he was one of the casualties of the worsening turf war.

Then, one Wednesday, in comes Minotti and takes his seat in the chair like normal. His hair was longer than I'd ever seen it. I guess when you're hiding out from your enemies and the cops, you let a little thing like haircuts go by the wayside.

Tommy didn't talk much that day and what he did tell me would make your hair curl. But the worst thing I found out: Delvecchio was gunning for him and swore vengeance for Tommy murdering his brother. I kept my mouth closed about knowing Jackie at all, but that was the first time I was ever really afraid befriending either one of those guys.

Next thing you know, the police come sniffing around the place. Joe and I were busy with customers and in walk two neighborhood cops looking like they were sharks at feeding time, all hungry and on the hunt. Now, I don't begrudge the cops their work. We always need more of 'em and seem to get fewer and fewer cops staying with the force very long. But these two guys, well, they seemed pretty intimidating to me. I could only imagine how my customers felt.

"You the owner?" the taller of the two asked me, a skinny rail of a guy with a snarl that would make his mother cry.

"One of 'em," I answered. "Joe back there is the other one."

Joe dutifully waved and continued working. His customer looked a little uncomfortable. Probably had an outstanding parking ticket or two.

"Have you seen either of these guys?" Tall cop pulled out two photos and they were pictures of, you guessed it, Delvecchio and Minotti.

"Yeah, I've seen them. In the paper." I pointed to the Daily News rolled up on the counter behind me. "You can't turn a page without seeing one of those goons."

"Do they ever come in here?" It was the second cop talking this time, a shorter, plumper version of his partner. He had the same sneer, too, a regular Clark Gable.

I shot a glance over at Joe, but he just kept his head down, probably praying those cops would get out of there. Joe didn't like trouble much.

"Nope, can't say that I've seen either one of them come in here. How about you, Joe?"

Joe mumbled something even I couldn't understand, and I knew the guy longer than anybody in the room.

"What was that?" the second cop asked, annoyed. "Speak up, will ya?"

Joe cleared his throat. "I said I never seen 'em here, either."

Tall cop looked at squatty cop and shrugged.

"Look, if either one comes here, give me a call, will ya? There's a reward for the capture of either one of these guys, triple for both. Here's my number."

He handed me a card with his name and phone number on it. I glanced at it briefly, then tossed it nonchalantly on the counter next to the newspaper.

"You, too," the second cop called out to Joe. My partner just raised his scissor hand, but didn't dare mumble another word.

I watched the two cops leave, then finished up my customer. As I expected, I got nothing for a tip, thanks to the two flatfoots and their heavy handed charm.

A few days later, Delvecchio checked in for a shave and a haircut ("two bits" … yeah, I know). Joe was out that day, so it was just me and him in the shop. I sat him down in my chair, not saying much. Normally, I'm pretty chatty with him, but he's a sharp character and sees I'm quieter than usual.

"Dame problems?" he asked me after a while. I laughed and shook my head, nothing more.

"Look, Tony, what's eatin' you? You're starting to make me nervous."

I took a deep breath and told the lie. "Oh, it's my ma. She hasn't been feelin' too good, you know? She lives in Jersey, at this home, and I can only get over to see her on Sundays."

"Is it bad?"

"Yeah, pretty bad. It's her heart."

Delvecchio didn't say anything for a while and let me cut in peace. But Jackie never stayed quiet very long. Empty spaces in conversations drove him nuts.

"Have you been reading the papers?"

Hell, I couldn't lie my way out of that one!

"Yep, I see you're a popular fellow, Jackie." I concentrated on trimming around his ears to distract him.

"Ha! Yeah, I'm popular. I got that guy Minotti gunnin' for me and the cops keep breathin' down my neck, hounding my crew. I just wanna be left alone, ya know?"

I just grunted and kept working.

"Hey, that reminds me. Do you ever see Minotti around here?"

I'm glad Joe wasn't around or he would've fallen over in a dead faint.

"Nope, he never showed up that I ever saw."

"Good. Do me a favor, will ya, Tony? If you ever do see him, give me a call. Hey, give me a piece of paper, okay?"

I peeled off a piece of the newspaper and handed him a pen. He scribbled something down and gave me the folded scrap.

"Keep this to yourself. Give it to nobody, got it?"

I nodded and finished off his cut. Delvecchio handed me a five dollar tip that time and shook my hand.

"Thanks, Tony, you've been a real friend. No matter what happens, don't worry. My boys will look out for you."

I watched him walk out the door and into the waiting car. From a distance, I could see he had two new goons. Those guys were even uglier than their predecessors. So much for the handsome mob guys you see in the pictures.

The next day, I told Joe all about my conversation with Delvecchio and asked him what he thought I should do. As usual, Joe didn't want to recommend anything. Instead, he raised his hand, saying something about it not being his problem, and sat down for his first round of solitaire for the day. Great partner, huh?

Later that afternoon, Officers Pete and Repeat came stomping into the shop like a couple of storm troopers. Just like with their previous visit, both Joe and I were busy with customers and didn't have time to deal with those two. This time, though, they were there to play for keeps.

"Tony, right?" Tall and skinny said to me.

"Yeah, I'm Tony. Any luck finding those guys?"

The shorter one looked at his partner and stepped forward.

"Look, Tony, you haven't been playing straight with us. We've had your shop staked out for the last week and our guy saw Delvecchio come in here just yesterday."

I tried to keep calm, more for my customer's sake than for anything else.

"So, what's the problem, Officer? Is it against the law for a guy to come in to get his haircut?"

"It depends," the skinny one said, stepping past his shorter half. "Our guy saw you and Delvecchio do an awful lot of talking."

"Nothing wrong with talking, is there?" I was starting to get pissed off. We're still living in the United States, right?

Slim saw I was getting agitated and took another approach. "Look, Tony, we have no beef with you. But Delvecchio's wanted for murder and we want to bring him in for a little questioning."

"Then why didn't you pick him up when he left here?"

The short one answered, a bit sheepishly. "Yeah, we wondered that, too."

"The plainclothes officer on the job said he didn't have back up, but the truth is Delvecchio had his bodyguards in high and tight. It was too risky." The tall cop looked apologetic like it was some skin off of my nose that he let a mob boss go. I just shrugged.

"Is there anything you want to tell us, Tony?" The short cop was trying to intimidate me again, I could tell. I wasn't budging.

"Nope, nothing. Delvecchio came in, we talked about my sick mother over in Jersey, sports, the weather. You know, the regular stuff."

"One other thing, Tony," the tall one said as both cops moved toward the door. "Our stakeout guy said Delvecchio handed you something."

Damn! He had me on that one. I desperately scanned the counter where I left the number. Next to it were a few local business cards I collected over the years.

"Sure, he gave me this," I said as I reached over and randomly pulled one of the business cards from the pile and handed it to the short cop.

"Diamanti's Tailors?" Shorty read out loud. "What's this about?"

"Oh, nothing really," I lied, hoping my nose wasn't growing at that point. "He told me that I should go there if I wanted a new suit made. The owner's a friend of his, he'll give me a good price."

Shorty looked at Slim for a second. "Best lead we've had in a week. Let's go check out Diamanti's."

I so much wanted the two cops to leave the shop then. When they were finally out of sight, I started breathing again.

"Are you done yet?" my customer asked me, staring nervously at the scissors pointing dangerously close to his jugular vein. I cleaned him up and sent him on his way. I was so shaken, I forgot to charge him for his haircut!

A week later, who came walking into the shop but Tommy Minotti himself. This place was starting to become a regular mob hangout. I didn't know if I should start charging admission to the local residents or not to watch the up close action.

Minotti looked haggard, more so than I've ever seen before. He just about fell into the chair. I placed the sheet over him and started his haircut as usual. Kneecap didn't say much for a while, which was fine by me. The way I looked at it, the less talking from these guys, the healthier I'd stay.

My luck didn't last long, though. Soon enough, Minotti was confessing his troubles to me like I was his neighborhood priest or something.

"Tell me, Tony, what would you do?" he asked me as I cut his ear hair. "I mean, Delvecchio killed my baby brother." He said "brother" like "brudda," the good old Brooklyn way. "Don't I deserve my revenge?"

I didn't answer right away. Minotti didn't like that.

"Well, don't I?"

The way he enunciated the words this time convinced me I should agree with him.

"Of course, Tommy, of course! He was your brother!"

"That's right," Minotti agreed. "You haven't seen that guy around, have you?"

Here I was, stuck in a squeeze play. I got Delvecchio wanting me to look out for Minotti and now I got Minotti pushing me to rat on Delvecchio. Hell, I was just a barber, for Christ's sake!

"No, Tommy, I've never seen the guy around this neighborhood."

Minotti looked at me hard like he was trying to read my mind or something. His face finally relaxed and he sat back in his seat.

"Yeah, I knew that guy wouldn't show himself in public. He's a yellow bastard and I can't wait to put a bullet in his fat coward head."

I was sure he meant it, too.

Minotti remained quiet while I finished his cut. He thanked me and gave me a good tip. He was about to walk out the door when he stopped and turned around.

"Hey Tony, thanks. You're a good friend."

I watched him get into the back of a black Cadillac and drive away. That was the last time I saw Tommy Minotti in my shop.

The cops kept stopping by, checking to see if I saw either of our mutual "friends." I kept giving them the silent treatment, but in Tommy's case, I had nothing to say. Delvecchio, on the other hand, must've thought he was bulletproof. He kept coming in every two weeks, usually in the middle of the day when it was slow. It's a wonder that the cops didn't figure out his routine.

Finally, the other shoe did drop. My two favorite cops made their regular visit, but they looked more unhappy than usual.

"Tony, we gotta talk to you," Shorty started out saying, not even waiting for his taller partner to open his mouth. Joe looked at me like we were about to meet the Clanton brothers at the O.K. Corral. I'm no Wyatt Earp, but I was in a smartass mood that morning.

"Good morning, gents. Haircut?"

"Cut the comedy, Tony, this is serious," Shorty said, his hand twitching near his holster. I didn't like the looks of that, so I kept quiet for a while.

"We got wind that there's going to be an all out war between Minotti's gang and Delvecchio's. And guess where the battlefield's going to be?" Shorty was talking fast, but that wasn't making any headway with me.

"Tony, be reasonable." Tall cop stepped in front of his partner, much to Shorty's chagrin. I couldn't suppress my smile.

"You may be thinking that you're protecting your friends, but there are a lot of innocent people who are going to get hurt if this war happens. You may be one of the victims."

"Or Joe over there," Shorty added. Joe looked like he was going to piss his pants, but I gotta give him credit, he didn't say a word.

I looked at the two cops and then back at Joe.

"Joe, didn't your wife tell you she needed help with moving that piano?"

This time, Joe didn't argue with me. He put on his hat and coat and rushed out the back door. I never knew the man could move so fast.

"Okay, officers, it's time to talk.

. . .

That was over fifty years ago this month. No all out war did break out in our Brooklyn neighborhood. Sure, there were plenty of other mob battles that raged over the years, but nothing on the scale of what was expected in the Minotti-Delvecchio conflict. I guess I had something to do with that.

Delvecchio was the easiest one to capture first. The cops had some guy call him at the number he gave me and pretend it was me. Told Jackie where Tommy was holed up. Delvecchio, not wanting to hide in the shadows from Minotti for the rest of his miserable life, decided it was time to take Tommy out. Instead of sending his goons to do the job, he wanted to do it personally. Too bad for Jackie that the cops were waiting for him instead. Later, I heard he died in a prison fight five years into his twenty year sentence.

Minotti wasn't so lucky. I didn't know how to lead them to Minotti, so they staked out my shop to nab him when he stopped in. The problem was Minotti never showed up again. Either he decided it was too hot for him to be seen in the neighborhood or he somehow knew I was going to rat him out. Either way, it didn't end up good for him. The cops eventually did find out where he was hiding, but Tommy wasn't going to go quietly. When they cleaned up the scene, they found about a hundred shell casings just from the cops alone. Twenty of the slugs were in Minotti's body. The poor sap never had a chance.

After that whole mess, Joe decided that being a barber was too dangerous. He left the neighborhood around Christmas that year and moved to Arizona. We kept in touch for a while, but his letters stopped coming one day. I never did find out what happened to him.

And me? Well, I knew I wasn't in a position to ask for much. Shorty threatened to charge me with obstructing police business or some such other nonsense. However, the D.A. was most appreciative of my cooperation and cut me a deal.

So that's what led me to California in 1956, a nice little town outside of Fresno. Thanks to the Feds, I got set up with a new shop here. Got a new name out of the deal, too. I insisted, so they let me choose my own. I'm now known as Tommy Delvecchio, the barber. Anybody, you got hair, I cut it. Just don't tell me anything I don't wanna know.

Slender Island

Naked balsam blue ascent,
Ebony, alabaster.
Untamed ire of red dissent.
Deftly defy disaster.

Coral crown of luminescence,
Verdant virgin caves.
Bedazzled jewel of iridescence,
Salty jaded waves.

Pitched eaves stand on blanched stone blocks,
Humanity averred.
Coiled in silent brocade locks,
Day's destiny deferred.

Antagonistic antiphon,
Lifts up the holy rafter.
Denounced by loyal Seraphim,
To silence Satan's laughter.

May humbled humankind prevail,
Upon her sandy shores.
Where eternity does unveil,
The heavens' golden doors.

Mr. Chang Is Missing

"When did you last see him, Mom?"

"Oh, yesterday morning around nine o'clock. He said he was going out for just a while," replied Edith with a sigh.

James pulled the car over on the shoulder. "Wait a minute. Dad left the house, didn't tell you where he was going and it's three o'clock a day later and you're *now* just calling me?"

"I told your brother."

"When did you tell Michael?"

"Earlier."

"Mom, stop playing around." James exited the Mercedes and walked over to the guardrail to sit down. Cars whizzed by him on the freeway and the resulting breeze blew road dirt into his eyes.

"Fine, James. I called him right before I called you."

James slapped his forehead. "So, basically what you're saying is Dad was out by himself all night for the first time in your sixty years of marriage and you didn't think to inform your sons?"

"Sixty-one years," Edit corrected.

"Mom, focus! Is there anything else missing? A suitcase maybe?"

"No, nothing that I saw."

"Did you look?" James began nervously pacing alongside his car.

"I guess not. Maybe I should."

"Good idea, Mom."

James walked back to his car and opened up the trunk. He reached into the grocery bag and pulled out a two liter bottle of Coke, drinking several long gulps while he waited.

"His golf clubs," his mother announced.

"What was that? His golf clubs are missing?"

"Yeah, it looks that way."

James rubbed his eyes and paused before screaming. His mother was eight-one and not as sharp as she used to be. He had to remind himself of that.

"Mom, who has he been playing golf with lately?"

"Oh, you know. His buddies down at the country club."

"You mean the senior squad he hangs around with."

"Yeah. Benny and the boys." Edit chuckled when she referred to the old geezers as "boys."

James took another swig of soda. "What about Uncle Bob?" Bob Yin was his father's best friend from childhood. James and his brother called him "Uncle Bob" ever since they could form coherent words.

"Your Uncle Bob doesn't play anymore. He's been in that convalescent hospital for so long now he can barely walk."

"Hey, I just thought of something. When was the last time you called his cell?"

"Just before I called you. I left another message."

James pulled out a pad. "What's the number of the cell he's using now?"

"Hold on, let me look."

James could hear his mother rustling around the room.

"I'm back. It's 555-555-1331. It's your Uncle John's cell phone. He can't use it anymore, so he gave it to your father."

"Do you know what carrier it is?"

"Carrier? You mean the phone company?"

"Yes, Mom, the phone company," James said through clenched teeth.

"Oh, I don't know the name of the companies these days. Your father handles all the bills, so I have no idea who charges him for that phone service. Why?"

"I thought if we knew this carrier, we could have them track where the phone is."

"They can do that?" Edith asked. James could almost see her jaw drop in surprise.

"Yes. But if we don't know the carrier, it's all moot. Anything else?"

His mother was quiet for several seconds before responding. "Nothing else, I guess."

"Okay, Mom. I'm on the 405 Freeway right now heading home from the grocery store. I'll try to call Dad's cell phone a few more times. Meanwhile, you said Michael's on his way over to see Uncle John and then he's going to go to the driving range?"

"Yes, that's what he said. You be careful and let me know if you hear from him."

James climbed back in the car and locked the seatbelt. "You do the same, Mom. Thanks."

It took less than fifteen minutes for him to get home. On the road, he tried his father three times and on the third attempt, the call went right to voice-mail. James remained hopeful because that could mean his father just turned off the cell with all the calls he was getting.

Once home, James called his brother to find out whether he found their father.

"Hey, handsome," James said when Michael picked up. Michael was his fraternal twin and was generally recognized the better looking of the pair.

"Hey, ugly. Where's your father?"

"I was going to ask you the same question. Any luck?" James asked, putting the groceries in the refrigerator.

"No luck. I went over to see Uncle John. He has no idea who he is, let alone Dad. His mind has deteriorated so much since Christmas, dude."

James pulled out a beer from the refrigerator and popped off the top.

"What about the driving range, Michael?"

"No luck there, either, bud. I had a picture of Dad with me that I brought around to show people and no one has seen him for a while. I even checked to see if he was on the course, but they have no record of him playing a round in recent days."

"Damnit!"

"You said it," Michael agreed. "Where are you?"

"Home, but I'm my way out to Pasadena to visit with Uncle Bob and maybe check out the course out by him."

"Do you think Uncle Bob will recognize you?"

"I don't know. I just hope he isn't as far gone as Uncle John. Otherwise, we may be screwed." James finished off the beer and dropped the bottle in the recycling bin.

"Well, I hope you can find him. I'm starting to worry at this point. I mean he and Mom haven't been apart since he retired."

"I know. I'll keep you in the loop, okay? Meanwhile, call me on my cell if you hear anything."

"Will do. Talk to you later, James."

After writing a note to his wife, James walked out the door and got back into his car. In ten minutes, he was heading north on the Pasadena Freeway to the convalescent home where his Uncle Bob lived.

Rush hour traffic was starting to get congested and it took James over an hour to get to the freeway exit leading to where his uncle lived. He was just about to pull into the parking lot when his cell phone rang.

"James, it's your mother."

"Did you hear from him, Mom?" James pulled into a space near the entrance and turned off the engine.

"No, I didn't. I'm sorry, did I get your hopes up?"

"Yeah, but that's okay. What's going on?"

"I just discovered something else missing. His medicine."

"Uh oh. All of his medicine?"

"No, just the pills he's been taking for the last month or two."

"What pills are that, Mom?"

The silence was almost deafening.

"Mom? Are you there?"

"Yes, I'm here, James. I'm so embarrassed."

"Mom, there's nothing to be embarrassed about. What pills?"

"Well, they're his ED pills."

"ED? You mean Viagra?"

"Well, Cialis, but the same thing."

"Oh, wow. I guess I never thought -"

"Never thought, what? That your parents would still fool around sometimes?"

James suppressed a snicker. "Yeah, I guess. I'm sorry, Mom, but I never think about you two in, you know, that way."

"James Ambrose Chang, don't you ever think that way, either. But I tell you this, your father took his Cialis pills with him, wherever he went. Now why do you think he would do that?"

"I really don't know, Mom, but I'm sure there's a logical explanation. Look, I'm at Uncle Bob's convalescent home now. Let me go talk to him and get back to you, okay?"

"Sure, James. Tell Uncle Bob I said 'hello', okay?"

"Sounds good, Mom. Bye."

James rushed up the stairs to the home and walked into the lobby.

"Hello, I'm here to see Robert Yin," he said to the receptionist. The woman pointed to the clipboard and pen, and asked him to sign in.

"Mr. Yin is in Room 323. Take the elevator up to the third floor and follow the signs. You can't miss it," the receptionist said.

James thanked the woman and walked quickly to the elevator. He paused to let several wheelchair-bound residents get into the car before him and waited impatiently as the lift rose slowly up the shaft.

On the third floor, James followed the signs as instructed until he was outside of Uncle Bob's room. He looked in and saw the old man lying asleep in bed. He walked in quietly and sat down in the chair next to him.

After several minutes a nurse breezed in past him, tray in hand. "Time for your medication, Mr. Yin," she sang. Uncle Bob opened up his eyes and held out his hands. The nurse placed the paper cup containing the pills in his left hand and a small carton of juice in his right. Someone had already inserted a straw in for him.

James waited until his uncle swallowed all the pills and handed the empty juice carton back to the nurse before he spoke.

"Hi, Uncle Bob, remember me?"

His uncle turned slowly in his direction and smiled. "James? James Chang? What a pleasant surprise."

"Nice to see you, Uncle Bob. You're looking well."

Uncle Bob chuckled. "You always were a bad liar, Jimmy." He began to cough, a deep rasping sound like nails shaking in a tin can. "But I'm glad you visited anyway. What brings you up here?"

"Well, Uncle Bob, it's Dad. I'm afraid he's gone missing."

"Missing? Your father? He's one of the most reliable people I know. What do you think happened to him?"

James shrugged. "Good question. I hoped you might have some ideas."

Uncle Bob looked out the window. The afternoon sun had just started streaming in the window causing shadows to move back and forth in rhythm to the swaying tree outside.

"Did you check the golf course?"

"Michael checked the one by his house and after I leave here, I'm going to stop by McCann and see if he's driving some balls."

Uncle Bob nodded. "Good idea. Besides that, I don't know where he'd be."

James paused a moment.

"Something wrong, Jimmy?"

"I'm not sure. Mom called me a few minutes ago and told me Dad's medicine is missing. Do you know about his 'special' medicine, Uncle Bob?"

Uncle Bob casually inspected his fingernails. "I might. I guess when you say 'special', you mean those pills that give you a, well, you know . . . a-"

"Yeah, one of those. Why would that be missing along with his golf clubs?"

"Help me to my walker, James," Uncle Bob requested. James did as his uncle instructed and followed the old man to the window. Both of them stared out the window silently.

"Jimmy, you see all that green out there? That's life in the making. You don't understand how profound that is at your age. When you get to be an old coot like me, you start to see things different. One thing you realize is that you squandered a lot of your youth doing foolish things. It's time that you can't get back once it's gone."

James nodded, but didn't interrupt.

"Your father and I sowed our wild oats, Jimmy, but we wasted much of them, too. I think your father found the Fountain of Youth in that medicine bottle and is sowing more wild oats."

James stared at his uncle, his mouth wide open. "You don't mean he's-"

"Playing around? Yes, maybe that's what he's doing. Hell, that's what I would be doing if I was in as good as shape as he is."

"But what about my mother," James stammered, face turning red.

"A fine woman, your mother, but they've been married a long time. It's possible your dad wanted to see if the grass is truly greener on the other side. Now that his lawnmower is rebuilt, he's taking it for a test drive."

James shook his head vigorously, trying to erase the image his uncle managed to conjure up. His father would never do that, James told himself.

Uncle Bob chuckled loudly. "Believe what you want, James, but your father and I go back a lot farther than you and he do. Neither one of us were angels before we met our wives. It could be he's out there one more time."

The old man turned around and walked back to his bed. James helped him get in and pulled the covers over him.

"Thanks, Uncle Bob. If you do hear from my father, please have him call home. We're really worried about him."

"Sure thing, Jimmy. Give your mom and your brother my love, okay?"

James left the room and made his way out of the building quickly. He drove halfway to the golf course before he called his brother.

"James, any word?" Michael asked.

"Nope, Uncle Bob knows nothing. But he thinks Dad is out sowing his wild oats."

James heard silence for several moments. "Did I lose you?"

"What do you mean, 'sowing his wild oats'?" Michael repeated. "Dad's eighty-one years old, for Christ's sake.

"Yeah, but he's taking ED meds."

"You mean, like Viagra?" Michael sounded incredulous.

"Something like that. I guess Dad was a player back in the day."

Michael laughed. "Our father was a player? Oh Lord, I could've gone my entire life without hearing that."

"Me, too. I'm going to have a difficult time sleeping tonight.

"Did Uncle Bob have any idea who he may be sowing his oats with?"

"No, he didn't say. I'm almost to McCann now. Where are you?"

"I stopped off to get some dinner at Burger King. Once I leave here, I'm going to check out the hospitals. I figured I'd drive around to those places rather than call them just in case he's in the ER somewhere."

"Good idea. I'll call you after I check out the golf course. Let me know if you find out anything, okay?"

"Okay, will do."

James hung up and then pressed the speed dial key for his parents.

"Mom, it's James. I just came from Uncle Bob's."

"Oh, that's nice, dear. I'm sure he was happy to see you. Did you tell him I said hello?"

"Yes, Mom, of course. He hasn't seen Dad recently."

"That's too bad. Did you talk to your brother?"

"Yeah, I just hung up with him. Nothing with Uncle John or the golf course over by you. Now he's heading over to the hospitals to see if he can find him.

"Oh dear. I hope he's not in the hospital."

"If something's wrong with him, Mom, I'd rather he'd be in a hospital than lost on the side of the road somewhere."

After several moments of silence, James spoke up. "Mom, did I lose you?"

"No, I'm here, James. I'm just worried about your father now. I wasn't until you mentioned the hospitals and now I don't know what to think."

"I'm sorry, Mom. Maybe I overreacted. We'll find him and he'll be just fine, okay?"

"Okay, James, you and your brother are good boys. You'll find your father, I'm sure."

"I'll call you later. I love you."

"I love you, too."

James slowed until he found the entrance to the golf course parking lot. McCann was a well-groomed public course and a favorite of retirees in the area. He kept his speed at the recommended ten miles per hour so as to avoid running down any late-playing senior citizens.

He parked his car near the clubhouse and trotted to the starter's window.

"Excuse me, I'm looking for my father, Adam Chang. You know him?"

The young man at the window shrugged. "Dunno. You have a picture or something."

James reached into his pocket and pulled out his wallet. He flipped through the picture windows until he found a family photo taken three years earlier in Hawaii.

"Here. That's him, there. The guy on the right."

The starter looked closely at the picture for several moments. "No, sorry, I don't know him. Why don't you check over at the nineteenth hole. They usually know the old guys who come through here all the time."

James thanked him and trotted over to the bar, quickly approaching the bartender.

"Hey there, can you help me? Do you know this guy?"

James held the picture in front of him, pointing to his father's picture. "It's my dad and he's been missing since yesterday morning. He sometimes golfs over here."

The bartender shook his head. "Nope, never seen him before. Why don't you check over where they rent clubs and balls. He may have been at the driving range lately.

James raced over to the pro shop and stepped up to the counter. "Hey, have you ever seen this guy?" He held his wallet open so the clerk could see his father's picture.

"This guy? Yeah, I've seen him here before. Not lately, though. What did he do?"

"Oh, he's my father and we're looking for him. Look, if he shows up, please have him call his son James as soon as possible. Can I have a piece of paper?"

The clerk handed him a pad and pen and James scribbled his phone number for him.

"Here you go and thanks. It would mean a lot to my mother if we can find him."

James ran back to the car and left the parking lot. He dialed Michael's number.

"Well?" Michael asked.

"Nothing, though the clerk at the pro shop does recognize Dad. He just hasn't been around lately, that's all."

"Damnit to hell!" Michael shouted. "I'm coming up empty here, too. I've been to three hospitals and no one has seen him. I'm running out of ideas."

"Same here, Michael. I think I'm going to head home and get on the computer. Maybe I can get inspiration there. God knows I won't find him tonight, it's darker than a coal miner's ass out here."

Michael laughed. "Dad taught us that, didn't he?"

"Yeah, you remembered."

"Don't worry, James, we'll find him."

"I hope so, dude. What am I going to tell Mom, though?"

"I don't know, but you'll think of something. I may be the prettier twin, but you're the smarter one."

"Bite me," James joked. "Okay, number one son, call me later. I'll see what's going on in cyberworld and if I have any leads, I'll call you."

James drove the surface streets back home, hoping that he'd find his father walking down some random road. He was three blocks from his parents' house when he decided to drive to the center of town and look around.

The city of Avendale was the perfect small town, complete with red light district. The ladies of the evening ran a very tidy business and never got in trouble with the local police. The cops, for their part, only wanted to keep the citizens calm and if that meant letting a few prostitutes ply their trade in peace and quiet, they were more than willing to do it.

James followed the cruising path most frequented by johns looking for feminine company, stopping every few minutes to let another call girl sashay in front of him, usually blowing him kisses. He parked the car on Maple Street and got out, remembering to lock the doors and set the alarm.

"Hey there, handsome, wanna date?" a blonde hooker oozed, her short skirt a perfect counterpoint to her thigh-high leather boots.

"No, not tonight. I'm looking for my father, though. Have you seen this guy?"

James held out the picture for the woman to look at.

"Hmmmm, I can't say that I have. However, old men usually don't go for me. I'm too slim, you know? Why don't you try Wanda over on Elm? She usually gets the senior citizen trade."

"Thanks, um, Miss. Have a good night."

James walked quickly down the street, occasionally sidestepping a particularly aggressive hooker. He neared the corner and approached three prostitutes standing next to a streetlamp.

"Are any of you Wanda?" he asked, looking at them eagerly.

"I can be 'Wanda' if that who you want me to be, sugar," one of them said to him, winking.

"Ignore her. I'm Wanda," said a heavy set woman. "What do you want?"

"I'm looking for my father. Have you seen him recently?"

James handed her the photo. The three woman huddled around and squinted at the picture.

"I don't know. He kinda looks like one of my johns tonight," Wanda admitted, handing back the picture. "But I need more encouragement to help my memory, ya know?"

James paused for a moment, but realized what she wanted when he saw her palm extended out to him. He reached into his wallet and extracted a twenty dollar bill, then placed it in her hand. She took the money and tucked it into her brassiere.

"I'm pretty sure he with me earlier this evening," Wanda told him, her hands on her hips. "Horny old man, too. I guess he took too many of those Viagras or somethin'. I was worried about his heart, he was so desperate."

James shook his head.

"There, there. You should be proud. Not every man his age has that kind of staying power. You probably got that gene, too."

James coughed nervously. "Um, thanks. Any idea where he went after you two, well, you know."

Wanda giggled. "Yeah, I know. The last time I saw him, he was walking down Oak toward the civic center."

James looked around. "That way?" he pointed.

"Yeah, just follow those signs to City Hall. Maybe that's where he parked."

"Perhaps," James said. "Thank you for your help, Wanda. Good night."

He crossed the street and walked quickly down Oak. He traversed Cypress Park and continued past the Civic Auditorium until he was in front of City Hall. There were a few cars parked on the side of the road, but none of them were his father's. He was about to walk back down Oak to find his car when he saw a transient shuffling his way down the opposite side of the street.

"Excuse me," James called out, crossing over to the other side. The transient ignored him and kept walking his slow pace down the sidewalk. "Sir?"

The transient glanced up and saw James standing in front of him. "Keep away!" he shouted. "I don't have anything for you."

"Sir, I just wanted to know if you've seen my father."

"Father? I have no father!" the man argued. "Go away."

"Not your father, my father. Have you seen him?" James showed the man the picture, pointing to his father's dour face.

"Chinaman, right?"

James nodded. "Yeah, he's Chinese."

"I thought so. You know, even though I'm a white guy, I can tell Chinese from Japanese from Korean. I bet you didn't know that, did you?"

"No, sir, I didn't. Have you seen my father?" James asked again, taking the picture back.

"I know faces and I think I've seen him before. Maybe tonight, who knows?" the transient said. "Who knows?"

James gripped the photo tightly, then calmed down. "If you saw him, where would that have been?"

The transient pointed down Oak. "Down there."

"There? Thank you." James started to walk away.

"Or down there," the man said, pointing in the opposite direction. "Or maybe there."

James looked and saw the man was pointing at the top of City Hall.

"Um, okay sir, thank you. I'll let you go now."

He took one more look toward the empty city center and then walked back to his car. All the way home, James kept thinking to himself that his father must've gone off the deep end. How were they going to handle a demented senior citizen on ED medication?

James pulled behind his brother's car parked in the drive. He saw Michael and his mother anxiously look out the front window.

"Any word?" James asked his mother when she opened the door.

"Oh dear, no," she replied, hand over her mouth. "We hoped you got some clue. Your brother wants to call the police."

James walked inside and sat down. "I think that's probably a good idea at this point."

Edith dabbed her eyes with a tissue. "Oh, your poor father. I hope he's alright. Excuse me, boys."

James waited until his mother was out of the room before continuing. "He was with a prostitute tonight."

"What, are you kidding me? A hooker? How do you know?" Michael slapped his forehead in disbelief.

"I went down to the red light district and nosed around until I found a hooker who thinks he was one her johns tonight."

"Holy crap, James, what's Mom going to say when-"

The front door opened. The brothers watched as their father walked in, golf clubs in hand. He looked up and saw their incredulous faces.

"What's wrong with you two?"

James was the first one to speak up. "Where the hell were you, Dad? You've been missing for two days. We didn't know what happened to you!"

"I wasn't missing, I knew where I was," Adam Chang said with a chuckle. "Don't make such a big deal."

"Dad! Are you crazy?" Michael screamed, standing in front of his father to prevent him from escaping. "In what reality do you think you live in when you just take off like that without telling anyone, the least of which, your wife? I'll repeat the question . . . where the hell were you, damnit?"

Adam looked at his golf clubs, then back up into his sons' angry eyes. "Isn't it obvious?"

"That's not an answer, Dad," James said, moving next to his brother. "If you were golfing, why did you need your, um, pills?"

"What pills are you talking about?" Adam asked, amused. "You seem to be awfully agitated, son, why don't you sit down? You, too, Michael. Both of you are a dangerously bright shade of red." He pushed between both of them and walked toward the kitchen.

"What about Wanda, Dad?" James asked him before he stepped out of sight. He stood facing him, arms crossed.

"Who's Wanda?" Adam said. "Is that one of your mother's friends?"

Michael approached his father again. "No, Dad, she's a hooker. She says you were with her." He marked the words 'with her" in air quotation marks.

"I don't know any Wanda," Adam replied simply, turning around again.

"Did someone mention a 'Wanda'?" Edith Chang said, standing in front of her husband. "Who is she?"

"Edith, these boys watch too much television. I don't know anybody named Wanda."

Edith looked at her sons. "Do you want to tell me?"

James and Michael shuffled in place, looking at their feet. "No one, Mom," James finally managed say.

"Whatever," Edit muttered. "Now you."

She focused her attention on Adam who was standing in the same place, waiting for the questioning to continue.

"If you went golfing, why did you need your pills?" she drilled, her hands poised on her hips.

Adam chuckled. "Everyone's worried about my pills. I'm not sure if I should be flattered or pissed off, to be honest." He reached inside his jacket pocket and pulled out a stapled pharmacy bag. "Don't you remember you told me to pick up my prescription when I was near the drug store?"

He handed her the bag with a smirk. Edith took it from him, a shade of a smile playing on her lips.

"Yeah, I remember. I guess we ran out a little early this month." She smiled a little wider and winked at Adam.

"Great, I could've gone the rest of my life without hearing that," Michael groaned, turning back toward the front door. "Look, folks, I gotta go home. Jeannie is waiting for me and I'm going to have to explain all this to her. She'll never believe it."

James followed him. "Me, too. You people may be my parents, but you're strange. Next time, Dad, tell Mom where you're going so we don't call out the National Guard or something."

"You got it, son. Good-bye, boys. See you at dinner next weekend?"

Both boys flashed the thumbs up sign and walked out the front door.

"Do you believe him?" Michael asked James, moments later. "I mean, it doesn't seem like he needs to look outside the house, you know?"

"Michael! Please, I'd rather not think about that anymore, okay?"

His brother chuckled. "Well, at least we have good genes."

"Yeah, exactly what Wanda said," James replied. "Neither time has that been as comforting to hear as it was supposed to be. Good night."

Adam and Edith watched their sons pulled away and walked hand in hand to the bedroom.

"Too worn out from playing golf?" she asked him, smiling.

"Never. Not as long as I have these, anyway," Adam said, holding up the bag.

City Slumber

Anthems play in hallowed halls
Crystals fall on snowy walls.
Winter left us, where is Spring?
Chill winds silence everything.

Vestiges of gray and brown
Nameless streets, an empty town.
Faces fixed with marble stares
Mask yourself in hollow prayers.

Disingenuous display
Frigid night, a gelid day.
Nature's rage at dreaded hour
Wrath that causes men to cower.

Conquer fear, the spirit cries!
Save your tentative good-byes.
Lift your sigh and look ahead
Reclaim the sun, the poet said.

Stand and face the new found world
Laugh at sullen insults hurled.
Embrace the iridescent spark
That comes to chase the endless dark.

Sweet Freedom

They arrived the same time every summer, their caravan of oddly shaped vehicles tumbling over the abandoned landfill and halting at a predetermined location in the scrub. Within hours, their descent into our world would be relayed from house to house, much like the jungle call on some primitive tropical island.

"They're here," my friend Grover said, almost breathless with excitement unbecoming a lazy summer morning. "I saw them drive by my house and down to the dump."

"All of them?" I asked, pulling the phone with me down the cellar steps, hoping to have an uninterrupted moment to talk. In a house with two adults and one annoying younger sister, private telephone time was a premium.

"Of course!" Grover answered, in that voice that wanted to know if I was really such an idiot. "I counted at least thirty huge vans. I'm surprised you didn't hear them."

Grover lived one street over from me, but in a subdivision that was vastly different than mine. Both were your typical suburban hideaways, but while mine was solely populated by white families, Grover's street boasted one of the few truly integrated streets in town, a first for the Deep South, especially in the late 1960's. You knew the world was changing when one of the local cops was both black and an immediate neighbor.

"What time are we going to meet down there?" I asked Grover. "I gotta mow the lawn this morning, then I'm free for the day."

"Can't that wait until later?" Grover whined. Grover was the school's biggest whiner. If there was a team for whiners, Grover would've made the first string and probably would've been an all-star. "I'm supposed to mow, too, but I told my ma this is more important."

I thought about it a second. It had been a long summer and I had been pretty good about mowing every Saturday morning without being told. I even took apart the mower engine once when the choke got stuck, using trusty machine oil to loosen the hinged flap. My dad didn't say anything, but I could tell he was proud of me. I might be able to use that goodwill to buy myself a delay from lawnmower detail.

"Okay, I'll do it," I finally told him. "I'll call Stephen and Trevor and you get Mickey. We'll meet at your house in an hour."

I could hear Grover on the other end of the phone almost straining at the leash. "Alright, just hurry up. And don't forget to wear your work clothes, it could get messy."

It took me only a few minutes to call the guys and make arrangements. I looked around the house for my father, finally finding him in the cellar, stubbornly trying to get his new sump pump working. The device was poorly installed, but worked just long enough to outlive its warranty. On exactly the three hundred sixty-sixth day since its installation, it died after a massive summer rain threatened to flood our always damp basement.

"Dad, can I mow the yard tomorrow? The guys want to do something today and I don't want to be the only one left behind."

My father knew if I wanted to tell him what I was doing, I would just come out and say it and let the truth be damned. However, if I was acting cagey like I was doing just then, he would have to decide whether to give me the third degree or not. Thankfully, he remembered being a boy once, so he normally would forego the questioning if I hadn't gotten in trouble for a while.

"Am I going to have to remind you tomorrow?" he asked me, eyes narrowing as he looked into mine.

"No, I swear, Dad! Right after church, I'll come home, change my clothes and get outside. I won't even lie around and watch cartoons like I usually do."

My father nodded. "How's your summer reading?"

Uh oh, my Achilles heel. He knew I usually spent my Sundays doing my reading, leaving Saturdays as my play day once I got my chores done.

"Dad, I swear I won't be out too long today. I'll do it tonight. I won't even watch television." I stood confidently in front of him as I lied through my teeth. He knew it, I knew it, and the whole neighborhood probably knew it.

"Okay," he finally said, never looking up from the balky sump pump. "Just try to not to get into too much trouble, okay?"

He knew! It wasn't until years later that I realized I never should've been surprised. He and I grew up in the same town and aside from more modern diversions, we both had the urge to run crazy sometimes. Summer invited crazy.

"Thanks, Dad," was all my eleven year-old imagination could muster in the way of gratitude.

I ran back to the kitchen to call my friends, but my sister was occupying it and from the looks of it, it was going to be another marathon conversation. The difference between my sister and me: I used the phone to communicate, she used it as an extension of her larynx.

Out the door I ran, across the street and in one bound, cleared the fence surrounding the Grange family's raised ranch. I hooked a left and jumped over the retaining wall down to the driveway. Mr. Grange was gassing up his pride and joy, a red, seventy horsepower riding mower that was the envy of every father in the neighborhood.

"Hey, Mr. Grange," I said with a wave and ducked into the garage before it even registered I ran by him. That was okay, because Mr. Grange didn't like the neighborhood kids much.

I ran up the stairs and knocked on the back door. Trevor's brother Pat answered.

"He's up in his room, Jim. Go wake him up, will ya? It's his turn to clean the kitchen."

The Grange family consisted of five boys and two girls, the largest family on our street. Trevor was the youngest and a couple of years younger than me. He was more spoiled than anyone that I ever knew, thanks to his being a surprise last baby among a group of siblings who were almost all in high school.

I bounded up the steps to Trevor's room and knocked on his door. "Trevor, it's Jim. Come on, we gotta go now!" I listened for signs of life, but it was as quiet as church in there. After a couple of jumps, I was able to retrieve the key from the top of the door frame, unlocked the door and went in.

The room was dark, but I was still able to make out Trevor's form huddled under a pale yellow sheet. He was out cold.

I whipped the sheet off him and kicked him in the ass. He stirred and then looked at me like I was one of his nightmares.

"What?"

"Come on, we gotta go. The guys are waiting for us."

He crawled out of bed, his red brown cowlick spiking tall above his head, and went to the adjoining bathroom.

"I'm using your phone to call Stephen," I yelled into him and dialed his number.

"Hello, Mrs. Stabler, is Stephen home?" I asked. The Stablers were the more recent transplants to our neighborhood with another six kids to add to our neighborhood hide-n-seek games. Like Trevor in his family, Stephen was two years younger than me, but we were thick as thieves from the very beginning.

"Yes, he is, Jimmy. I'll put him on." Mrs. Stabler liked me and thought of me as a member of the family I was there so much. She kept Stephen on a short leash, but if I was involved in an activity, she lengthened it considerably.

"Stephen, today's the day," I told him breathlessly.

"Really? Geez, I have to do my reading today and can't go anywhere until it's done. I can't believe I'm going to miss it!"

"Let me talk to your mom. She likes me."

"Well, good luck. I got a C in reading on my last test and now I have to read ten pages a day or I can't do anything. Here she is."

Ten minutes later, Mrs. Stabler put Stephen back on the phone.

"How fast can you get over here?" I asked him. He was knocking on Trevor's door before the phone even cooled off.

"I don't know how you do it," he muttered as the three of us ran down the street to Grover's house.

When we got there, Mickey and Grover were throwing a football around. Grover looked a little peeved.

"Took you long enough."

"Hey, we did the best we could. Are you ladies ready or are you going to play with your dollies instead?"

Grover didn't answer. We marched down the street, eyes fixed ahead. Mickey was the first one to break the silence.

"What are we supposed to do?" he asked. Mickey was new to Tandy Lane. His family was the most recent one to break the color barrier in our neighborhood, having moved from a mostly black community a few miles away.

"Look, let me do the talking," Grover insisted. "I've been doing this the longest and I know what to say."

"Sounds good to me," Mickey assured him. "I try to keep in the background anyway."

Stephen chuckled, but didn't say anything. Instead, he chose that moment to tackle Trevor from behind, throwing him on someone's front lawn. The two of them tussled around while we continued our steady movement to the dump.

"Ladies," Grover called out, all sing-song and teasing. "Are you going to hug each other all day or are you coming with us?"

Stephen and Trevor rolled to their feet, sufficiently chastened, and caught up with us. As we turned the corner, we could see the eighteen wheeled trucks parked in rows outside the designated area. They had already started unloading the poles and canvases.

"Follow me," Grover commanded. We saluted him in response, laughing in derision at our self-nominated leader.

We approached the first adult we saw standing on the outside of the chaos. "Excuse me, sir," Grover began meekly. "Can I ask you something?"

The man, a well-muscled, hulking bruiser, took the cigar out of his mouth and flicked off an ash. "What's up, boys? Looking for work?"

"Yeah!" I shouted, earning a withering glance from Grover. The kid certainly took his leadership role seriously. Years later, it would serve him well in the Marines.

"All of you healthy? Nobody with bad backs or anything?" The man inspected each one of us, staring particularly long at Mickey. "What about you?"

Mickey looked at Grover for guidance, but seeing none forthcoming, just shrugged. "I'm as strong as an ox, sir."

The man laughed like this was the funniest thing he heard all day. "Fine, then, let's see if we can get you kids something to do."

We watched him wander over to where a large group of men were huddled. He singled out one man in particular, pointing toward us as he discussed our fate. After several minutes, he walked back to us.

"Okay, boys, the boss says you guys can help us set up the side show tents. Go over there and asked for Shorty. He'll show you what to do, okay?" He pointed off toward a separate area behind the main clearing.

"Thank you, mister!" we all shouted and raced over to find Shorty.

We encountered a group of men and women, all milling about and conversing casually.

"Hello, boys," one of the women cooed, stroking a six inch beard. "Looking for me?"

"Franny, watch yourself! They're just kids," warned another woman. She must've weighed close to five hundred pounds and gasped after every few words.

"We're looking for Shorty," Grover said, all business. The rest of stood there like the slack-jawed yokels we were, so the negotiations fell on our presumed leader, at least for today. Kid leadership changed depending on a number of factors, including the given activity of the moment.

"Shorty! There's some kids here to talk to ya," shouted Franny to the trailer behind her. The door popped open and a guy no taller than three feet jumped out and headed towards us. Grover shot us his patented "don't act like jackasses" look, but such subtle warnings were lost on the likes of us. We held it together, though, but snickering was imminent and could be set off with the wrong word.

"What do you guys want?" the charming Shorty demanded, a stub of a cigar tucked into the corner of his pursed lips. He wore a porkpie hat that looked like it had once been a chew toy for a lion cub.

Grover stared dumbstruck at the little man for so long that all of us started getting nervous, especially Shorty. He turned back disgustedly toward his trailer when I spoke up.

"We heard you're looking for some guys to do some heavy work," I growled, trying to look tougher than my seventy-five pound frame suggested. I even curled my upper lip like I saw Bogart do in *To Have or Have Not.*

"You don't look so strong to me," Shorty said with a sneer. "How much can you lift?"

Mickey interrupted. "I could lift you and carry you around this whole lot!" he said. The four of us boys took a step back from him, afraid the taint of his of his braggadocio would rub off on us. I shot a furtive glance at the fat lady, but she was too busy trying to figure out if Mickey could do it.

Shorty stood chin to breastbone with Mickey and blew smoke up in his face. "Show me."

"Do it, Mickey!" we shouted. "Come on, show him how strong you are!"

Mickey got down on his knees and waited until Shorty straddled his neck. Once he felt the short man's legs wrap around him, he slowly rose to his feet, keeping his passenger astride and balanced. We watched while Mickey started walking, then jogging, all around the area that would be home to the side show tents.

Shorty's cigar remained securely in place throughout the entire tour. He waited several minutes before directing Mickey to return to where we stood. Exhausted, Mickey fell to his knees as the short man dismounted from his neck.

"You're hired," he announced. "Go see Clyde and tell him I said to put you all to work. Remember, you don't get paid until the work is done. None of this 'lift one pole and tell me your mommies want you home for dinner' crap. Got it?"

"Yes!" we shouted, then rushed over to find Clyde. Mickey stood up and half-trotted to catch up to us and when he did, he had the biggest smile I ever saw on an eleven year-old, even on my own kids years later.

Grover assumed the lead of our little troupe again, stopping before each adult we passed and asking where Clyde could be found. Finally, the tallest man I ever saw pointed out our new boss. I was almost disappointed that Clyde was a normal, if not surly, looking man.

"Clyde? Shorty sent us to find you. We're here to work," Grover announced. We all stood around looking expectantly as Clyde inspected his temporary help.

"Yeah, I know you from last year," he said to Grover. "But the rest of you don't look so familiar to me. Especially you." Clyde pointed accusingly at Mickey, a sneer on his lips. Mickey just stood there, but I could tell he wanted to tell the guy off.

"Are all of you strong?" Clyde asked us with a growl. "I need strong workers here. And you're not just going to just lift one box and complain you're tired or you have to go home to do babysit your sister or something like that. You got it?"

"Yes, sir!" we cried in unison, at least all of us but Mickey. He moved his lips, but not a sound came out. I could see him trying to hide his smirk.

"Fine. Follow me."

Clyde led us to a stack of twelve foot iron poles. He pointed to an empty area just beyond us. "You see that area over there squared off by ropes? I need you to carry each pole and set it in front of one of the stakes pounded into the group. There are eight poles, eight stakes. Got it?"

Grover and Stephen began struggling with one pole, while Trevor, Mickey and I took on another. Thankfully, the poles were hollow, but they were still heavy. We laid the first one in front of a stake as directed, then moved on to our second one. Grover and Stephen were still struggling with theirs, so I ran over there to help them.

"How long are we going to work?" Stephen asked me quietly. "You know I can't stay here past four o'clock."

"Don't worry about it," I told him. "Aren't there laws about making kids work too long or something?"

Grover looked at us like we just grew extra noses. "What are you talking about? It's not like they're making us work here, right? Geez, you guys, stop acting like babies. We're supposed to be strong guys, remember?"

We nodded sullenly and dropped the pole on the ground. Meanwhile, behind us, Trevor and Mickey were struggling with their load. Stephen took his turn and ran over to help them, leaving me with Grover.

"Ready to do one by ourselves?" he challenged me.

"Sure, let's get to it." I wasn't going to back away from a thrown gauntlet.

We heaved the pole up with a large grunt and crept our way to an empty space near the designated area. I could feel the metal cylinder slipping from my sweaty grasp, but was able to find a rougher spot on the surface to grab before it fell. I could see Grover in front of me having trouble as well, but he struggled to maintain his tenuous grip, perspiration beading on his forehead.

Grover steered us to an empty stake and guided his end in front of it. On the count of three, we dropped the heavy pipe on the ground and jumped out of the way. The landing made a satisfying clang that caused our other three friends to quickly turn our way.

Grover and I high-fived each other, then walked back over to where the remaining unmoved poles laid.

"Come on, you slugs, let's finish this job before Clyde gets on our ass," Grover blustered. With that encouragement, it only took us a few more minutes to finish our assignment. We walked around to find Clyde to find out what was next.

"You boys done already?" he exclaimed, seemingly impressed. "Hell, I didn't think you'd be back for another hour at least. Follow me."

He led us to a mountain of traveling boxes of varying sizes and colors stacked just beyond the poles we moved.

"There are about one hundred boxes or so in this pile, all painted in one of six colors. I need you to stack the boxes by color in front of those signs over there." Clyde pointed to the signs along the perimeter. "Each sign match one of the box colors. Pile them up neatly in front of the signs and then come back to see me when you're through."

We spent the next three hours moving the boxes in the prescribed places. They were too heavy to carry alone, so we had to work in pairs or threes, depending on how big the box was. It was tiring work and by the time we moved the last box, all of us were panting and a little sore.

Clyde laughed when he saw us limping over to where he stood. "So now it looks like you boys have worked. What do you think? Like it?"

The five of us gave him a half-hearted "yes" and he chuckled again. "Okay, you look like you've had enough. The professionals now need to finish setting up everything and we only have a few hours to do it before sunset."

We looked at him expectantly.

"I guess you wanna get paid or something, right?" He reached into his back pocket and held up five pieces of paper. "Here are all access passes for tomorrow's show. That's everything under the big top and the side shows, too. How does that sound?"

"Great!" we shouted, despite our near exhaustion. We gratefully took the tickets, thanked him profusely, and headed home.

"I'm so dead," Stephen whispered to me. "I was supposed to be home an hour ago, remember?"

"Yeah, I know. Leave it to me," I told him.

Stephen and I said our good-byes to the other guys at Grover's, then jumped the fence and made our way to my house.

"Mom, I'm home. I'm here with Stephen," I called from the kitchen.

My mother walked out of the laundry room to join us. "Hello, Stephen. Your mother called here about fifteen minutes ago wondering if you were here. I told him you boys were together so she wouldn't worry so much."

"Thanks, Mom. Stephen needs to use the phone before he leaves, okay?"

"Of course. We'll be eating dinner soon, so after Stephen goes, you need to wash up."

I handed Stephen the phone near the cellar door and we walked down the stairs, closing the door behind us.

Stephen tried to sound casual when he talked to his mother, but I could tell he was floundering in a hurry. I pointed to the phone and then to me and finally understood and handed me the receiver.

"Hi, Mrs. Stabler. Oh yes, I'm fine. I'm sorry Stephen's late today, but we were busy riding our bikes around and didn't think about the time."

I covered the mouthpiece with me hand and snickered for effect.

"What's that? Yes, exercise is a great way to stay healthy. Whenever I get in from playing, I always can study better. Yes, I know Stephen needs to concentrate more."

Stephen punched me in the arm, as much a show of affection as a way to get even.

"Okay, I'll put him on, Mrs. Stabler. Nice talking to you."

I handed the phone back to Stephen and hit him in the arm in response.

"Yeah, Mom, I'm heading out now. Okay, bye."

We walked back upstairs and I hung up the phone.

"You did it again," he said to me with a grin. "I just have to read when I get home."

I nodded. "See, just stick with Jim and all your problems will soon disappear. But I was thinking, will you be able to go to the show tomorrow? It starts at two in the afternoon."

"I should. I'll just have to get up early and get all my reading done."

"Okay, call me tomorrow when you're done. Maybe we can get there early and eat something first."

I walked him to the front door and returned to the kitchen. My mother was there waiting for me, a concerned look on her face.

"What's wrong?" I asked her.

"I just heard a newsflash on the radio. They said a prisoner escaped from the county jail. He may be anywhere in the vicinity."

I laughed. "Come on, Mom, don't worry. Nothing exciting ever happens around here. The guy's probably long gone and into the next state already."

She walked over to the oven and checked on her roast. "You're probably right. Besides, your father will be home soon and then I won't care so much. Well, go get washed up now. We'll talk more about this convict later."

Two hours later, we were sitting around the kitchen table, listening to the radio, when another newsflash interrupted the evening program.

"Police believe that the inmate, Richard Atchison, who escaped from the county jail today, is still within the county proper. Authorities request that all residents be on alert for the convict, said to be six foot two, two hundred pounds, brown hair and blue eyes. He is considered to be armed and dangerous. If you see this individual, do not try to apprehend him yourself. Instead, please contact the sheriff's department immediately."

"I don't want you kids going outside tomorrow," my mother decided. My sister and I looked at each other in dismay, then appealed to our father.

"Dad!" we whined in unison. My father just rolled his eyes and prepared for the onslaught.

"That's not fair," I continued. "Tomorrow is the circus. We worked down there today to get passes to go and I want to go!"

I asserted myself a little more forcefully than intended, but hoped the passion in my voice would hide the fact I may have overplayed my indignant hand. My sister stared at me with her mouth open, a barely contained smirk on her lips. She lived to see me get in trouble.

Instead of rebutting me, my father closed his eyes to think. We all knew that during the "closing of the eyes" ceremony, all extraneous input was blocked out while the man processed all of the information he was willing to work with.

He finally opened his eyes and looked at me. "You worked hard today, you should go to the circus." He looked at my sister. "I want you to stay home tomorrow like your mother said. You don't like the circus anyway. You're only interested because of the cotton candy."

"Mom!" my sister complained, but one sharp look from my mother cut her off in mid-whine. How I kept the smirk off of my own face then can only be attributed to my resolve in enjoying the fruits of my labor.

"Thanks, Dad," I managed to say without gloating.

"Just be careful," my mother warned.

§

Stephen called me early the next morning.

"I can't go to the circus today," he started.

"Why not? You have plenty of time to get your reading done."

"It's that escaped prisoner. My mother won't leave me leave the house until they catch him."

"What about all that work you did?"

Stephen sighed. "I know, but what am I going to do. You know how my mother is."

Mrs. Stabler's overprotectiveness was legend in the neighborhood. I shuddered involuntarily, thanking God and the stars above I didn't have to bear that burden.

"Do you think you can talk to her?" he asked me hopefully. How could I turn down one of my best friends?

"Sure, let me try," I told him, bracing myself for the conversation.

"Hi, Mrs. Stabler."

"Jimmy? Did you hear about the convict? It's very scary."

"Yes, we heard about it on the radio. I guess it's a little scary."

"Well, I know you boys were planning on going to the circus today, but I'm going to keep Stephen inside. I'm sure you're mother's doing the same."

"No, she's not, Mrs. Stabler. She wanted to, but my dad thought that I worked hard today, so I deserve to go. They didn't pay us in money, only in tickets."

I could almost hear the wheels turning and waited for her response. One thing that Mrs. Stabler has is a good sense of fair play.

"No money? So, if Stephen doesn't go, he worked for free?"

"That's right."

"Well, I wish I could forget about this escaped prisoner, but he's armed and dangerous. No, my mind is made up. Even if you two were together, I'd still be worried to death. I'm sorry, Jimmy. Here, I'll put Stephen back on."

"Hey," he said, sounding more dejected than I ever heard him. One thing kids don't like is working for nothing. It goes against our understanding of how the world is supposed to revolve around us.

"I'm sorry, man. I tried."

"I know, don't sweat it. Look, I better go read now."

I tried to sound optimistic. "Hey, maybe they'll catch the guy before it's time to head down there."

"You think so?"

"Sure, anything's possible. I'll call you before I leave, just to see if you got out of lockdown."

I hung up the phone and ran outside to do my chores.

§

Around one o'clock, I turned on the radio and listened as the newscaster announced the convict was still on the loose and the state troopers were brought in to help find him. More about the prisoner was revealed. He was a convicted murderer who was picked up for suspicion of assault with a deadly weapon. The police were holding him in the county jail until his arraignment. He broke out before he was to appear in court.

I dialed Stephen's number.

"Hello?" he answered.

"Hey, it's me. I just listened to the radio. The guy's still out there. Did your mom change her mind yet?"

Stephen laughed bitterly. "Are you kidding? She's been walking around with the portable radio all over the house. There's no way I'm going anywhere today. I'll be lucky to get out even after the guy gets captured."

I kept quiet for a few seconds.

"Are you there?" he asked me.

"Yeah, I'm thinking. Listen, how bad do you want to go to the circus?"

I could feel the tension through the phone. "Are you *nuts*? I wanna go to this more than anything else in my life."

We both realized that was an exaggeration, but neither one of us acknowledged that out loud.

"Okay, look. Here's my plan."

After a few minutes of explaining, he caught on and enthusiastically agreed.

Fifteen minutes later, his bike slid into my driveway. We ditched it in the garage and took off for the Grover's.

"How'd it go?" I asked him.

"Fine. I did what you said to do and told her your mother won't let you go to the circus after all, so I was coming down here to spend the afternoon with you."

"Do you think she'll call my mother?"

"No, she trusts you. If it was one of the other guys, forget it. In fact, I didn't even mention them because if I did, she'd get suspicious and keep me inside anyway."

We met up with Grover and Mickey, but Trevor was nowhere to be seen.

"He had to stay home and help clean the house. His mother's on the warpath again," Grover explained to us as we walked down to the dump. Trevor's mother would get on intense cleaning jags, involving the entire household in a top down scrubbing of immense proportions. She chose this one Sunday of all days to flip into super-clean mode.

The dump had been transformed overnight into a huge entertainment center. The big top was most prominent, towering proudly over the landfill. We could see a long line of trucks, vans, coupes and sedans making their way to the designated parking area.

"There must be a thousand cars," Mickey exclaimed. "I hope we can get in."

Grover chuckled knowingly. "Don't worry. These passes guarantee us the best seats in the place. Last year, one of the clowns threw a bucket of glitter right on me as he rode by on his unicycle."

We threaded our way through the crowd and walked up to the side entrance of the big top. A big, burly guy dressed in a red and white striped shirt and a bolo tie stopped us.

"Tickets, boys," he growled. He looked like he had a rough night of carousing. His eyes were bloodshot and I swear I could see his vein pulsing in his temple all the way from where I stood.

We all handed him our passes and proceeded to walk through the flap.

"Hold on there, gentlemen," another man said, holding up a cane to block our way. "Where do you think you're going?"

"They have passes," the gruff man explained. "What's the beef?"

The man with the cane pointed it directly at Mickey. "He's the problem. This boy can't go into the reserved section. He'll have to go sit in the colored section with the others."

I shot a glance at Mickey, fully expecting him to argue, but instead he just hung his head. Stephen wasn't having any of this, though.

"Look! We all worked our asses off yesterday, especially Mickey, so we all deserve to sit in the reserved section. Got it?"

Even Grover took a step back or two, not knowing what would happen. The man with the cane walked right up to Stephen and thrust his face within an inch of his. Mickey watched the two of them warily.

"Look here, kid, I have no problems with you or those other two white boys going in, but your colored friend has to do what I say if he wants to see the circus. Those are the rules. I didn't make 'em, but I have to enforce 'em. So what's it going to be?"

I looked up at the gruff guy, but he was busy taking tickets from other visitors and ignored the little drama behind him. Good to see we have allies, I thought somewhat bitterly.

Stephen remained quiet, trying to stare down the man who was almost swallowing his face. Finally, he turned toward us and said, "I'm not going in if Mickey can't sit with us. Anybody with me?"

I immediately stepped over to Stephen's side and stood in front of the cane man with my arms crossed over my chest. I must've thought I was one tough hombre planted there like some skinny statue. We all turned to look at Grover who seemed to be frozen in place.

"Well?" Stephen called to him.

"Shit, I don't care about the circus anyway. Last time I'll work for free at this place," he grumbled out loud and followed us as we walked to the side shows.

Mickey brought up the rear. He didn't say anything, but the look on his face was all the thanks any of us needed.

We wandered around the side shows. When we passed the bearded lady, she was quick to blow us all a kiss. Her friend, the fat lady, was seated in the next booth down and clucked disapprovingly. She had a broad smile for all of us and waved like we were old friends. We even saw Clyde. Instead of just being a regular circus worker, we found him swallowing swords, much to the pleasure of the crowd that surrounded him.

It took us an hour to see everything worth seeing at the side shows. Meanwhile, we could hear the circus audience cheering wildly for some unseen act under the big top. Grover looked absolutely miserable after each roar, but I had to give it to him, he never said a word about his disappointed he was.

Stephen was the first one to speak up. "Why don't we go back over to the side entrance and see if we can get in now?"

Grover perked up when he heard that and agreed, as did I and Mickey. We sauntered casually over to where the gruff man still sat.

"Hi, it's us again," Stephen said. "Do you think you can let us sneak in now?"

The man glared through half-lidded eyes at him, obviously further along in his hangover recovery. "Look, kid, I want to help you. But this is the first regular job I've had in years and I can't risk losing it or I'm back on the street. Sorry."

We huddled together, planning our next strategy. The crowd noise was almost deafening. Suddenly, the pitch of the screams rose to frantic levels. We looked at each other, wondering what act inspired such a reaction, angry we weren't inside watching.

Without warning, five chimpanzees stormed through the flap and headed right for us. We scurried out of the way, unsure if this was part of the act or something that had gone terribly wrong.

Our question was answered when a crew of circus workers ran out of the tent and tried to corral the escaping simians. We stood several feet away, but still close enough to watch the action.

Three of the chimps were caught immediately, shrieking in dismay at their recapture. A fourth one bit an attendant and ran off in the direction of the woods. Number five was close on his fellow escapee's heels, but got caught at the tree line by an alert trainer. The lone success in the chimp breakout soon disappeared from sight and ran deep into the thick vegetation.

We witnessed this vignette with a mixture of excitement and amusement. Who would've thought we would've been in the exact right place at the right time to see one of the oddest things to ever hit that circus?

After animal control arrived and the police were sent out to comb the woods for the missing chimp, we decided it was time to head back. Stephen was afraid his mother would hear about the circus ruckus on the radio and call down to my house to make sure we were inside or even worse, would drive down to pick him up.

Stephen and I said good-bye to Mickey and Grover and ran the rest of the way to my house. When we walked in, my father was on the phone and for a minute, we both were ready to panic because we could tell right away he was talking to Stephen's mother.

"I'm a dead man," his whispered, shaking his head. "Looks like I'll be locked in my room until Labor Day.

I was about to disagree when my father hung up the phone and walked into the living room. We held our breath and awaited the verdict.

"Stephen, that was your mother. She was wondering if you heard about the chimpanzee escape at the circus."

I hesitated for a second, then squeaked "What did you tell her?"

"That you boys were in the backyard, playing and didn't hear about anything that happened down there. That's where you two were, right?"

My father looked at me expectantly, knowing full well this was a make-or-break moment for both of us. I sighed, then as I opened up my mouth to tell one of the biggest whoppers of a lie I ever told, Stephen spoke up.

"Mr. Benson, we weren't in the backyard. We were at the circus. I'm sorry." He hung his head like he was standing before the executioner. I stood quietly by his side, wondering how badly we were both going to be punished.

"I know," my father finally said. "I wondered what story you were going to concoct to get out of it."

"Are you going to tell Mrs. Stabler, Dad?" I asked. Stephen looked over at me, then at him, then back down to his feet.

"No, I'm not. That's not my job. Stephen should do what's in his heart, but if he's the kind of guy I think he is, he'll tell her the truth. That's not for me to decide."

"Thank you, Mr. Benson," Stephen said, shuffling to the front door. "I know what I have to do."

I walked Stephen to the garage to get him his bike. He sat astride the oversized Peugeot and paused. "Your father's a good guy, but he's right. I have to let her know or I don't think I can look him in the eye again."

"I know, man. Hey, it won't be so bad. We'll be able to hang around after school until you get off of probation."

"Sure thing," he said. I watched him pedal down my street and up the hill toward his.

§

It took close to two weeks for all those professionals to finally find where that chimp was hiding. It managed to elude capture by living off the wild berries and water from the small streamlets that crisscrossed the woods he called briefly its home. They cornered it about five miles from where it ran off, in the woods behind where my cousin lived. A tranquilizer dart brought the beast down and it was cared for by animal control until someone from the circus claimed him.

Meanwhile, the circus picked up stakes and left town the day after the big breakout. The details of the escape graced several editions of the local newspaper, reporters analyzing every nuance of the event. The two patrons and the worker who were bitten by the crazed chimps were all released the same day, none of whom would end up with more than a small scar and a strange tale to tell someday.

The story about that escape convict weaved its way into the whole circus affair. As it turned out, police thought they had cornered the wayward simian up in the treehouse that some kids from a nearby apartment building had built. Instead of finding a scared chimpanzee greeting them, they instead discovered the missing prisoner, who had been able to live up there for several days, subsisting on nothing more than candy bars, soda and potato chips courteously left behind by the apartment kids.

Stephen went home that very day and confessed to his mother, though he altered the tale a little. In order to protect me as his reliable cover story, he told his mother I wasn't with them and that I tried to talk him out of going. Mrs. Stabler never asked me if that was true and I certainly wasn't going to tell her anything different. As it turns out, he was only grounded for a week, mostly because he told the story of the chimpanzee escape so well, he had his mother in stitches for days.

I also got in trouble for my part in the whole affair, though it lasted all of two days and consisted of cutting off my television privileges. I wasn't going to complain, though. That left me with plenty of time to read about the further exploits of the chimp and the convict and also gave me time to reflect on our small part in defying the racist sentiment that still engulfed the South, even at the time of great social change. It was a crazy summer for all of us and one I'll never forget.

www.ingramcontent.com/pod-product-compliance
Lightning Source LLC
Chambersburg PA
CBHW020613310726
48979CB00008B/1458/J

* 9 7 8 0 6 1 5 2 1 6 7 9 9 *